A
MODEL
LIFE

ISBN 978-1-908318-86-2

This is a work of fiction but was based on real events. The names, dates, places and people may have been changed.

www.acornindependentpress.com

A MODEL LIFE

Muriel Rodriguez

Based on a true story

Acorn Independent Press

To my beloved husband
and our beautiful children

PROLOGUE

The weather was perfect. It was a lush early summer afternoon with a clear blue sky. Ensconced in a chair on the sunny terrace of a popular café, Emmanuel scanned the seafront. He glanced at his Rolex. One o'clock. He nibbled at the aubergine and tomato stew, drizzled with lumps of melted feta, but could feel nothing. The amphetamines were still rushing through him; each mouthful seemed bland. His awareness of the people surrounding him was enhanced: naked legs, dark sunglasses, impeccable white teeth, mirth, and laughter. Emmanuel stroked the tumbler in front of him with his thumb and middle finger and a few ice-cubes floated amidst the aniseed-flavoured translucent Pastis. He readjusted his dark Gucci sunglasses with the tip of a half-bitten nail and gently pressed his fingers again around his cool drink, throwing the ice cubes anti-clockwise against the glass.

Legs, he thought, *preferably frail. Thin, wispy legs, yep, that's what we want.* His thoughts became as agitated as the icy rocks in his drink. *As frail as those of a new-born fawn.* He curled his upper lip, revealing sharp canine teeth. *Never-ending sun-kissed legs, where each bend takes one down the highway to narrow hips and budding breasts.* His trembling hands brought his glass to his lips; some of the sticky liquid spilled onto his shaking fingers. His tremors stopped at once as Amirit and Eden strutted past him.

Emmanuel reached for his cigarettes, lit one quickly, and inhaled deeply. He savoured the warmth of the smoke sprawling on his cold, wet tongue, held it for a moment, and then released it through his nostrils. He could just see jutting cheekbones and cryptic pale eyes through the curls of smoke. Her wild strawberry blonde locks bounced around her and her white skirt lifted lightly as she walked. Emmanuel pictured the perfect white page, the immaculate canvas on which she would be printed, in due time. *A diamond in the rough*, he thought. As Amirit neared his table, she gave a quick glance towards Emmanuel, as if she had felt his pressing gaze upon her. He made her uncomfortable, so she shyly looked away. Excitement suddenly erupted in Emmanuel and a familiar sexual tremor ran through him.

***

Emmanuel was not your average sleazebag; he was actually working – trying to scout his next recruits. It took solid intuition, or so he believed, to pluck out the perfect pearl – the rare beauty that gave him his solid reputation as a successful talent-hunter.

His previous catch had taken him all the way to Russia, to a small village called Kholui, set against a backdrop of old, tipsy-looking white monasteries with green onion domes. He knew there was serious demand for that wispy but powerful Baltic look and where there was demand, there was money. He had first noticed Elena as she walked down the dirt path along the winding river, holding her father's arm, and at times leaning into his shoulder. She was *It*. Her unusual beauty had scored serious points with his boss and his bank balance.

***

He followed her down to the market where she stood out among the thickset women wrapped up in several layers of clothing, with their hair covered by dark shawls. Elena took no notice of him as he leaned against the wall of the building opposite the market place, surrounded by smoke like a dragon poised to spit fire. He observed her habit of flicking her silky long brown hair behind her shoulder and twirling it into a bun, thus revealing her perfect glowing skin and almond-shaped eyes. He meditated on her long delicate fingers as she manipulated the vegetables that her weather-beaten mother had cultivated with grace. She had accentuated her narrow waist by fastening a large leather belt around her coat, under which Emmanuel pictured were a pair of long pale-skinned legs.

After a few days staking her out, Emmanuel, the top Icon agency scout that he was had decided to approach his target. He felt that thrill of fresh blood as he stood on the front steps of her family's house with an interpreter by his side. They both wore dark suits and shiny shoes, which might have been inappropriate in such a small Russian village community. The interpreter wore thin-rimmed glasses, which he repeatedly pushed up the bridge of his nose. His small moustache twitched and undulated as he spoke.

'Emmanuel represents a famous modelling agency in Paris and he would like to have a chat with you regards to your daughter,' the interpreter had said.

'I saw your daughter last week at the market with you. I believe she has true potential as a professional model and I would like to discuss her future with you.' Emmanuel spoke in French and the interpreter translated.

Elena looked over her father's shoulder, clearly confused.

Dmitri had cleared his throat and said, 'Come in, have a seat.'

The house was small, and the kitchen, where they all sat uncomfortably around the stove, was even smaller. A few lacquered objects and plates that Dmitri had made were displayed on the shelves above their heads. The sour smell of *solyanka* filled the room. Dmitri poured two glasses of medovukha for his guests and one for himself.

Emmanuel's speech was well-practised, and he delivered it with ease.

'Icon is the largest modelling agency in the world and represents models from across the globe. There are not many Eastern European girls on the market, and I truly believe that Elena could have a great career. Let me show you some of our recent campaigns,' he said placing an armoury of glossy magazines on the peasant family's table.

Elena stretched out her hand and took one of the magazines. Emmanuel noticed how she gawped at the women on the glossy pages – they were wearing expensive clothes the likes of which she had never seen before. They were probably far more graceful than the beauties in her father's folktales.

'Most of the girls you see in this magazine are represented by us,' Emmanuel said.

Dmitri turned to the interpreter with frowning eyes. 'What is this? Human trafficking? Who are you? What do you want?'

The interpreter and Emmanuel exchanged a few words in French. Elena was at a loss, and didn't quite understand what was going on. Emmanuel frowned and toyed with the small glass he was holding.

'We're not human traffickers,' the interpreter translated patiently. 'We work in the fashion industry. The girls mostly pose for clothing or cosmetic companies. It's advertising, plain and simple. There is no need to get worked up about it.'

Elena listened to her father arguing in Russian with the interpreter as they quickly exchanged words. Emmanuel did not budge. Beads of sweat pearled on his brow while he stood watching their conversation with his mouth open, his lips darkened by too many cigarettes.

'OK,' had said Dmitri reluctantly. 'Keep talking.'

Emmanuel tapped on the empty glass. 'With all due respect, your daughter could make as much money in a few days as you make in a year, maybe more.'

Elena only had the faintest idea of what kind of money he meant. But Dmitri's attention had been well and truly regained. 'My daughter is only sixteen,' he said, darting glances at Elena's mother. 'I'm not sure I am comfortable with sending her away.'

'We don't expect her to come on her own.' Emmanuel crossed his legs and swept the dust from the tip of his shoe as the interpreter translated his words. 'You're very welcome to come too. I understand your concerns and I won't insist if you're not happy with the idea. Why don't you have a think about it? In the meantime I'll leave these magazines for you to go through at your leisure.'

Emmanuel pulled the Russian version of Icon's standard rookie contract out of his briefcase and pushed it across the table. Dmitri started reading, silently.

'Take your time, read through what we're offering. I'll come back next week and we'll chat some more.'

Emmanuel sensed that it was a done deal and that the opportunity he had offered would be hard to decline.

***

Emmanuel pulled a couple of banknotes out of his pocket and carelessly threw them on the table. He quickly gathered his belongings and ran after the girls. He slowed down his pace, cleared his throat and tried to look as composed as possible.

'Hello? Hi! Excuse me? I hope you don't mind me calling out to you like that,' he looked around him as if about to disclose a secret, and took off his sunglasses. 'My name is Emmanuel, I work for Icon Models in Paris,' he paused, half-expecting to see awe in her eyes. Instead, she stared in a questioning manner. He extracted his business card out of his wallet, totally ignoring the other girl. 'I saw you walking by. I think you're very pretty and I was wondering if you'd have time for a coffee so we could talk about your career as a top-model.'

To his great surprise, Amirit interrupted his spiel. 'Actually,' she paused, 'there is somewhere I need to be right now. Can I call you later?' she asked, waving his card.

Eden gawped and elbowed her. She could not believe she was letting such an opportunity go by. Amirit dragged Eden away. Over the next few yards, the girls occasionally looked back at Emmanuel who gave them a confident smile.

Emmanuel turned on his heels, rolled his eyes and slouched back into his chair, determined to persevere with his prey. *I must think of a better opening gambit with the Israeli women*, he thought. *They're a bit of a challenge.* His left eye twitched, and his fingers resumed their dance around the empty glass.

***

Amirit casually tossed her keys into the crystal bowl by the door, and grabbed the letters stacked next to it.

'Honey, there is one there for you,' said her mother, busy in the kitchen.

As Amirit sorted through the letters, her eyes caught sight of the escutcheon of the Israeli Defence Forces, Tzahal. She felt a sudden pang in her stomach; military service had now become a reality. She knew this day would come, but she'd been dreading it. In a few months' time she would be forced to join the army for two whole years. It meant no more shopping, no more beach, no more coffees with friends, and no Christmas holiday at her parents' chalet. While her family considered it an honour, Amirit had always regarded military duty as a barrier to the freedom of youth.

She couldn't face her mother just yet, so she went upstairs, lay down on her bed and held Emmanuel's business card. She flipped it over a few times, rolled on her back and sighed heavily, staring blankly at the ceiling. The curtains swelled and flapped gently as the breeze blew through the open windows. Amirit shut her eyes and focused on the familiar sounds of the house: the rattle of plates and cutlery in the kitchen, the muttered voices on the radio, and the humming of the cars driving along the boulevard. She rolled over and reached for the phone.

'I just got the enlistment papers,' Amirit sighed.

'Don't act so surprised, did you really expect special treatment?' Eden laughed sarcastically. 'Well, my friend, unless you quickly get pregnant or married or both, I don't see how you're going to get out of it!' Eden laughed. 'We've all got to do it.'

'I wish I could be as pragmatic as you are,' Amirit muttered and rolled on her back again, feeling rather limp.

'Well, just accept that there is no way around it. It's just how things are.'

'Do you think I should call that guy?' Amirit asked, changing the subject.

'Which guy?'

'You know, the dodgy French guy with the sandals. Oh, come on, you know... the guy we met earlier at the beach, with grey teeth and yellow fingernails. The walking ashtray who works for the modelling agency!' Amirit said impatiently.

'Of course, I do. And I still can't believe you brushed him off! Walking ashtray or not, had he come up to me – which he didn't, by the way, you lucky bitch – I would have taken him at his word.' Eden paused before adding 'It doesn't hurt to call the guy and have a chat with him.'

'You may be right,' Amirit sighed.

'See! Things are looking up already! Us ugly people have a normal life to continue,' Eden joked as she hung up.

That evening during dinner Amirit told her parents about Emmanuel. Ben, her father, almost choked on his food.

'A-mo-del-ling-ca-reer?' Her father turned to Amirit with raised eyebrows. He then looked at his wife who shrugged and started clearing the table. She had already discussed it with her daughter and knew her husband's position perfectly well. She left them to debate.

'Why not?' Amirit shyly replied. 'It would only be during summer—'

'I am not sure I like the sound of you going away... What's modelling anyway? It's not a real job, is it?' Her father retorted. 'You know very well that your uncle needs your help in his restaurant this summer. Don't let him down.'

Amirit pushed her food around her plate with her fork and pouted.

'But it's so boring...'

'You just don't know your own luck young lady.'

'I don't see what's so lucky about smelling of fish all day and being surrounded by sweaty cooks and ungrateful customers.' Amirit replied dismissively.

Ben thumped his fist down on the table making the plates jump a little. He lowered his voice and screwed his eyes. He pulled no blows with his words as he shook his right index finger menacingly. 'I have worked very hard to win a place on the Labour Party's list for the next elections. I gave up my job as a journalist, and got us into a huge amount of debt so that you could study and have a future. Now is not a good time to leave the track and make me look bad. You will do your military duty. You will do as you're told. Too much is at stake!'

Amirit pushed her plate away, folded her arms on her chest and heaved a long sigh.

'So… because of your career move, I can't travel this summer?' she said, looking at her father from the corner of her eye.

'That is not what I said,' Ben spoke calmly, trying to defuse the argument. 'I don't want you involved in the fashion industry because I know full well that you won't be gone just for a couple of months. No one turns into a top-model overnight!'

As Amirit remained silent, Ben added, 'Working at your uncle's restaurant may not be glamorous, but it will give you a secure income and ensure that you stay put in one place before you enlist. Not to mention the fact you should do your bit to support your family.'

Amirit's chair screeched as she pushed it back violently and left the table. She stormed off and slammed her bedroom door behind her.

***

Amirit had heard the murmurings of discussion below, and half an hour later, her father knocked on her door.

'Amirit, I am sorry, but you have a tendency to overreact every time I disagree with you. It is absolutely impossible to talk to you without causing a stir.'

'It's not me—'

Amirit was interrupted by her father putting his arm around her and rocking her affectionately.

'Your mother and I have discussed this and we've come to the conclusion that if this is something you would really like to try, I will take you to Paris personally for a week and make sure that you are taken care of properly.'

Amirit hesitated, turned towards him and threw her arms around her father's neck.

'Thank you!' She exclaimed struggling with the mix of extreme emotions the last hour had brought.

Ben gently pushed her away and held both her hands in his. He looked into her eyes and added, 'This is of course, on the one condition that you return for your military service in a few weeks' time.'

A couple of weeks later Amirit was sitting next to her father on a plane to Paris. She looked sheepishly at him, hoping he would turn his head towards her so that she could confess her scheme. Being deceitful didn't come naturally to her, but she knew that he would do everything in his power to prevent her from going to Paris if he knew – including coercing the pilot into turning the plane around.

Blissfully unaware and filled with trust and high hopes for his daughter, her father was engrossed in his newspaper. She felt ashamed for shutting him out of her plans. She turned towards the window, fidgeted nervously and prayed that her father would find it in him to forgive her somehow.

PART ONE

SOUTH OF FRANCE AND
THE ICON MODELS CONTEST

CHAPTER 1

Marion, Ardèche and Avignon, Summer 1995

My body was tossed around like a ragdoll. I was trapped underwater, hitting one rock after the other, not sure when I would be able to gasp for air. *I should have worn that ridiculous red life jacket after all.*

One thing was certain, if I made it, I would not set foot in a canoe again and I would certainly not sit in the front and do all the paddling. At this point, unbelievably, all the years of competitive swimming seemed totally irrelevant.

After what felt like hours, the furious river let me go. As I bobbed out of the water I let out a loud cry, then I lay motionless in the shallow waters, belly up, panting while I gathered my thoughts. I was disorientated. All I could remember was the loud bang, the tip over and the endless tossing. It was clear that another canoe must have hit ours from behind. An acute pain suddenly seized both my leg and lower back. My whole body felt as if it had been chewed up and spat out.

Do not move, I told myself, trying not to succumb to terrifying thoughts of permanent damage and spinal paralysis. I thought of the forthcoming National French Swimming Championships. Why had I been so foolish about not wearing a life jacket? *Wait for the others*, I thought.

'Are you OK?' Still trapped in the canoe we were sharing, Lucie rested her oar and peered down at me. Stones from the riverbed had lacerated my back whereas Lucie was unhurt and her white-blonde hair was still bone-dry. When we hit the rock, the canoe had tipped propelling me into the water, while miraculously Lucie had remained unharmed and still safely aboard.

'Do I look okay to you?'

A few minutes later the others caught up. Vincent removed his helmet and jumped out of the canoe he was sharing with Charles. Visibly upset, he waded towards me and tried to lift me out of the water.

'Don't!' I said, feeling frightened. 'I can't move. My back is sore and I can't feel my right leg.'

'Get help!' he urged Charles. 'You'll be fine, Marion. Just stay nice and calm for me, okay?'

As Charles raced away up the riverbank, Vincent took off his life jacket so he could move more freely and held my head above the water. Looking unconcerned, Lucie jumped out of the canoe and dragged it ashore. She took off her life jacket and lay down on the riverbank to dry herself in the sun.

'If Lucie cared a bit less about sunbathing and more about paddling properly, I would still be on that bloody canoe,' I hissed at Vincent, gesticulating above the water.

'Don't get all worked up about it. It was an accident. Can you try and sit up for me? Looks like you're able to move and get angry – I'll take that as a good sign!'

By the time Charles came back with a paramedic a few minutes later, I had managed to sit up on the riverbank. The paramedic was young and presumably inexperienced, but he rolled his sleeves up and deftly examined my wounds.

'You seem to have a few nasty cuts in your lower back,' he concluded. 'Were you wearing your life jacket?'

I felt sheepish. 'No. I thought it would be OK as the water wasn't deep. The heat is unbearable in those things.'

I winced as he applied the butterfly stitches to my lower back. He looked unimpressed.

'Maybe so, but you wouldn't be in this state if you had worn one. Let me have a look at your leg.' He carefully examined my bruises. 'You want my advice?' he said at last, sitting back. 'Call it a day and find yourself a physiotherapist.'

Once the medic was gone, Lucie sighed heavily. 'It looks like we can kiss our little trip goodbye.'

I looked up at her in dismay. 'Come on, how can you accuse me of spoiling your fun when you were the one steering and guiding the canoe? I couldn't have possibly avoided the rocks while paddling in the front,' I replied, with a frown.

'Let me stop you right there,' interrupted Vincent. 'There is no point in arguing about it. In any case we have to continue the trip.'

'What…what do you mean by that?' I stammered.

'We don't have a choice,' he said with a shrug. 'You can't walk and the car is parked much further down the river.'

'Maybe we could ask the medic for a lift? Surely he wouldn't refuse; he was the one suggesting I shouldn't continue,' I said looking up at my three companions as they formed a circle around me.

'Oh come on, don't make such a fuss. It's just a few scratches. Lucie will paddle down the last stretch on her own and you can ride in our canoe,' Vincent concluded, avoiding my disappointed look.

I was so stunned by the decision that I could not react. Getting back on a canoe was the last thing I wanted to do at that point but, as I was clearly outnumbered, I was left with no choice. They had taken the decision to continue the canoe trip without a care in the world for my injuries.

***

In the tent that night, I didn't get a wink of sleep. I certainly did not enjoy the thin mattress given the circumstances, nor the mosquitoes dancing above my head. What should have been an idyllic summer holiday camping trip turned out to be an unbearable nightmare. The night dragged on as I lay there, aware of every single noise surrounding me: the wind rustling the leaves, the owls hooting, and the sounds made by the less familiar creatures creeping in the woods, which are all the more terrifying at night. I lay on my back as if trapped in a cobweb, wondering when I'd be on the menu for the squadrons of mosquitoes that had taken up residence in my tent. I pressed my right hand into the ground, shifted my left elbow underneath me and tried to lift my sore body slowly onto its side. My arms and legs shook as my toes pivoted and I heaved. I pressed my head on the mat, straining my neck muscles and twisted, then winced as my body slipped, falling onto the mattress with a thump. I could feel my eyes welling up as the pain renewed. I wailed and mumbled unintelligibly.

Conveniently my injuries had been all *my fault*.

What troubled me more than my discomfort was that the friends with whom I so wanted to be sharing more than school memories had seriously let me down at a critical point. Along with their friendship, my chance of qualifying for the National Junior team during the Summer Swimming Championships in three weeks time had swirled past me, flushed down the Ardèche River – for good.

CHAPTER 2

Marion, Marion's bedroom, Avignon, Summer 1995

While other kids of our age hung out aimlessly after school in the town square, my brother and I were devoted swimmers. Swimming had played a pivotal role in both our lives and that of our parents', especially since they were always the ones having to chauffeur my brother Patrick and I to and from the pool every day. It took up our whole lives; we were utterly committed to the sport and we loved every minute we spent in the water. There wasn't a day that went by when we didn't stink of chlorine or fall asleep on our homework (which as a result was always completed long after it was due). Swimming filled our weekends, some of our summer holidays, and most of all, our Olympic dreams. Everything else seemed rather trivial to us.

Summer had just started and there I was, bedridden with a huge lump on my right thigh. With too much time on my hands, I grew frustrated. I wasn't used to being inactive and it didn't suit me. I began to dwell on the painful memories of my first love, Christophe as frustration turned to depression.

I had met Christophe at the age of twelve during a swimming competition in the tiny island in the Indian Ocean where I had spent most of my childhood with my family before we all moved back to France. For my local swimming mates hosting the French National Team had been quite an event to look forward to. Nothing much ever happened on the island apart from the occasional volcanic eruption and sharks killing some poor soul in the bay. To us these events were so habitual as to be completely mundane but to see the French National Swimming Team; well that was really something.

Christophe had nudged everyone to come and sit next to me during lunch break and swept me off my feet with one sentence. To be honest, it had taken slightly more than a few words; his charisma had been crucial to the beginning of our romance, coupled with the fact that he was a real Olympic swimmer. That he was five years older than me didn't matter. He was a muscular dark-haired young man with intense brown eyes, who lived miles away from me, much to my parents' relief. They knew all along that their baby girl was taller than average and would likely attract the attention of boys at an earlier stage in life than was perhaps normal. As long as I kept my head under water -literally speaking- I was safe, or so they thought.

'Will you wait for me?' Christophe had asked. He wanted me to wait for him until I was old enough to be his. What I perceived as a chivalrous question struck me as the beginning of a fairy tale only *I* lived in and I gladly played the part for years. I waited for his letters which came parsimoniously but ravished me every single time as I read them again and again under the cool of the bougainvillea trees, giggling and sighing like the young innocent girl that I was. Our epistolary romance was enough to fuel his desire and fill me with the bliss of being in love. I wasn't training for the Olympics any longer; I was training to swim for France by his side. He had become my leitmotiv, my raison d'être. My parents did not approve of such heedless romance but decided to ignore the underlying sexual tension to focus on the positive side of the situation; it kept the other boys at bay.

Christophe's athletic career took a bad turn when he started suffering from numerous back hernias, which not only caused him some considerably agony, but also triggered his fall from swimming superstardom to average Joe. After a few unsuccessful surgeries, he was quickly set aside by the swimming selector, and eventually dismissed from the French National Team altogether. Consequently his sponsors severed their contracts while I powerlessly read of him sink into an ever more destructive depression. His letters became scarcer and the distance separating us prevented me from truly measuring the depth of his distress.

Soon enough, I was going to be confronted by the full force of his fall from grace and his inner torment -much to my detriment- as I had finally qualified for the winter French Nationals in Paris. I was set to try out for the European Junior Championships in March. Instead of rescuing me on his white horse as I had dreamt of all these years, he took me to his apartment on the first day of the competition. Without saying a word, he casually put his beer bottle on the floor, pinned my arms down, and thrust his penis inside me before I could even react. Some people say that when one dies, one's life story unravels; I must have died that day as what I had called 'love' was pillaged by the same man who had planted it in my heart. I hadn't expected love to be so painful, I hadn't expected sex to be so violent and I certainly hadn't anticipated how much damage it would do. Within quarter of an hour, the eternal love he had promised me in all his beautifully-written letters over the past five years was shattered. And I was falling apart inside. I went to school, with music blasting in my ears, thus shutting myself completely off. My heart had been pulled out of my chest and torn to shreds; I felt numb to the world. As I recollected the scene, my eyes reddened with tears, my eyelids fluttered, and I looked up to contain my tears while my lips trembled with sorrow. I wiped my tears with the tip of my fingers and stared blankly. My family couldn't see me like this.

I still longed for the young promising swimmer I had met when I was twelve, but loathed the myopic monster he had become when his dream of Olympics was crushed. I remembered how his mouth had not met mine, how I had suffocated under his weight and cried silently as he dug inside me. What I had so preciously kept for him was taken violently.

I remembered how he had driven me back to my hotel and dropped me off like an unwanted package. I remembered how loud silence could be and that the radio played Gainsbourg's song *Je t'aime... moi non plus* – French for "I love you... me neither"- a contradiction in terms only Christophe understood. I remembered how time had stopped, how I could not breathe and how I had wept and wept in the shower, soiled and broken-hearted.

Christophe had prolonged my agony as he walked up to me the following day while I was sitting in the calling room, waiting to swim the 200 metre freestyle to find the strength left in me to qualify for the French Junior Team. He pressed his face into my ear and threatened me with more harm if I turned him in. My whole body trembled as I stood on the starting block and as if the blood had drained out of me. I dived in and seemed to become a spectator of my own race.

I returned home a failure and a disappointment. My parents noticed that I had lost my appetite and I became withdrawn. I had lost the faculty to laugh or even smile and woke up in sweat at night, smothering my terror in my pillow. I couldn't really tell them the whole story, but I did confess to losing my virginity, for which they punished me severely and that only served to make me feel worse and to even consider swallowing all of my mother's sleeping pills. Because I never told them about the rape, only the fact that Christophe had left me, they never understood my suffering. I never shared the rage, the implosion, and the hollowness in my heart, only the sadness of a lost love.

The pain now throbbing in my leg was an acute reminder that after my first failed attempt to qualify for the Junior Team in March, the canoe accident would be putting an end to my swimming career at seventeen. Swimming one hundred metre freestyle in under one minute had been quite an extraordinary achievement at such a young age, but it wouldn't be so during next year's French Championship. I had gone from the gifted young swimmer to just-another-swimmer for my coach. I guess I would have to see my older brother Patrick off to the Summer French Swimming Championships without me.

Later that summer my older brother Patrick came back from Paris where he worked as a trader, to stay with us. He was tall, blonde and looked nothing like me or our young brother Matthieu. Patrick had always been the odd one out – the blondest but also the most ambitious. He was chatting with our parents and setting the table for lunch outside when the phone rang.

'Marion! Phone call for you!' my mother yelled from the corridor.
'Hello?' I said.

'Marion, it's Lucie! I was wondering if I could borrow your helmet and your bike for next week's triathlon... now that you don't need it, that is!' Lucie's voice was cheerful.

'Sure, why not? Come and pick it up whenever!' I replied, as I leaned against the side table.

I limped along the corridor and out onto the narrow terrace where my brothers and parents were having lunch in the shade. The cicadas were singing and my brothers had removed their t-shirts and were by now already bent over their plates, devouring the healthy, colourful food with gusto.

'Who was it pup?' my father asked.

Patrick dragged my chair back so I could sit down. I rested my crutches on the floor and hopped to my seat.

'Oh, it was Lucie. She wants to borrow my bike and my helmet for her triathlon next week.'

I helped myself to some melon and my parents looked at one another in disbelief.

'Well, you're going to call your friend Lucie and tell her that she's not borrowing anything from you,' my father stated plainly.

My knife stopped half way through cutting the melon. I looked at my father quizzically.

'Not only do your so-called *friends* make you sleep in a tent in the middle of nowhere when you're clearly in bad shape, they now have the indelicacy to borrow your stuff and rub your face in it? You have to stand up for yourself a bit more,' my father spoke firmly and I looked down. 'Blame it on me, I don't care. Tell this 'friend' of yours that your father didn't want you to lend your stuff to anyone and that's final. Your mother is a teacher, and as a teacher's daughter you should know to handle your school friends better,' he added as he agitated his knife in circles round his plate.

I noticed how my father's grey hair had been gaining ground and thinning out. My mother was showing signs of aging too, wearing her pink dress and matching braided scarf in her hair to fight off the stray locks and hide the white ones. My parents seemed to have shrunk while my brothers seemed to have exploded, displaying their muscular chests through their thin t-shirts at the table.

***

Summer dragged on inexorably. All day long screaming children were jumping into the neighbouring private pools while adults cheered them on and ate late into the evening on their terraces. What should have been a matter of days turned into weeks of dragging my weakened body between the bed and the physiotherapist, with way too much mindless television in between. Unable to pull myself together I felt I was slowly turning into a poor imitation of a lazy housewife; watching cooking shows and soaps all day long. My boredom usually came hand in hand with eating, so I managed a few trips to the fridge in between one mind-numbing TV series and the next. I was slowly devouring a small tub of pecan and vanilla Häagen-Dazs when modelling came knocking. I looked up mid-snack at a tantalising commercial for the national Icon modelling contest.

Long-legged Amazonians were strutting down the runway with a mesmerising aura that overpowered the clothes and made my jaw drop to my knees. They were all skin, perky breasts and floating hair. They were surrounded by an army of makeup artists and hairdressers who touched them up to perfection. Melinda, Brittani and Julia paused before a bank of famous photographers.

'If you think that you could be the next top model, send us a picture of you in your bathing suit, a headshot, your measurements, and your age.' The voice was enticing and introduced Icon Models' chairman, Paul Newhouse, towards the end of the presentation.

'We represent pretty much all the best working models on the market. Most of them have signed multi-million euro contracts and achieved worldwide recognition. It has not only propelled them to the rank of supermodels, but it's also empowered them to take over the only industry where women clearly earn more than men,' he summed up, with a strong American twang.

I had never really thought of modelling as a career choice nor considered my looks an asset. Being pretty may have helped me to get away with a few things in life, but it had never made me swim faster or get better grades. However the ad got me thinking and, eventually, I decided to send a few pictures to the address on the screen to test the water.

When my mother came back home from work, I armed her with a camera and a measuring tape.

'I've always thought you had potential. When you were twelve, Paco Rabanne had already spotted you during the holiday, foreseeing a successful modelling career. I remember—'

'I know Mum,' I interrupted, 'you've told me that story over and over. But Paco Rabanne also said that the world would end and that is very unlikely to happen.'

'Let me just put the groceries away, darling,' my mother said.

'Can you measure my chest, waist and hips? They need to be 90-60-90 centimetres for the competition,' I explained once my mother was done.

'92...62...90, and with a squeeze, 90-60-90!' she chuckled. 'Perfect!'

I smiled for the first time in a long while. I could feel the pulse of life being slowly rekindled.

The possibility of becoming a model had given me a renewed sense of purpose. Once my application was sent off, I looked out for the postman every single morning. Strangely enough, my crutches didn't pose a problem when it came to rushing to and from the letterbox. Apart from the occasional flyer most days, I returned empty-handed. As the days went by, I started to lose hope. I had to face up to the fact that I was probably not model material after all. I was a tad too tall and way too muscular. My curly hair was out of control and my teeth were slightly too big for my face, but being only seventeen, I was hoping that with time I would grow in proportion.

In August the news I had been waiting for didn't arrive by post, it came by phone. I picked up the receiver absent-mindedly. 'Yes?'

'May I speak to Marion, please?'

'Speaking.'

'This is Esmeralda from Icon Model Management in Paris. You have been selected to take part in the first stage of our modelling contest.'

Silence. I was speechless. Pause. Rewind.

'Marion? Are you there?'

I realised the person on the other end of the phone couldn't see my nodding head. 'I…yes. Yes, I am…I—'

'You have been selected out of three thousand girls. We now have forty-eight contestants including yourself who are to be invited to attend this next stage in the competition.'

I stuttered and finally managed to find the words. 'I…what?'

'I know that it's a lot to take in. We would like to know if you're able to come to Paris and meet us in September?'

CHAPTER 3

Marion, Round One, Paris, September 1995

Out of the two of us I wasn't sure who was the more excited about the trip to Paris, my mother or me. I was already off school convalescing after my disastrous canoe accident and I welcomed any opportunity to get away, even if for a day, from my life at home and my 'friends' Vincent and Lucie.

***

There was a very large queue at the taxi stand at Gare du Nord. It was like nowhere we'd ever been before. It was as if we'd been parachuted onto the surface of another planet. People seemed to rush and push, huff and puff, more than the French average. 'This is all so exciting! I can't wait to see you made up.' My mother was almost breathless with pride, 'I wonder what the other girls look like. I am sure you'll be the prettiest!' My mother's opinion was always one to be taken with a pinch of salt when it came down to her children.

'Hold your horses Mum, we're not there yet!' I interjected, 'There's the taxi stand, come on!'

My mother gasped as the wind caught her by surprise and tousled her blonde hair. 'Oh my God, look at the queue! We'll never get there on time!'

I finally pulled my mother into a cab at last, feeling dishevelled and tired. It was just gone 1 p.m.

Finally the taxi dropped us off in front of the warehouse where Canal Plus had its recording studios. We stood there alone, for a couple of minutes taking it all in, before a pretty brunette with headphones and a clipboard came to greet us.

'Where is everybody?' My mother looked around, flabbergasted.

'Shh Mum. I think that must be the person we're supposed to be meeting over there.' I had just caught sight of the hostess.

'Good afternoon! Are you Marion?'

'Yes!' I said in relief.

'We've been waiting for you. Follow me and I'll take you to the make-up studio. Once you're ready, someone will come and take you to the set.'

Feeling like the new kid at school, I grabbed my mother by the arm and followed the brunette through the maze of corridors and into a brightly lit and smoke-filled make-up studio. We were met by the makeup artist and hairstylist who sat giggling and gossiping on facing chairs, with their legs crossed.

'I swear it's true!' Rene, the hairstylist was saying, bursting into laughter, 'She literally flipped out and tore off all of her clothes!'

The make-up artist was nodding vacantly like one of those distasteful dog toys you sometimes see in the back of people's cars at traffic lights. As we walked in, they swivelled their chairs toward us. Their grins suddenly faded when they saw my mother wriggling her nose and waving her hand in front of her face to fan away the cigarette smoke. Rene was wearing tight jeans, a neatly buttoned up shirt and a silk scarf around his neck. He had unkempt hair and a scruffy beard, which made him seem like a walking contradiction.

Two big suitcases lay open on the grey-tiled floor, teeming with a vast selection of hairpieces, hair products, brushes of all shapes and sizes, curlers and more. The make-up artist propped her case against the mirror, with its blinding rows of lights, in pursuit of eye make-up in every colour and shade of a rainbow.

'Hello darling,' said Rene, looking me up and down with contempt. 'Have a seat and let me look at your hair.'

He pulled off my hairband and ran his fingers through my entangled curls, tutting as his fingers got caught in several knots.

'What are we going to do with this mess?' He then shook his hands free. Clumps of hair fell limply to the floor. I cringed. In the corner of my eye I saw my mother half-ready to say something from her seat.

Please Mum, stay still, I thought to myself, *and please for the love of God don't say a word*! I prayed she would not embarrass me.

An hour and a half later, the curls were tamed into straight sleek hair, falling as far as my lower back. My hair always sprung back up to the same height, no matter the length. I looked at myself in wonder for the first time as I stroked my unusual hair.

I look like a model!

'Much better!' Rene concluded.

He lit up another cigarette and filled the room with smoke once more. My mother sprang up from her chair like a jack-in-the-box and opened the door pointedly.

"Please Mum!" I frowned at my mother, hoping she would sit down again, as Rene glanced across at his colleague and stubbed out his cigarette.

'Your turn, Elsa' he said.

Elsa was short and plump. She put her glasses on, took my face in her hands, and turned it from one side to the other.

'Let's see what we have here.'

She inspected me through her half-moon glasses, which allowed her to look both through and over the neat little lenses. She swept her gaze from the top of my head to my chin. From the moment I saw her, I had the feeling that her head had a life of its own and was somewhat disconnected from her body. Ill-at-ease, I tried my best to avoid eye contact. She then started to pluck almost every single hair of my eyebrows, thus widening the gap between my eyes and my eyebrows.

What on earth has she done? My eyebrows had become a ridiculous thin line that gave me a permanent look of surprise.

'Big eyebrows are *quite* out of fashion, darling!' The make-up artist said and applied a thick layer of foundation on my face and a dark hue of blue onto my eyelids.

The stylist appeared, armed with a white bathing suit. I wriggled into my costume, and looked into the mirror. The low-cut bikini bottom made my legs look shorter, and the colour itself didn't do justice to my pale skin with its millions of freckles. The bikini top looked tiny against my broad swimmer's shoulders, the gleaming body oil emphasised my muscular body, and my long, dark, unrecognisable straight hair framed my shocked, over-painted face.

I thought to myself, *I look like a transvestite!* My seventeen year old self was horrified.

'She's gorgeous,' said the hairdresser in approval. 'What a change! She is ready', the hairdresser spoke about me in the third person as if I was not in the room. My mother was asked to wait for me in the dressing room, which was probably a good thing.

'Alright Marion, I'll take you to the set now,' the stylist said.

I was ushered on set in my bikini. I felt rather uncomfortable in front of the crew of technicians and kept my arms across my chest to try and hide as much skin as possible. A lady with short hair approached me.

'Hello Marion! My name is Lydia and I am the director of photography. I need you to stand still for me and look into the camera while we do a close-up of your face. Please don't smile, it's always nicer not to. Much more elegant, far *sexier!*' She said as she raised her shoulders and pouted.

I was not sure what she meant by sexier but surely she must have realised how uncomfortable it felt to be in the skimpiest bikini in the world. I tugged hopelessly at my tiny bikini.

'We'll do a full-length body shot. Walk from right to left and come back to the middle of the set. Then turn around and look back at the camera.' Lydia moved her fingers as if they were legs.

'Got it!' I nodded apprehensively.

'Alright darling, let's go.'

Lydia turned around and walked away behind the lights, where I could hardly see her anymore.

Two hours later, thirty seconds' worth of footage was in the can, and without further ado, I was sent back to the changing room. My mother was eagerly waiting for details, pacing like a lion in a cage.

'There you are! How was it?' My mother was so giddy with excitement that she could barely contain herself.

'It was good… I guess,' I said carefully. 'I'm not sure. It was a combination of an extraordinary experience and having absolutely no control over my body. Being the centre of attention made me feel special on the one hand, but also quite raw and exposed'.

My mother frowned, in miscomprehension. 'Well, I am sure you looked good.'

'I am glad at least one of us thinks so,' I said, sighing a little.

'It'll be fine,' said my mother bracingly. 'Chalk it down to experience and the same with whatever happens next.'

There was something annoyingly defeatist about her comment but deep down, I knew she was trying to undermine any potential unhappy outcome. What really mattered to me at that point was that after spending months feeling sorry for myself, I was finally renewing with a sense of purpose in life dangling in front of me. I secretly hoped that Icon would take me on as a model whatever the results. I tried not to imagine my disappointment should I fail once more.

Before we knew it, my mother and I had taken a taxi through some busy traffic, bought our tickets and were on the train home. As I leaned my head against my seat and gazed out of the window, the whole world seemed to be quickly unravelling in one long ribbon of concrete buildings, cottages, cows, open space, blue sky, wind and teenage ennui.

***

At school the next day, I felt totally disconnected. I couldn't concentrate during class and spent most of the morning daydreaming, unsettled by what I had experienced. The teacher's voice filtered through like a weak radio signal: alternately distorted, clear, and then inaudible once more. I glanced at my classmates and then at Vincent, Lucie and Charles, whose lives were continuing as normal while mine veered sideways.

'What happened to your eyebrows?'

No superficial detail ever escaped Lucie. Charles and Vincent wouldn't have noticed if my head had been shaved. I wanted to tell them about Paris, but I wasn't sure if I should share the news with them. I was also unsure that they could relate to anything else but sports. I gave it a shot anyway.

'Remember that modelling contest I told you about?'

'Yes, I remember, the Icon contest. Did you hear back from them?' Vincent grew a sudden interest in the conversation.

'Yes, they replied and I went to Paris to meet them!'

Vincent's face lit up. 'No way! Awesome!'

'Really?' Lucie said with a suspicious look. 'When did you go? What did you do?'

'Last weekend. I didn't meet anyone from the agency, but they shot a short video of me and it's going to be on TV.'

'TV? When?'

'It'll be on *Une Histoire Extraordinaire*, some time soon.' I said with a note of pride.

The conversation was put to an end as the bell brought us back to class.

***

Sure enough a month later my Paris footage was on *Une Histoire Extraordinaire* presented by their up-and-coming presenter Jacques Connelli. Every day the public were given a choice of three girls to vote for.

The day after I was on TV for whole of the country to see me in that embarrassingly immodest bikini, Vincent came running towards me. 'I saw you! I saw the show! I hardly recognised you! It's amazing what they can do!'

'Did I look okay?' I blushed.

'You looked different, but you looked good!'

Different but good. It was etched in my memory.

Shortly after the programme was over and the votes were in, I received another phone call from Esmeralda.

'Marion! I've got good news! You have been selected for the final!' Esmeralda announced.

I shut my eyes. It was too much to comprehend.

'It took a while to introduce all the girls, but we got there in the end. You're now one of just sixteen finalists. You should feel proud of yourself!'

'Thank you so much!' I managed to reply, still in a state of shock.

Hovering in the hallway, my mother did her best to understand what was happening on the other end of the phone.

'The next stage will take place in Cannes, in May. We are hoping that the weather will be perfect. We'll be shooting a short film.'

'A film?' I gasped.

'We are doing a black and white remake of the Cannes Movie Festival newsreel from the fifties. It'll be fabulous darling, you'll see. I'll call you later with more details. Bye darling.'

I hung up carefully, turned to my mother and squealed, 'Un-be-lie-va-ble! I have been selected for the final *and* I am going to Cannes!'

My mother screamed louder than I did, 'How wonderful! See, didn't I tell you that you looked great and everything would be fine?'

We hugged and jumped as if the floor had suddenly become too hot to stand on.

'You're going to become a star!'

My mother was hysterical, but I loved it. I loved rediscovering my dreams of success. Being a model would help me show the world and especially Christophe, that he hadn't utterly destroyed me after all.

CHAPTER 4

Marion, Round Two, Cannes, September 1995

One weekend my mother came with me to the French Riviera. It was only two hours away from our hometown, but it wasn't somewhere we'd ever been. We'd never really felt glamorous enough to fit in. We were put up in the Majestic Hotel, in a beautiful suite with a view of the world-famous palm-lined seafront avenue and in the distance, the twinkling turquoise light of the Mediterranean.

First thing in the morning we ordered room service, choosing from the menu all sorts of things we never indulged in at home: salmon, bagels, eggs, croissants, pains au chocolat and freshly squeezed orange juice. We sat out on our balcony in the sunshine wearing our hotel dressing gowns, admiring joggers running along La Croisette and laughing at the local fascination with tiny, uncontrollable dogs. Determined to enjoy every single minute my mother and I decided to misbehave and jump up and down on the bed like a pair of over-excited children.

'I could get used to this lifestyle,' I said, as I finally collapsed onto the big bed. Almost immediately the phone rang.

'Mum, I've got to hurry. I have to meet everyone in thirty minutes!' I shrieked as I hung up.

'I'll be here when you get back, Honey. I think I am going to stay by the pool and do absolutely nothing at all!' she said with a mischievous smile.

'Excellent plan!'

I took a quick shower and, with no time to dry my hair, I slipped into a short denim skirt, a black tank top and black flip flops. My mother was still lying on the bed. She had apparently already put her plan in action. I kissed her goodbye and ran out the door.

By the time I made it downstairs, all the contestants were already in the hotel's reception area, which was an oasis of majestic golden columns, heavy chandeliers, and soft brown velvet sofas. The girls looked very different, but they were all very thin and very beautiful. Some were shy and stood beside or behind the others, while the more confident among them were more poised and waited patiently, legs crossed, noses pointing towards the ceiling.

The air was electric with anticipation. Models were sizing each other up and I rapidly worked out who I would and wouldn't get along with. In particular there was a dark-haired girl called Amber, who nudged me as she made her way to the front with an arrogant pout.

'Don't mind her,' said a pretty blonde on my right, with a friendly smile. 'The contest hasn't even started and she already has an attitude! I'm Sophie by the way.'

'Pleased to meet you.' I smiled back.

'At breakfast this morning, Amber overtook me as I was waiting to be seated. She pretended I wasn't even there!' Sophie suddenly turned around. 'Look, there's Emmanuel! He's the talent scout for the agency and our chaperon during the contest.'

A short man with black hair in his late thirties walked in wearing a pale blue shirt, white shorts and a pair of Versace glasses. He lifted his shades for a few seconds and looked at us carefully. The girls looked at one another in disbelief while Emmanuel ran a hand through his brown hair.

'Emmanuel's job is to spot and approach the agency's next recruits,' whispered Sophie, 'He's done it for the past five years and he's made quite a name for himself.'

'It must be hard for him – travelling around the world and being in the presence of beautiful girls.'

'Yeah, no kidding – just look at the way he poses, he thinks we're all his,' Sophie continued.

Emmanuel gathered the finalists around him and quickly ran through the schedule before he assigned us to our different teams of makeup artists and hair-stylists.

'Girls, welcome to Cannes and welcome to the 1995 Icon modelling contest,' said Emmanuel, once he had everyone's attention. 'You have all been selected by the public vote and by a team of renowned fashion professionals and we hope that you will make the most of this unique experience. Today, you are going to be filmed by a number of different teams in a variety of different situations and locations. Listen carefully to your respective directors as we don't have much time and, as you will soon learn, time is money. I hope you have a great day – and don't forget to have fun.'

***

Having been divided up, joining designated teams of hair and make-up artists, I was taken to a nearby swimming pool with a film crew. Despite the July weather, the water was too cold for most of the locals who were lounging on the grass and enjoying the sun. The film crew caused quite a stir.

The stylist, Sabine, was in her fifties. Her hair was bright red and cut in a bob with a straight fringe, like a Playmobil action figure which made me wonder what exactly she'd be doing to my hair. I didn't have to wait long as she handed me a fifties-style bathing suit and a swimming cap covered in flowers. *Is this really how they see me?* I thought to myself, *Retro? Old-fashioned and out of date?*

The stylist took a big towel out of one of her numerous bags and stretched it out between her arms.

'You can get changed now. Hide behind this towel.'

I grew anxious. 'There is a changing room in the building over there. Can't I use that?'

'We don't have much time and no one will spot us,' the stylist reassured me.

I looked at her bright red hair anxiously. Apparently, I seemed to be the only one troubled by this lack of modesty. I looked around, squatted and slipped on my bathing suit as quickly as possible.

Once dressed I was told to wait for Alain, our director of photography who spent a great deal of time examining his megaphone and his camera. He finally walked up to me, belly first.

'I need you to climb up the ladder and sit on the five-metre diving board for five seconds or so and then stand up and dive into the pool.'

I looked up and tried to picture myself on that board for a few seconds. My throat tightened and I felt suddenly terribly dizzy.

'I don't think I can dive from up there,' I said.

Alain tutted. 'They told me you were a professional swimmer!'

'Yes, but not a diver,' I pointed out. 'That's pretty high and I... I can't do it. I'm sorry.'

He rolled his eyes at the rest of the team. 'Fine! We'll only make you dive from the side of the pool and do some underwater shots, but we still need some shots of you up on that diving board.'

I could feel everyone watching me as I reluctantly climbed up the ladder and sat down as he had asked. Just as I did so the silliest idea ran through my mind. *I like it up here. What if I stay up here? What if I don't come back down?* I tilted my head back and let the warm breeze caress my face.

Alain waved at me and put both his arms out in a questioning manner as I refused to move.

'You're a bit pig-headed, aren't you?' he complained when I eventually came back down, then stomped off and grumbled "*Merde alors!*"

I walked to the edge of the pool, squeezed my feet together and gave a jerk with my upper body, which threw me momentarily up in the air and then straight into the water.

'Perfect!' Alain said. 'Let's do a few more of these please!'

After a few takes, he had a look at what had taken and picked up his megaphone.

'Can you try and make fewer bubbles when you dive into the water, please?'

I was taken aback. I had never heard such nonsense.

All the diving and underwater swimming had ruined my make-up so the make-up artist spent another half an hour touching me up before Alain deemed me fit to continue. Finally, we shot the last bit of the film – the part where I bobbed out of the water, smiling at the camera.

'Very good!' Alain cried. 'You're pig-headed, but you're good!'

They called it a wrap and I hid once more behind Sabine's towel to change back into my clothes, briefly exposing my naked self to the passers-by. I wondered whether I would ever get used to the casual attitude this industry had towards bodies and nakedness.

'Alain, could I see the reels do you think?'

'French girls are so nosy!' he grumbled. Alain grumbled a lot, but in the end he relented and showed me. 'Look at this, it's beautiful: the position, the underwater shot, and the headshot. A bit of slow motion there, a bit of skin and a nice smile. *Nice and easy*.' I wasn't sure what had happened to the old Alain, but I certainly preferred the happier version.

Eventually, Alain was so pleased with the rushes that he gave me a big hug, and I forgot about the disgustingly dated bathing suit and terrible swimming cap.

So far, modelling had been fairly easy. It wasn't great, but it wasn't too far out of my comfort zone.

CHAPTER 5

Marion, Paris, October 1995

The day of the final was drawing near, and the sixteen contestants had been asked to gather in Paris. My mother could not come along this time as she was too busy teaching and was unable to take time off. By now, my parents trusted me to be sensible.

On the train, I was desperate for someone to ask me about where I was going, so that I put my emotions into words and share my excitement with a perfect stranger. No one did. I opened the magazines I had bought and flipped through page after page of different girls, colours, garments, make-up styles, and perfumes until my head started to spin. My brand new world felt as though it was so nearly within my grasp yet at the same time still so improbable. I stretched my legs and closed my eyes and thought about it allowing myself to be gently rocked by the rhythm of the train.

At Gare Montparnasse I jumped in a taxi and gave the driver the address of a small hotel in the fourteenth district, close to Alesia. Cars streamed down the avenue, spitting and sputtering while the taxpayers huddled together at the bus stop on their way to work. We pulled up to a small four-storey hotel with a white façade, which had greyed from the car fumes. The entrance looked impressive and I was beginning to feel much better. Two precisely pruned trees stood proudly on each side of the front door, lit up by two wrought-iron lanterns. The area seemed much nicer too, next door old ladies gathered around a fruit stall displaying perfectly arranged colourful waxed apples and vegetables. On the other side of the hotel Parisians were crammed into a smoke-filled Brasserie, enjoying the last of their pastries and one final espresso before the day's kick-off.

I walked into a rather impersonal reception: the walls were beige and the furniture was off-white, which created a sterile ambiance.

'Good evening!' said a voice. I turned and saw the receptionist standing behind a very large, very white desk.

'Good evening, there should be a room reserved under Marion Durant,' I said.

The receptionist quickly typed in my name.

'I am afraid we don't have that name on our records.'

'Try Icon Models,' I enquired, worried.

'Most of our rooms are occupied by Icon Models tonight but I am afraid I don't see your name,' the receptionist said as she looked up.

I heard footsteps behind me and I turned around. It was Sophie arriving in the lobby. We hugged and kissed on both cheeks.

'Have you just arrived as well? My train was delayed, I should have been here hours ago!'

'I only got here two minutes ago but there seems to be no room under my name.'

'Oh, that's strange,' Sophie then turned to the receptionist. 'Could you please check if you see Sophie Pottin on your record please?'

'Yes, Sophie Pottin, you are in room 4, on the first floor.'

'How many beds are there in that room?' Sophie asked.

'Just one bed.' the receptionist replied.

'And how big is it?'

'It's a king size bed mademoiselle.'

'That's perfect, then. We'll share the bed!'

'Are you sure?' I asked raising an eyebrow. I was beginning to feel very prudish by modelling standards.

'Do you have an alternative? It's pretty cold out there tonight, you know!' Sophie laughed.

We walked up the stairs to her room. My first taste of the hospitality models can expect was not what I had expected. We were sharing a small off-white room that consisted of a large bed and one cupboard. The bathroom was about the size of the cupboard and had a faint musty smell.

'This place is like a mental hospital! Everything is white! Where do they keep the straight jackets?' I joked.

'You don't need a jacket, you're not mad enough, well not quite!'

When we finally went to bed, we lay there, sleepless, listening our own thoughts, our own nervousness, the steady stream of traffic and beyond, the hubbub of the rest of the city. After what felt like only a couple of hours of sleep we woke up bright and early to prepare ourselves to be photographed at Pin-Up Studio by a leading fashion and portrait photographer called Marco Tutti. I had never heard of him, but judging by Sophie's excitement, he was a big deal.

***

Pin-Up Studio was bright with daylight flooding in through the skylight. Across the room, four receptionists were clustered behind a small desk frantically answering calls. After what felt like hours, one of them finally looked up.

'Hi there! We have come for the shoot with Mario Tutto,' I grinned proudly.

'You mean *Tutti*,' snapped a skinny young man whose bleached hair covered half of his face. 'He's not here yet. Go to the restaurant with the others and wait.'

'Friendly guy!' I said as we made way towards the studio restaurant.

'Do you think we got the time wrong?' Sophie asked.

When we got there the other girls were sitting on benches around a big glass table, waiting. I noticed a buxom mannequin standing on the counter, overlooking the room from the bar. It had been positioned in such a way that the arms of the mannequin were stretched above its head and it boasted a large bosom clad in an old-fashioned blue bathing suit. Surrounded by a sea of metal and white space, she looked rather lonely. Spotlights ran across the ceiling and framed black and white photos hung on the walls. The pictures were a reminder that this was the hub of everything; the essence of the most famous Parisian fashion studio. A daunting feeling overwhelmed me as we all sat there in silence and I wondered if the others felt the same way.

One of the receptionists ushered us into Studio 1. We all sprang to our feet. A bit of nudging here and there later and we entered a spacious studio. A white backdrop held up between two black poles was unfolded from a holder like a giant roll of toilet paper creating an entirely white space.

By the entrance croissants, pains au chocolat and various hot drinks were laid out on a long table. Ignoring the temptation, the others all walked straight past it and headed towards the make-up room. Reluctantly, Sophie and I did the same. I was beginning to realise I would have to seriously change my attitude to food. As a swimmer, I'd had a large but healthy appetite to fuel my daily two-hour training sessions. Now I was inactive in a world where keeping 90-60-90 was everything.

Marco's numerous assistants bustled about, setting up lights and lining up a collection of reels and Pentax cameras for the shoot.

Joseph, the stylist walked into the changing room dressed in combat trousers, army boots, and a military jacket – it seemed as if the US army was his main supplier.

'This guy looks like a total fascist!' Sophie whispered.

'Good thing he's not carrying a rifle, he'd have me worried!' I smirked.

Joseph was holding a rack of clothes. He gave each of us a white shirt and made-to-measure leather trousers.

'Girls, most of the trousers are slightly too big and will be altered for the final shoot,' Joseph said, running his hand over his freshly-shaven head.

A Belgian girl began struggling with her trousers.

'Well, well, it looks like *you*'ve been eating too many waffles lately, young lady!' Joseph snapped. Florence's face went crimson as all eyes were drawn to her. 'Since this is all I have, you'll have to breathe in! Come on, harder!' Florence gritted her teeth and breathed in as hard as she could, trying not to faint.

But Joseph had more ammunition. 'My advice, if you want to last more than two minutes in this business, is drop the carbs and stock up with veggies and water! You'll thank me later!' With that he turned on his heels and walked away.

There was a lull in the conversation as we each digested what we had just heard. I thought that modelling would give me a new life and freedom but it was starting to feel very strict and oppressive.

The make-up artist summoned us into a line, execution style.

'Girls, I am Adrian. I am not going to do much to you, as Marco would like you to be as natural as possible. I am going to limit the preparation to a bit of base and powder only. No eyes, no lips. We want to capture your natural essence!' he pouted. He then brushed everyone's hair jumping from one model to the next as if on a spring, while the mischievous stylist helped the girls into their clothes. I felt like some sort of toy on an assembly line waiting to be displayed in a shop window.

One by one unmade up and dressed down each of the contestants sat on a stool and posed in front of the camera. One of the assistants brought a light meter close to my nose a few times while Marco stood upright behind his camera and his lights and camera were adjusted to perfection by a second assistant. Marco pressed the shutter without even looking into the lens. He had such a large staff that I couldn't help but wonder if he could function without them. Lending a detachment to the whole process, Marco devoted only a few seconds to each shot.

By the end of the morning, it was a wrap. I felt completely deflated when I was handed a Polaroid at the end of the session.

'What's wrong? You don't like it?' asked Sophie.

'The make-up around my eyes narrows them to slits and my hair is frizzing around my face— it looks like I've just put my fingers in an electrical socket!' I complained.

Sophie laughed. 'Stop being such a grouch. I think you look great.'

'Well, it's easy for you to say,' I replied gloomily. 'Your hair's nice and sleek. For some reason they don't seem to know what to do with mine. I heard Adrian actually calling it 'seaweed'.

Two hours later, after a lunch consisting of salads and sushi, Emmanuel introduced us to our walking expert, Constantine. A few girls started giggling when Constantine barged in wearing a skirt and high heels, but his deep voice reminded the girls that he was very much a man, and his fierce, professional manner wiped the smirks off their faces within seconds.

'Right girls, I am here to make your life a living hell,' he said proudly. 'Over the next couple of days, we will entirely devote ourselves to the choreography for the big final in the hotel conference room.' I was not looking forward to what he had in mind.

***

The day arrived, and the taxi dropped me off a couple of streets down the Cirque d'Hiver. The hundred-and-fifty-year-old building looked rather small from the outside, but if the Cirque had previously squeezed in horses and elephants, then surely it would be up to the task of showcasing sixteen tiny aspiring models.

Everything backstage seemed quiet and empty at first and I was easily disorientated. I followed the wires that ran along the ground of the winding corridor in search of our dressing room. I passed a beautiful woman wearing dungarees who was pacing back and forth in the badly lit space, warming up her voice.

Oh my God, it's Neneh Cherry, I thought as the famous singer turned towards me. She was so close, so real. I was surprised at how tiny she looked.

Emmanuel startled me as he grabbed my arm. He looked at me wide-eyed, stress emanating from every pore. He was squeezed into a tight jacket and drops of sweat glistened on his forehead like dew.

'What are you doing here? Where were you? You're late. Your seat is over there. Let's move it!'

'Am I really? I'm sorry I hadn't realised...'

He sighed and pointed at an empty seat at the row of make-up tables. I must have taken too much time admiring the building and wanting to absorb every last detail about Neneh Cherry. *I am so scatterbrain*, I thought to myself, hurrying to my seat. *Knowing me, it'll get me into more trouble than I'm worth.* I kept my head down, trying to make myself as inconspicuous as possible. The other girls were already in the process of having their hair done. Amber was sitting up straight, smoothing her long brown hair. She twisted her head slightly, gave me a scornful look for showing up late and resumed smoothing her hair. I sat down next to Sophie whose legs were shaking. She took her headphones off and smiled.

'Can you actually hear anything in this hubbub?'

'It helps me relax,' Sophie smiled nervously.

We spent the next two hours amongst a racket of chatter and hair dryers going full blast. In the mirror I could see acrobats warming up and juggling, trying to avoid the men on stilts who were stalking back and forth behind them. The world really had gone mad. It was swirling all around me. In a strange way, I felt as if I were in the call room before a swimming race; the same feelings of anxiety flooded through me.

My hairdresser and make-up artist introduced himself. Nicholas was thickset and wore baggy jeans and a tight shirt revealing his love handles. Happy to have some company at last, he tried to ease my concerns with small talk.

'How are you holding up?'

'A little stressed I suppose,' I admitted, with a nervous smile. 'This place is amazing, isn't it?'

Nicolas agreed enthusiastically. 'I come here regularly during show season. It's magical, you'll see. Try to relax and enjoy it as much as you can. You'll be fine.'

Easier said than done, I thought. I winced as he pulled at my hair with a round brush and jerked it about so much that I thought I was going to be sick.

Nicolas kept chatting away. Every other word was muffled as he drew the noisy hair dryer over my head again and again.

I swallowed my nerves as best I could. 'How long till we go on?'

'An hour and a half, give or take. Beautiful hair, by the way. It's like Italian hair: thick at the root and thinner towards the ends.'

He took a curl, stretched it and let it fall again.

At last someone likes my hair! I thought in delight.

'We are going to make it nice and straight,' went on Nicolas. 'Curls tend to refract the light in all directions. A sleeker look will make you look more sophisticated.'

I felt deflated, but I let him get on with it.

He battled with my hair for the next hour and then sat down on a stool to start my make-up. After covering my face with a light base, he pressed the bottom of his palm against my chin and worked for the next twenty minutes on my eyes. His proximity forced me to withdraw, to close my eyes and become less aware of my surroundings. When I reopened her eyes, I caught sight of Lulu.

Lulu was a famous transvestite and he looked extremely flamboyant in a blonde wig and with his chest was squeezed into a sparkling narrow corset, giving the impression he had breasts.

'They're called man boobs,' Nicolas enlightened me as he saw me staring at him open-mouthed.

Lulu strutted about, trying to exorcise some of the tension by joking with the girls. The bizarre reality of what was happening all around me would not have been complete without him.

Making their way backstage through the crowd of models and artists, the technicians took their positions, ready for the show to begin. A live video feed had been linked up to a large projection screen, so that no one in the audience would miss a thing. A small TV screen on the wall backstage allowed us to peek at what was happening on stage.

Raised rows of velvet chairs encircled the stage. It was buzzing with well-dressed people. Everyone was looking down at the white T-shaped runway in anticipation. The judging panel were seated in a booth on the right hand side. Fashion designers, fashion magazine editors and top models – the upper crust, would decide our future careers.

Jacques Connelli, the TV host of *Une Histoire Extraordinaire*, was standing in the centre of the front row, facing the runway with his back to the audience. He wore a black suit and was perfectly groomed with short black hair and thin-rimmed glasses. On his left side, Lystelle Holly, the top French model with a not-so-French name, was hosting the show with him. She looked like a mermaid with her long blonde hair, and her generous bosoms clad in a sea blue sequinned dress.

'Girls, may I have your attention please! Jacques Connelli is about to start the show.'

We all stopped chatting and turned to see what the show's producer Romain was telling us. He had piercings and he was extremely handsome with deep blue eyes that I just wanted to dive into.

'The audience is seated and is expecting a great performance. I am going to ask you to stay in this room and get dressed as quickly as possible. Follow my instructions as you come out on stage, and everything should be OK. I know that you are not very familiar with the venue, but you have been practising very hard with Constantine in last few days at the hotel, so tonight should be a piece of cake. Good luck!' We were as restless as horses pawing the ground before a race; the tension was palpable.

Our military stylist Joseph despatched his assistants to help the finalists slip into the leather pants and white shirts they'd worn during the photo shoot with Marco Tutti. Joseph barked orders to his underlings and whistled between his teeth when he wanted to get their attention.

'I can't bear him!' I told Sophie.

'Don't worry about him, he's not worth it,' Sophie said as she put her boots on.

The stage was suddenly plunged into darkness. A giddy murmuring ran through the venue. The area above the artists' entrance suddenly lit up and a small figure appeared, swimming in light. It was Neneh Cherry, still in her dungarees. She stepped forward and warmed up the auditorium by breaking into *Buffalo Stance* with all her might. It was unbelievable how such a powerful voice was coming out of so small a person.

Backstage we were now wearing all dressed in our leather pants and white shirts. Even the Belgian girl had been prised into hers.

'Girls, stand in a line, please,' said Romain. 'You know which order you need to exit. As soon as Neneh's song is over, the show's hosts will announce the beginning of the contest. Run to the end of the stage and pose in front of the camera. Only when the hosts announce your name, should you turn around and run backstage. It's not a race; remember that you're wearing very high heels. Don't trip up on the cables and don't run into the next contestant unless you want to make a fool of yourself.'

My heartbeat grew louder and louder and seemed to fill my head, making my skull vibrate. My tongue felt furry and I was finding it difficult to breathe.

We lined up in a row and Romain kept an eye on the small screen showing the stage and put his hand on Florence's shoulder. As Jacques Connelli announced the beginning of the show, Romain tapped her shoulder once.

'Go!'

'She is named after an Italian city, lives in Belgium and she has a French boyfriend; everything points to an international career. Florence!' Jacques Connelli announced, as Florence ran up stiffly to the end of the runway in her tight pants.

She looked into the video camera and turn around when Jean thanked her. Out went Florence. In came Amber, swishing her hair.

'She believes that modelling is slightly superficial. In the event of victory tonight, she will have to take 'ficial' out of the word. It's Amber!' Lystelle Holly announced with a mellifluous voice.

Amber lingered in front of the audience for a few seconds longer, enjoying her short moment of glory and ran back out, haughtier than ever.

The other girls were pushed out one by one like pinballs. Sophie nervously stood in front of me. Romain put his hand firmly on Sophie's shoulder. His beautiful fingers were covered in silver rings. As I leaned forward to have a closer look at them, Romain patted Sophie's shoulder, which caused me to start and pull back.

Off went Sophie. As she stepped out, she tripped on a cable but just about managed to keep her balance. Sophie tried to appear composed as she stepped onto the mark on the floor, staring into the camera. I was the next in line, facing the dark curtain that separated me from the audience. Romain put one hand on my shoulder and another one on the curtain opening onto the stage. I got distracted from the show for a moment as I felt the warmth of Romain's touch.

'She believes that the other contestants are far more beautiful than she is. Should the jury contradict her tonight by giving her the lead, she won't bear them a grudge – Sophie!' Jacques Connelli announced.

Romain gently tapped my shoulder again and I ran out on stage. As I crossed paths with Sophie, I noticed the tears in her eyes.

'If the main selection criterion was the speed at which she swam 100 metres freestyle, she would cross the finishing line first, tonight. Marion!' Lystelle announced.

I was so high with excitement that I could barely fathom what she had actually said. My heart was about to explode.

As the last contestant left the stage, on went the Russian acrobats. I was almost totally absorbed by the gymnasts as they jumped and flipped across the stage. It was magical, but I wanted to check on Sophie. I found her sitting on a bench in the small staging area, crying. I dried her tears and tried to reassure her.

'Don't worry about it, you have other chances to appear on stage and show them what you're made of.'

'Everyone saw me. I have made a fool of myself in front of absolutely everyone! This is so embarrassing!' Sophie said.

Romain came up to us. 'Sophie, try not to let it get to you. It can happen to anyone, even to top models. So, come on, chin up. Put your bathing suit on and show them just how good you can be.'

Ten minutes later, we were in our flesh coloured underwear getting changed. It was neither the time nor the place to be shy. As I put my foot into my bathing suit, I looked up and met Romain's eyes. I lost my balance as my foot got stuck in the bathing suit and I hopped onto the other foot, affording him a good view of what I so desperately wanted to hide. I was mortified but soon in my uniform bathing suit and pink afro wig. Our designated make-up artists smeared our cheeks with bright pink blusher to complete what seemed to me like an utterly ridiculous look.

While the acrobats neared the end of their perfectly orchestrated show, we sneaked out unnoticed and stood on our marks. Sophie and I had to climb up the side stairs to a higher platform. When the acrobats left the arena, the spotlights swept the stage and revealed the girls' positions. We were poised on platforms in each corner of the stage.

The lights went off, thunder rumbled and the spotlights were suddenly directed towards the big top where Constantine sailed down from the roof on a trapeze in a cat suit.

'Good evening girls. Remember what I have taught you. Follow me!' he said after landing, on the firm ground, visibly relieved. Just as in our rehearsals, he started swaying his hips and arms to excess as he balanced his feet along an imaginary line. All the girls left their positions in turn and followed him with as much grace as possible.

I focused as hard as I could while I walked down the stairs urging myself not to fall. We glided to the end of the runway one after the other. As one contestant turned around, the next one skipped up the steps and eventually off the runway.

Once backstage, we ran to our make-up seats. More make-up was slathered on our faces and hair extensions were added giving me a long, thick ponytail. We ran back to the changing room in our underwear to put on our next outfit. Joseph stood with his bowed legs apart, staring at us with contempt as we scurried along, his arms folded across his chest in his habitually unimpressed-military-commander stance.

In the next sequence, I traded my swimming costume for a cat suit and sat astride a Harley Davidson motorcycle behind a topless male model. By now, I couldn't care less if Romain or any other man for that matter saw me half naked. I was now aware that my body did not belong to me anymore; it was a tool and I was learning how to use it.

Two cameramen, in seats on tracks were sliding across the floor. One was driving the dolly while the other one filmed the contestants on their roaring motorbikes. All the girls posed with attitude and ran their hands over the male models' bare torsos. My hunk was American. He was roughly my height and as blonde as I was dark. His skin was soft and it reacted to my touch with goose bumps. The notion of sexiness which had been a blur for the past seventeen years was becoming clearer by the minute. I was growing up fast.

The male models put their feet down and drove around the stage making a terrible noise. One by one, we drove out, trailing heavy fumes behind us.

Five minutes later, the lights grew dimmer. Musicians appeared on stage while we changed into our next outfits. When the lights returned, where the runway had been sixteen round platforms slowly rose from the ground. We walked in for the finale dressed in haute couture dresses. The male models came on wearing tuxedos, guiding us to our plinths. They kissed our hands and left the stage.

We stood still for a few seconds as the music started. The platforms rose again and started to spin slowly, as if we were ballerinas inside a huge music box. The male models appeared once more and showed all the contestants out for a final exit that was met with rapturous applause.

As the jury deliberated, more magicians and acrobats appeared, stunning the audience with their skills. Backstage the suspense was unbearable.

'That was amazing!' I exclaimed to Sophie, who had now cheered up a bit.

'But I am glad it's over. It was so stressful!'

'Champagne, girls! Good job everyone,' Romain announced.

He seemed relieved. His smile revealed a perfect set of teeth. We gathered around a small TV screen to see what was happening on stage. Everyone was busily trying to decipher what the jury might be saying to each other through their lip or eyebrow movements.

My heart was racing. *I have just lived the most exciting day of my life*, I thought. It was a very different feeling altogether than the one I felt during the swimming nationals where I was caught up in the anger and disappointment of failure. During the final I had felt beside myself with excitement, transformed into a beautiful Cinderella for one night of my life. I still could not believe my own luck to be part of the fashion world, even if it only lasted until the end of the show.

At last, top models Melinda, Brittani and Julia walked to the middle of the stage. They were dressed in knock-out couture dresses and were ready to announce the three lucky winners. We all wriggled nervously as we awaited our fate.

Melinda took the microphone to her lips. 'Ladies and Gentlemen, good evening. In the light of tonight's contest, the third place goes to… Florence!'

Beaming, Florence stepped out onto the set to thunderous applause and stood next to Julia who congratulated her. Backstage we all looked at each other desperately.

'Second place goes to… Sophie!' Melinda said.

'Sophie! Well done!' I hugged my bewildered friend.

Sophie walked out onto the stage with a faint '*Amazing*!' muttered under her breath. Brittani took her hand and kissed her.

'In first place...'

Melinda paused.

'The winner of this year's Icon Model Competition is...'

She paused again.

The wait was unbearable.

'Marion!'

If felt as if a ten tonne weight had just hit me square in the stomach. My legs gave way. I could hardly stay standing up. I took a moment to just sit and a wide grin split my face in two. My arms went limp at my side and, my feet felt as if they were stuck in quicksand.

Lystelle Holly had to venture backstage to drag me out onto the stage.

'Well done, Marion!' Jacques Connelli's words boomed around the auditorium. 'You have won a one-year contract with Icon worth two hundred and fifty thousand francs!' He handed me a pair of car keys. 'And a car!'

'She is too young to drive, she's not yet eighteen,' Lystelle commented, eliciting a laugh from the audience. 'She hasn't even finished school yet!'

My heart was pounding and my temples throbbed. I kept a firm grip on both Lystelle's and Jacques' hands, and felt that if they let go I would fall over. I was like a puppet held upright by two strings. The world around me was muffled and someone had pressed the slow-motion button. I tried to take it in as all the other girls embraced me and patted me effusively, even Amber, much against her will.

As I returned backstage, laughing with the other contestants, someone tapped me on the shoulder.

'Can I please have my car keys back?'

Before I was able to process the question, a lady plucked the keys from my hand.

'What's going on?' Sophie asked.

'Am I not getting a car? Was it just part of the show?' I suddenly felt like a fool.

'Did you really expect that the car would be parked outside and that you would drive straight off home?' the lady said.

I was speechless. The magic was shattered.

Sophie took me by the hand and dragged me away to the after-party. Black-clad waiters stood up straight with their hands tucked behind their backs in front of a display of ramekins, canapés, sushi and other delicacies. Rows of crystal glasses formed a perfect square on each side of the white tablecloth waiting to be filled with bubbles and delight. Waiters circulated trays amongst the thick crowd of designers, magazine editors, and other fashionistas. I wished my mother could have been there to see it.

Still disoriented, I followed Sophie as we sidled up to the bar. People held their breath and nodded in consent. Squeezing myself through steamrollers of people, I felt as if I had been squished into a fine spread by the time I reached the bar. I gulped down my fruit juice and reached out for a porcelain spoon filled with sushi and foie gras. The pan-fried liver coated with caramelised sugar melted in my mouth and the effect on my taste buds was scintillating. I had never tasted food like that before. As I turn around, Lulu was towering over me, batting his eyelashes.

'Darling, you were the most beautiful tonight. I knew it would be you.'

His laughter echoed in my head.

PART TWO

PARIS

CHAPTER 6

Marion, The Adventure Begins, Paris, September 1996

When I had first set foot in Paris, I had been overwhelmed by the sheer size and dirtiness of it. The air was stuffy and the sky was sunless. Now the sense of feeling lost amidst the flow of grey people rushing in and out of metro stations was still as present as it had been the previous year on that astonishing, life-changing trip as a contestant in the Icon Modelling competition.

Paris was like a heart whose blood pumped day and night. At 5 a.m. sharp every morning the sweepers rhythmically cleaned the streets in preparation for the millions of pairs of feet that were due to step on them. Then the lorries took over, beeping and belching smelly fumes from their exhaust pipes. Deliveries had to be made, bread had to be kneaded and baked, the newspaper stands had to be filled to display the morning news.

Each day I was soon out among the hustle and bustle, taking the metro to every corner of the city, and occasionally getting lost trying to navigate my well-worn map of the Parisian metro right and wrong. I was swept across Paris for my casting with a map in one hand and my bag in the other. The wind once snatched away my list of appointments, hurling the fragile paper into a puddle, mixing my meetings into a soggy blur.

An average day for me went something like this:

8 a.m. : Board the metro.

9 a.m. : Yves Saint Laurent fitting, Avenue George V, thirty minutes wait, two minutes fitting. I'm too big.

10 a.m. : Casting on Villa Verte in the 11th District for an ice cream company. I'm late. Fifteen girls of every shape and size are there before me.

12 noon: Glamour Magazine, Central Paris. Twenty-five girls have arrived before me and many more are still to come. They feel I'm too 'new'.

1.30 p.m. : Photographer's agent, the suburbs. One hour wait, two minutes on my portfolio.

3 p.m. : Casting at Icon. I'm starving. More waiting.

4.30 p.m. : Casting for L'Oreal. They want straight hair, mine is curly.

5.30 p.m. : Another photographer's agents. Thankfully they are just around the corner from my flat. Another waste of time.

6.30 p.m. : Finally, I get home, eat what's left in the fridge: ham and tomatoes. Not much of a dinner. My stomach rumbles as I lie down in bed.

All in all seven castings. Ten hours rushing around the streets of Paris. No call-backs. Time to try again tomorrow.

***

As the days went by, I realised that the agency was shooting me in all directions with no strategy in mind. It would have been better to choose selectively and save their ammunition. Despite her second place in the Icon Contest, Sophie never started a modelling career and instead she went to University. I was the lucky winner and yet I was beginning to see her point of view.

The agency decided to put me up in Emmanuel's flat while he was at his sick mother's. It was a big empty bachelor pad that smelled of mould and cum. Past a certain time of night, I tended to watch over my shoulder as I approached the main door. The pavement that ran alongside Boulevard Brune was always empty in the evening, giving the street an eerie feel. After the turmoil of the day, time ground to a halt around 10 p.m. I would slip into bed, stretch my sore limbs, reassess the day and gather my thoughts for the next morning and its attendant battles.

It was the evening before my first photo test. I desperately needed decent pictures for my portfolio, which I would show at castings. It was a necessary but costly evil. Icon had selected an American photographer called James, another one of Emmanuel's finds and we all met for dinner the night before at La Grande Coupole, a famous Parisian brasserie. James was a former male model who had wound his way into photography not so much out of passion, but necessity. You couldn't rely on modelling forever if you could even rely on it at all. I tried hard to perceive his model's characteristics but couldn't find any as his bad skin and sparse hair did not strike me as particularly attractive.

Judging by the way he dressed and carried himself Emmanuel must have thought himself ten years younger than he actually was. He and James ostentatiously ordered a seafood platter to share and I stuck to something I could eat without using my fingers, not wanting to risk sending a claw flying across the restaurant.

I didn't understand how Emmanuel could eat oysters, to me they looked repulsive and smelled like the worst part of the ocean, and, I was told, they are alive!'

'If you close your eyes,' said Emmanuel, 'they taste of seaside, sun burn, waves, holidays…' and he proceeded to swallow oysters whole one after another.

My throat tightened in disgust.

'I have just had the most excellent idea,' said Emmanuel between slurps of oyster, 'Since we're shooting at my place tomorrow, James why don't you come over and we can all sleep there, so we can start bright and early, with no commute. What do you say?'

'Good idea, Manu,' James said as he broke the crab's claw with a pair of pliers.

I was too busy focusing on the breaking, the gulping, the dripping and the belching to really take it in but somewhere in the back of my mind a distinct sense of unease had crept in.

'Shall we go to *Les Bains* for an hour or so and then go home? What do you say Marion? It's still early.'

My watch said 11 p.m. Emmanuel's second genius idea made me realise that I had a total misconception of what being fresh for work meant in the fashion industry.

Les Bains Douches was the best club in town; a home from home for the famous and infamous and the exceptionally wealthy. I felt special to be even going there. I hoped this was a taste of the glamorous things to come. When we arrived there was a huge queue building up outside. Despite his short stature, Emmanuel walked straight up to the doorman, snubbing the queue.

'We're three tonight.'

The bulky doorman let us in with a nod. It was not only my first night out in Paris but also my first time in a club ever. I wasn't quite sure what to expect and the imposing bouncer played an intimidating role. Emmanuel kissed an older blonde lady standing next to the bouncer. They exchanged a few inaudible words and laughed heartedly, which led me to think that Emmanuel had some form of stake in the ownership of the place.

'This place used to be an old Turkish bath,' Emmanuel explained.

I trailed after Emmanuel and James as we were being escorted directly to what we had been told was a VIP area. The dimly lit ground floor had a smoke-filled bar and restaurant area which was buzzing like a beehive even though it was close to midnight. Glamorous waitresses dressed in black walked by with their platters up in the air, which looked as if they might fall at any minute on the immaculately coiffured heads of the crowd.

Emmanuel, James and I walked down a staircase studded with blue lights towards the club and they looked amused by my open-mouthed expression. We passed giggling girls in high heels and flattering dresses and impeccably groomed boys smoking cigarettes. In my simple black dress and no make-up, I felt slightly uncomfortable, very under-dressed and utterly provincial.

We could see people looking at us, trying to fathom who we were and whether my companions and I were famous which served to make me feel even more self-conscious. The thumping music was so loud that talking was out of the question and the dance-floor was packed wall to wall with a crowd jumping and throwing themselves around in a trance. I found myself feeling vaguely envious of the others who were able to so easily and naturally stalk through the crowd, but I was still entirely distracted by the size and strangeness of the place. The VIP area was a small separated space delineated by red ropes where models and men in suits lounged on velvet red sofas, sharing champagne.

'What would you like to drink?' Emmanuel asked.

I tore my gaze from the dance floor. 'Thanks,' I said. 'Could I have a juice of some kind?'

'You don't drink?' asked Emmanuel.

'Not alcohol, no.'

When it came, my juice tasted sharply of vodka and after a few minutes I could feel my head start to spin and my hands felt moist.

'You'll be fine here,' James said comfortingly. He put a long-fingered hand on my thigh. 'You can drink in peace with no risk of anyone dropping a funny pill in your glass and no nasty morning surprises, like waking up in a strange bed,' he smirked.

My head suddenly cleared. I pushed his hand away from my thigh. James laughed, put his arm behind me on the back of the sofa and started moving his head to the beat.

***

Day was breaking by the time Emmanuel, James and I crawled back to the flat. Emmanuel staggered as far as the living-room before passing out drunk on the floor.

'Should we help him to his room?' I asked.

'He's alright, he's fast asleep,' James said as he lumbered slowly down the corridor behind me.

When he got to me, he took hold of my arm and pulled me against him. The alcohol had made my body limp and clumsy, but I stiffened as he grabbed me.

'What are you doing?' I asked as we stumbled down the hall. James pinned me against the wall and started groping my breasts. 'Get away from me!'

I panicked and called out to Emmanuel but James suffocated my screams by clamping his mouth onto mine. I moaned in disgust. He reeked of alcohol. I tried to turn my head away but to no avail, it was caught in his vice-like grip. I squirmed, kicked and wriggled but could not free myself; he was pressing me hard against the wall. James trailed his hand over my body and jammed his hand between my legs while he rubbed his body against mine.

Tears rolled down my cheeks and my pulse was thundering in my head. I gathered all my strength and kneed him below the waist. He grunted and fell to the floor in pain, cupping his hands over his groin. I rushed to my bedroom and locked myself in. With my back against the door, I slid down it, trembling with my hands over my face. Then my whole body started almost shaking and I was panting and trying to get in enough oxygen. My mind was a mess of images and feelings of what had just happened and what Christophe had done to me at the beginning of the year. Being sexually molested twice was too much for me to process and I prayed that if I pushed both their attacks to the back of my mind, I would find the strength to face James.

Beyond the door, there was no sound. *There's nothing better than a good old last resort kick in the nuts* I thought, and although I was in shock, the giggles set in.

A few hours later, there was a knock on my door. Startled, I sat up in my bed and drew the sheets around me. *Please God, not James.*

'Marion! Time to get ready!' came Emmanuel's voice. 'We'd like to start the shoot soon. We're in the living room, alright? I've made coffee. Hell, I need it.'

I struggled out of bed, dreading seeing James. Last night was like a bad dream, but the pain in my heart told me it was real. I took a quick shower and put on my jeans and t-shirt. Barefoot, I walked stealthily into the living room, studiously avoiding eye contact with him.

James was busy preparing his cameras and pulling the reels out of the packages.

'Good morning! Did you sleep well?' James asked innocently.

'Not great,' I said pointedly.

'Here, have some of this while it's still hot,' Emmanuel said, handing me a smoking mug of black coffee.

'I'll fetch some milk and sugar. I have this horrible after taste from last night,' I said searching James for any kind of reaction.

'It's probably the alcohol!' he replied, unabashed. His cigarette drooped limply from his lips and the smoke hindered his vision.

I leaned on the kitchen counter and stirred my coffee that seemed to get larger and larger as I could feel myself zoning out as my body struggled to rationalise what had happened in the cold light of morning. It seemed almost as if little push would be all it would take to fall into the mug and drown in the black swirling hole. I breathed in, got a good grip of my coffee mug and walked out of the kitchen with murder on my mind. I neared James at a brisk pace, boiling coffee in my hand, ready to hurl it at him. As I reached him, my hands started shaking.

'Careful! Your coffee is dripping on my carpet. You'll burn yourself!' Emmanuel hurried to take the mug from my hands.

'You wouldn't want to get burnt today, darling,' James said, without flinching. 'Take your top off and put on this poncho. You can keep your jeans on.'

'That's too kind of you, James!' I finally managed to say.

'My pleasure! Now sit down on the table. There is some good daylight right there which should erase your dark circles,' he tutted as if he was in no way responsible for my tired looks.

I stood silently. My eyes were throwing spears at him.

'Very good! I love your angry look. Turn your head this way for me, please. That's my girl.'

A couple of hours and outfits later, Emmanuel called it a day. I wanted James gone and would have gladly thrown the sleaze and his camera out of the window if I could have. I left him to pack up and went back to my bedroom.

'We're off!' Emmanuel said as he had popped his head round the door. 'Well done, Marion, I think we have some nice shots. James will bring a selection of pictures in a couple of days. Come to the agency tomorrow. Take the rest of the day off, alright?'

When I heard the front door slam, I rushed over to it and bolted it. Then I grabbed the phone and dialled the agency's number.

'Icon Models, good afternoon!' said Florent, my temporary booker. While I was building my portfolio, I was stuck in the New Faces department where I was in limbo before my career as a model took a serious, professional turn. .

'Florent, it's Marion.'

'I'm sorry, who is it?'

'Marion! Marion Durant'

'Hello, darling, I'm sorry I was distracted with some paper work. What's up?'

I rolled my eyes and explained my ordeal.

'Are you sure that you didn't lead him on?'

I couldn't believe he was being so laissez-faire about this. I was seething. Maybe it was because he was a man that he wasn't taking this seriously.

'Would I be calling you to complain if I had led him on?'

'I'm sorry to hear that. It's never happened before. I'll make sure I speak to him—'

'I want to move out!' I interrupted him. 'I want to move out now. I cannot bear to stay one minute more in this hell hole.'

'Where will you stay?' Florent said, absent-mindedly.

'Put your damn paperwork down and listen to me. Check what's available in the models' flat. I'm on my way to pick up the keys.'

I slammed down the receiver, my hands were shaking. I sat down for a minute to catch my breath, then sprang to my feet and rushed to my bedroom to pack up my belongings.

CHAPTER 7

Marion, The Agency, Paris, September 1996

When I walked into the agency, shortly after six in the evening, the office was largely abandoned with almost all bookers away attending shows as part of fashion week. I stormed past the main booking desk, which was strewn with papers left in haste and made a beeline for the New Faces department. Florent was thin, boyish man with a bookish look about him. When I arrived he was sitting upright in his chair drumming his fingers nervously on his desk. He certainly didn't look like he'd had much experience. After a few seconds, he pushed his round spectacles up his nose and looked up at me with an affected smile.

'As it's show season most of our flats are full. There is one left, but you'll have to share with Betina, Elena and Amirit. That's the only option I have right now, I'm afraid. Betina's Danish – she's very nice, you'll see. I'm sure you'll get along well. Amirit is Israeli. She joined the agency this summer. You're very lucky – she's never around, always travelling. And Elena arrived a few days ago from a little town in Russia. Her mother stayed with her for a few days but had to go home to attend her market stall. Elena is very discreet; she hardly speaks French or English. I should imagine it's a major culture shock for her to come to Paris, it could be good for her to have someone like you around. You'll probably meet her when she's back from her castings.'

'Fine. Where is the flat?'

My face was inscrutable.

'Rue de la Sourdière, in the first district,' Florent said as he handed me the keys. 'Betina has been working today but should be back anytime now.'

Not long afterwards I was sitting in a taxi with my suitcase was in the boot, heading towards the heart of the city. Something had been stirred within me. I felt somehow older and wearier. I rolled down the window and let the breaths of cramped Parisian air fill my lungs while the driver honked his way through traffic.

'There you are Miss. Forty five francs please. Plus two francs for the luggage,' the taxi driver said as he turn around towards me. 'Do you need a receipt?'

I was too weary to argue about the extra charge. I handed him a fifty francs banknote. 'Keep the change.'

Rue de la Sourdière was located in Central Paris. It was a dark narrow street, winding up towards a small market place, away from the luxurious boutiques of Rue Saint-Honoré. I opened the narrow door of the building and dragged my suitcase up the tight staircase and after a few moments struggling with the lock, I let myself into the flat.

When I finally got in, every wall of the small open-plan studio was covered with mirrors which were plainly designed to give the illusion of space. In one corner of the studio were two bunk beds. One was made up and was clearly intended to be my bed as it had a fresh towel on the end. I resigned myself to the fact that there would be little privacy in this new home.

The narrow doors of a closet beside the bathroom door hid a kitchen with two hotplates and a small fridge under the sink, which was bare apart from one lonely carton of milk. A few dirty spoons and bowls with dried cereal flakes were piled up in the sink. Across the other side of the studio was a bathroom crammed full with beauty products. It was going to be cramped but *home sweet home*.

I squatted in front of the small TV and pressed the on button. Black and white confetti danced on the screen but I could discern the voice of Georges Orleans, a news journalist through the static. I looked at my watch – it must have been the eight o'clock news. I tried to move the antenna around in order to find a decent picture but to no avail. At that moment, I heard someone's keys jangling and as I turned around with my arm up brandishing the TV antenna, a gorgeous red-headed girl walked in, wearing a summer dress. Her face was heavily made-up which jarred with her girlish body. She frowned for a short moment as she saw me, but her deep green eyes quickly softened as I smiled at her.

'Forget about the TV. It's a lost cause unless you're willing to stand with your arm up in the air all night!' Betina said as she kicked off her sandals and dropped off her grocery bag, she couldn't have been more than sixteen years old. 'I'm Betina, by the way,' she said as she stretched her hand out. 'Florent didn't tell me you'd be there, but welcome anyway!'

'I'm Marion... Sorry to intrude on your space,' I replied, uneasy.

'Don't worry about it at all, I'm used to it!' Betina was busy rummaging through her bag. She took out some milk and cereal along with a few cans of Diet Coke.

'Want one?'

Betina threw a can at me. I hadn't anticipated the move and I caught it just as it was about to hit the floor. I took the can to the kitchen in case it was too shaken to open. When I did open it the Coke overflowed everywhere and Betina took the towel that was on my bunk and casually mopped the floor with it. Dumbfounded, I looked at my bath towel being smeared with dark, sticky Diet Coke.

'Have you been in Paris long?' Betina asked.

'A week,' I replied as she sat down on the sofa. 'You?'

'Six months, more or less,' Betina sighed, as she massaged her sore feet.

'Do you like it so far?'

'It started off well enough, but now I feel like I'm stuck in first gear, unable to move any faster, if you know what I mean.' Betina gazed silently to the ceiling for a few seconds then sprang to her feet. 'Right! I'm going to take a quick shower. Make yourself at home. You can share Amirit's chest of drawers – that's the one on the left hand side over there. You can't miss it. Amirit has loads of pictures of her family on top of it,' she said as she pointed at a dilapidated chest of drawers with its contents hanging out at odd angles.

Unabashed, Betina took off her dress as she walked away, revealing her frail figure. She threw her dress on the floor and left the bathroom door ajar while she took her shower. Five minutes later, she walked out of the bathroom wrapped in a towel. Betina slipped her knickers on and let the towel drop down to her feet, flashing her small breasts.

'What do you think about them? Should I have them done?'

Betina pushed her breast upward and sighed at her sad little boobs.

'Personally, I find surgery scary, I wouldn't…' I replied, slightly taken aback by her openness.

'The surgeon said that at sixteen the tissue will scar easily, but getting a boob job is really quite a common thing to do now,' Betina replied.

Betina took a small bottle out of her bag and shook out a little blue pill. She then sat down next to me and swallowed it with a sip of Diet Coke.

'What are those for?' I asked.

'They help me relax and sleep better,' Betina replied, as she put her bathrobe on and opened the kitchenette doors. 'Have you eaten yet?'

'I was planning to go and buy some groceries, but it's getting late and I am too tired to go out again. It's been a long day.'

'I know exactly what you mean. I just bought some cereal if you want some?' Betina said over her shoulder.

'Is that your dinner?'

'It's quick, filling and not fattening. Or at least, that's what's the box says!'

As we ate our cereal, I thought about my family and pictured the lovely meal they were probably having that night. I could smell the roast chicken in the oven, the scent of basmati rice and slow cooked ratatouille. I remembered how my dad religiously caramelised the onions, and added in tomatoes, aubergines and courgettes in a strict sequence. I sighed and made a promise to myself to have something more substantial than cereal the next day.

Betina climbed up the ladder to the top bed across from mine and pulled an envelope out of her handbag. Lifting her mattress, she tugged a wad of banknotes out of a small black purse studded with sequins. She wrapped a few banknotes in a white piece of paper, tucked it into the envelope, and sealed the flap. She then put everything away and rested her handbag against a pile of books on a shelf above her head, on top of which sat a small red-headed doll. She selected a book and started reading. I took this as my cue and decided to unpack my things so she could have some quiet time.

Amirit had lots of framed photographs of her family and friends: Amirit with her father, Amirit at the beach, Amirit with her siblings or friends, Amirit with a girlfriend. A beautiful strawberry-blonde girl with long curly hair smiled out from nearly every picture. Amirit's presence was pervading the bedroom, even in her absence.

Amirit's clothes had been rolled up into balls and carelessly thrown into the drawers. Like a dutiful housewife, I spent the next half hour folding her clothes into the lower drawers, to make a bit of space for my own. As I fumbled at the bottom of one drawer, my fingers brushed against what felt like paper. I pondered for a moment, gave a quick look over my shoulder in Betina's direction – she was lying on her side, facing the opposite wall – *all clear* – I extracted the sheets of paper, feeling like a trespasser. They were Amirit's monthly statements from Icon Models. I wet my index finger and flipped through. Each monthly statement added up to thousands. I was flabbergasted.

I heard someone at the door and hastily hid the papers under my jumper. Elena walked in gracefully. She looked like a ballerina; her beautiful thin legs carried her lightly and her hair was up in a perfect bun. Small pearl earrings dangled from her ears and swayed gently. She had brown almond-shaped eyes, high cheek bones and satin-smooth skin. Her lips parted in a faint smile as I stepped towards her.

'Hello Elena, I'm Marion,' I began. I pointed pathetically at my bags, which were still lying on the floor.

Betina leaned over and waved at Elena.

Elena waved back and smiled. She batted her eyelashes gently, looking for words. There was an awkward silence. She placed her bag on top of her bedside table next to a black lacquered box and a small mirror. She folded her denim jacket on her colourful bedspread where a teddy bear sat amongst the pillows.

'That's a beautiful box!' I commented, trying to make conversation.

'My father made it,' Elena replied shyly in her thick Russian accent, looking for words. 'This is Snow-maiden, daughter of Fairy Spring and Father Frost,' she pointed at the lady with the skin as pale as salt and hair down to her waist. 'One day, in the forest, she hears a beautiful melody. Lyel's flute. The Snow-maiden could not step out of the shade because the Sun God's er… rays would kill her.' As she told her story, her eyes lit up and words unravelled more easily in a disjointed manner. She had very little inflection in her voice, rolled her 'r's and hissed the other consonants. 'Until there is this one day when, her growing love made her walk out of the forest and into the open fields where he was playing. The sun lights up her beauty at its fullest for one great and perfect moment – and in front of Lyel's eyes she melted.'

She softly smiled as she put away her box and made her way towards the bathroom, which I came to realise was the only place of retreat in the flat; the place where we could remove our make-up, pray, cry or just sit and think quietly.

***

The next morning I was keen to get myself sorted out, and I was famished. Betina had just gulped down another bowl of cereal, close to half a litre of Diet Coke, and had gone back to bed. I jerked on the window handle and popped my head outside. A soothing breeze swirled down from the clear blue sky and caressed my face. I took a deep breath and closed my eyes for a few seconds.

'I'm going out to buy some groceries, do you guys need anything?' I told my roommates.

'I can't think right now,' Betina mumbled, still half asleep, ruffled up in bed.

As I came out of the bathroom few minutes later, ready to start my day, Elena was standing by the front door with an empty hessian bag.

'I guess you're coming along!' I said with a smile.

I grabbed my handbag and ignored the habitual mess of the flat.

Elena led me to the nearest supermarket. We had underestimated the late September temperature, which had dropped significantly in the last week. Elena wore a flowery dress and her denim jacket. I had opted for stone-washed jeans and a long beige silk V-neck top.

My Roman sandals revealed the only sign of my coquetry – my red toenails. My curly untamed black hair bobbed around my face and it felt good.

Communication was difficult given the language barrier, but I found Elena's company comforting. She was a sweet girl and I was growing fond of her.

As we reached the supermarket, Elena came to a sudden halt and gawped at the colourful window display. I followed her through the entire food department; she couldn't believe her eyes. Eventually, she stood, arms limp at her sides, staring at the fruit and vegetable stall, paralysed by choice.

'Do you need some help choosing?' I asked.

Elena nodded.

'Right. Why don't you take some courgettes, carrots…?' I paused as I realised that Elena's attention had been distracted by the melons and nectarines. 'These are yummy, sweet. You should have some,' I lifted the fruit up in front of Elena. Elena carefully placed them in her bag. Forty minutes later, after much hesitation and dawdling, Elena was walking with me to the till with cheese she had never eaten, ripe bananas that she had never tasted and bread and milk she did not have to queue for and without having to get a stamp in a ration book.

'I'm sorry but your card has been declined,' the cashier told me as I gazed at the jar of ratatouille, the fruits and rice I had placed on the counter.

'Declined?' I asked, surprised.

'Insufficient funds, apparently. Do you have another card?'

Embarrassed, I slowly put my card back into my wallet and took out my last banknotes.

As soon as I was back in the flat, I dialled the agency's number. The phone rang, and Florent picked up.

'Icon Models, good morning!'

'Hi Florent, it's Marion Durant. Can I be put through to accounting please?' I said while nervously tapping my fingers on the desk.

'There is no one at accounting at this time, Marion. You can have an appointment with them tomorrow when you come in,' Florent replied in a honeyed voice.

I stopped tapping my fingers and hung up, fulminating.

'What's wrong?' asked Betina, getting out of bed.

'Everything's wrong!' I replied. 'I am so fed up with Florent. He's absolutely useless.'

I was still feeling a little taken aback by apparently having no money in my account at all and I still hadn't heard anything about how far he had got with James. Elena was standing close to me, holding two cups of hot tea. Her hair was down to her shoulders and framed her beautiful face.

'Thank you for... help earlier!' she said with a hesitant voice and a reassuring smile.

'You're welcome, Elena,' I replied as I cupped my hands around the mug.

***

After a thirty minutes subway ride, Elena pushed the heavy door of the building where the agency held its headquarters and pressed the button for the elevator. We stood in silence on the way up to the second floor. Then she put her hand on the agency's door knob, took a deep breath and pushed it open.

The agency bustled with people; models chatted amongst themselves or with their bookers while they waited for their daily schedule. Gus, the head booker, swivelled on his seat as he caught sight of Elena. He held up one hand to get her attention and cradled his phone in the other.

'Elena!' He waved at Elena. 'This way please!'

Elena walked toward Gus, the booking prodigy with greasy scraggly hair and leather trousers. He stood up and walked towards her; his thick legs were squeezed into his tight trousers and each button of his white shirt was threatening to burst free.

He put his hand on Elena's shoulder and walked with her towards the wall next to his desk. I stood by the entrance for a moment and watched Elena being scrutinised like a racehorse. Gus grabbed his Polaroid camera and took a few shots of her against the white background. He then reached out for the tape measure and took her hip, waist and breast measurements.

'85-60-85' Gus told his assistant, a red head with freckles who willingly jolted down the numbers in Elena's file. 'High cheek bones, beautiful skin, sticking to her measurements,' Gus commented while his assistant stalled, wondering whether she should write those details down. Elena looked at Gus and his assistant in a daze, while they exchanged words about her in French. 'I am thinking of sending her to the Chanel beauty casting. Is it still on today?' Gus asked.

His assistant checked her file. 'It is!' she said with a grin.

'Perfect! Call them and tell them Elena is on her way. Don't take your Book along. It's not strong enough to secure a booking like Chanel, but in person you might just do it.' He released Elena by patting her on her shoulder.

Elena waved goodbye and told me she was off to her first important casting.

***

Elena had been to many other castings but they hardly paid anything. Despite her innocence she realised that modelling for Monoprix supermarket wasn't going to launch her international career. She was not sure whether she should be excited or scared. Everything had happened so fast and the language barrier did not make things any easier.

She walked towards the subway station and down the stairs with a natural elegance. Her long thin legs moved gracefully. People hurried to work, elbowing her as she stood on the train at a loss, looking for directions. She extracted her subway pass from her bag and gently made way towards the turnstiles. A young boy wearing baggy jeans and a baseball cap bumped into her as he ran past her, jumping over the turnstile and before disappearing off into the hoards of people. Once Elena had recovered her balance, she tucked her shirt into her skirt and blew a stray lock of hair away from her face. Having regained her composure, she fumbled in her bag for her subway pass.

She suddenly realised that her wallet was missing. Panic-stricken, she looked inside her bag once more, only to confirm that the young boy had stolen her purse. She threw her arms limply down by her sides and, bewildered, looked around for help. Reluctantly, she made her way towards the platform and waited for the green and white subway, holding her bag tightly against her chest.

When she reached her destination, the casting was almost over. A few girls sat with their book on their laps, waiting to be seen by the photographer and the art director. As Elena entered the room, the photographer, Greg Salome, whispered a few words to the art director's ear. Greg was a tall dark man with curly hair and a friendly smile.

'Let's have a look at the girl who just arrived,' he said as he waved Elena to come closer.

She gave a sheepish glance to the other girls and made hesitant steps towards the photographer. He looked up at her with relish.

'High cheekbones, almond-shaped eyes, and a beautiful figure. She has that unusual Eastern beauty. What do you think?'

The art director, a skinny blonde woman with short hair, nodded and asked Elena for her portfolio but Elena did seem to understand.

'*Book*? Do you have a *Book*?' The art director insisted with a stern face.

'She doesn't have a Book, Laurie, Gus called and said she was new,' Greg interjected and smiled at Elena.

Greg stood up and asked Elena to follow him. Once she was sitting on a stool, he put his hands on her shoulders and turned her sideways.

'Please put your head down and look into the camera. No smile.' He twisted her shoulders gently so she would understand. Turned sideways, Elena shyly looked at him. He pulled her chin down gently. 'Stay like that please. Don't move. Yes, that's it. Very nice!'

Elena felt blinded by all the light boxes that flooded the set. She couldn't see a thing and could only guess that the photographer was now positioned behind his camera.

'Good, thank you. Come with me,' He waved her towards him.

He went back to the table followed by Elena. He showed the Polaroids to the art director and looked at Elena once more.

'Thank you Elena. Thanks for coming.' He smiled and nodded.

Elena smiled back shyly and turned around hesitantly. As she walked out, she tried to avoid any eye contact with the other girls waiting to be seen by the photographer and made her way back to the agency to sort out the problem of her stolen purse Paris could be such a rough city, she thought, hoping the agency would give her a stipend to help her out.

***

I returned home from an uneventful day of castings, to find Amirit sitting on the floor, unpacking her bags. Her suitcase was wide open and her clothes were strewn all over the wooden floor.

'Hi! You must be Amirit!' I said, a little uneasy as I hadn't been expecting her.

Amirit startled and turned around. 'Oh, hi! And *you* must be Marion,' Amirit replied without a smile. 'The agency told me you'd be coming' Amirit continued with a cold unfriendly tone.

I sat down on the bed, at a loss for words, feeling unwelcome as Amirit twisted up her hair into a soft bun and continued rummaging through her bags, totally ignoring me. Her skin was naturally tanned and contrasted nicely with the colour of her hair. She wore white jeans and a white tank top that gave her a really healthy complexion.

'Are you going to stay for a while?' I asked, hoping to lift her mood.

'I have nothing planned for the next two weeks, which freaks me out. I might go to New York soon and try the market there for a few months. Paul Newhouse, the founder of Icon is flying over from New York this week to select a few girls to introduce to the American market. I hope he'll take me along,' Amirit replied without turning around.

'I'm sure he will!' I said reassuringly, not really quite sure why going to the US meant so much.

Amirit stood up, put a pile of folded clothes in her drawer and kicked the dirty ones into a heap to be washed later. As she didn't seem to be very open, I decided to leave her to it and walked towards the kitchenette where Elena had started cooking. A spicy smell emanated from the stove, which ignited our appetites. It smelled like a proper meal. I leaned against the wall by the kitchenette and watched her deftly handle the knife.

'You're a much better cook than me, that's for sure!' I said as I poured the canned ratatouille I had bought that morning out onto a plate.

'No one can beat your canned veggies or my cereals!' Betina added with a giggle as she poured some milk into her bowl.

'No Betina, that's for sure!' I replied with a laugh. 'You should be careful though, I don't see how a cereal diet can be healthy in the long run. You need veggies and proteins.'

'Yes, Mummy!' Betina said as she put her free arm around my shoulder. 'But it's much easier to eat cereals when four people are fighting over a stove in such a crammed place!'

'Point taken,' I replied with a smile and kissed Betina on the cheek.

Amirit walked over to the fridge and stood there blankly for a few seconds. She mechanically took out some cheese, pickled gherkins, and some salad and made herself a sandwich.

'Are you having cold veggies?' Amirit asked, wrinkling her nose in disgust.

'Ratatouille can be eaten cold. It's pretty good, want to try some?' I offered with a smile.

'No thanks, I think I'll pass,' Amirit said coldly as she devoured her sandwich. Amirit seemed to be determined to kill the friendly spirit. We all ate quietly while Elena continued stirring her dish. Elena turned down the flame and went to the bathroom for a moment and Amirit took advantage. She leaned over the stove, lifted the lid, stirred the contents with the wooden spoon, and took a generous helping of Elena's goulash.

'Amirit! That's Elena's food!' I exclaimed in a high pitch voice, stunned by such boldness. 'You can't just go ahead and help yourself!'

'She won't know, there's plenty left,' Amirit said unphased as she wolfed down what was on her plate.

A couple of minutes later, Elena came back out of the bathroom and noticed that the spoon had been removed from the pot and licked clean. She turned around in a questioning manner but Amirit was busy looking down at the apple she was peeling. Elena's eyes locked onto mine for a moment and she turned back slowly towards the stove. She put the wooden spoon into the sink and took another utensil. I stared angrily at Amirit who stood up, knotted the rubbish bag and stormed out of the flat. I ran after her hoping to catch her in the corridor.

'Why didn't you just ask her?' I asked Amirit as she walked stealthily towards the staircase. 'She would have given you some!'

'Communists are used to sharing, aren't they?' Amirit said with a smirk as she rushed downstairs.

I was shocked. 'How can you say something so awful?' I hissed, running behind her.

'Come on, it's not the end of the world, I was hungry and she doesn't understand anything, so I couldn't ask her, OK?' Amirit retorted in a clipped voice.

'She understands more than you think and she doesn't deserve to be derided like that!'

'Well, at least, *she* doesn't have to be in the army for two years risking her life!' Amirit sputtered.

I grabbed her arm to stop her, 'What does that have to do with anything?' I asked Amirit who was now facing me on the doorstep.

'You seem to know about *communists*, but do you *know* that *I* can't go back to my country, for fear that they'll force me into the military service for two years. I'll probably be punished for running away in the first place.' Amirit was on a roll. 'It doesn't stop there, I married an old man so I wouldn't have to do the military duty… my parents don't even know about all that, of course, because I'm such a coward… they even expect me back next month!' Amirit paused and stared at me. 'How is that for a shocker?' The veins of her neck had swollen.

'Who did you marry?' I asked softly, no longer thinking of the goulash.

Amirit's lips started trembling and I wondered if she'd ever told anyone this before.

'Emmanuel found him for me,' she said in a small voice. 'It all started when he scouted me in Tel Aviv, on the beach and promised me a wonderful career. I saw it as the perfect opportunity to flee my responsibilities. The only way I could escape the military service was by being either married or pregnant.' Amirit paced back and forth, wringing her hands nervously. 'As there was no way I was going to get knocked up by some random guy, I married a husband of convenience. He's Emmanuel's friend; he's a widower. Whatever his motive was, I don't have to see him anyway. I travel all the time and he doesn't really care.'

'I can't believe Emmanuel hooked you up with some old guy! What about when you really meet someone you love and truly want to marry?' I was growing concerned.

'Emmanuel said I only had to stay married to him as long as I wanted.'

I frowned.

'That doesn't sound right to me.' I thought for a second and added, 'But does it mean you will have to do the military service if you get divorced?'

'I'll be too old then. Rest assured, what really worries me is my father's reaction,' Amirit explained. 'He's a politician; he's working hard towards being part of the next government. The last thing he needs is bad publicity.'

I wasn't convinced at all.

'What are you going to do about it?' I asked as I leaned against the wall.

Amirit was looking down, fiddling with rubbish bag handles.

'I haven't figured it out yet. I'm keeping myself busy, hoping that my career will take off. If I'm successful, my father won't need to find out about the old guy and won't be too mad at me for running away.'

'Your career seems to be keeping you very busy already!' I said brightly.

'The agency said I had to lose some weight. Clients have complained lately.'

'You're not overweight! Well, if you continue taking other people's food you might be!'

Amirit smiled back. 'Well, when I signed up with the agency, they made it very clear that I should stick to the 90-60-90 measurements stipulated in the contract. So now, they are putting extra pressure on me!' She stood up and pointed at the entrance door, 'Do you mind if I get rid of the rubbish?'

***

Later on, Amirit came out of the bathroom wearing a bathrobe. Her Medusa-like fiery locks contrasted with her white bathrobe. Half goddess, half monster, her ice blue eyes looked through me as she walked past, treading on the strewn clothes. She climbed up onto the bed above mine.

I had a shower too, but clumps of long red hair blocked the plughole. I took some toilet paper, gathered the hair and threw it in the bin. I opened the cabinet above the basin, hoping to find some cleaning products, but as I rummaged through Amirit's numerous vitamin bottles, I came across a small bottle filled with blue pills. I read the label. They were appetite suppressants. They must have been the pills that Betina was taking the other day. I was growing more and more suspicious of this so-called medicine.

'Are these yours?' I asked Amirit when I came out of the bathroom brandishing the bottle filled with pills. Amirit put down her book and nodded. 'Did the agency give you the appetite suppressant pills that are in your cupboard?' I asked.

'I only started taking them a couple of days ago. They don't work.' She put her book upright and resumed her reading.

'Then don't take them,' I was genuinely concerned.

'I want to give it a shot and see if it kicks in eventually. I don't really have any other option,' Amirit mumbled behind her book.

'Gym and diet – there you go, two options for you.'

'I hate gyms,' Amirit lowered her book again. 'And I hate diets, they depress me.'

'You're a lost cause,' I laughed and got ready for bed.

CHAPTER 8

Marion, Professional Model, Paris, October 1996

Over the next few days, I underwent more uneventful photo test shoots. By the end of the week, I was so exhausted that I spent most of my weekend resting, reading, getting to know my new flatmates and doing my laundry in the small laundrette on the market place with Betina. We really got to know each other well and I was glad to have someone to hang out with who knew the city well. Somehow, even though I had only known her for a few weeks, I felt much closer to her than to Lucie and Vincent back home. My old life seemed so far away. Strangely enough, being cut off from the real world was making our friendship blossom. While our clothes spun around, we sat in a café, sipping coffee and freshly squeezed orange juice and discussed everything from modelling to our families.

'Can I ask you why you keep your cash under your mattress? It's not the safest place you know,' I enquired.

'I just don't like to leave too much of it at the agency,' Betina replied.

'Why the agency? What about a bank account?'

'I am not eighteen yet. I would need my mother to co-sign the papers.'

'Can't you open an account when you're home? Have your parents visited you yet?' I asked.

'My dad left when I was eight, for a younger woman, which resulted in a flock of children and more debts. He wrote a "forgive me" note and left in the middle of the night, which tells me what a brave man he was on top of being extremely moral.' Betina looked out for the waiter, 'Can I have an espresso please?'

'I am sorry I brought it up. I didn't mean to stir up the past.'

'It was a long time ago. Now that I think of it, my mother is probably better off without a drunken, unhappy husband, but it seems to have spread like a disease. My mother has been drowning her sorrows in whisky ever since. But I do what I can for her now I'm old enough.'

'So, the money you send every week is for your mother?' I asked.

'Fifty per cent probably goes towards her booze. But I am hoping that what's left of it helps her take care of my little sister, Mia. My mother lives off welfare. She is too damn lazy to shake off her sorrow and get on with her life.'

'How old is Mia?' I asked as she leaned forward to stir her coffee.

'She's twelve. She was only little when my father left; she doesn't remember him.'

***

Back in the flat, Elena had propped an easel in the middle of the room where she sat, humming a soft song. She had mixed pastel colours on a large pallet and looked dreamily outside the window for inspiration.

'This is absolutely gorgeous!' Betina exclaimed as she stood behind Elena and looked at her painting. 'Marion, come and see this!'

Both Betina and I stood there in admiration. Elena could express so much beauty on canvas.

'I didn't know you painted so well!' I said softly.

'She must be a true optimist as she's the only one who's able to see pastel colours while looking out of a Parisian window... all I see is grey and bloody pigeons!' Amirit joked. She was sitting on the floor by her bed, removing pictures from her Book and rearranging them.

'Being an optimist is precisely what you should aim for,' I joked back. 'What are you doing anyway with your pictures lying on the ground? Are you throwing them away?' I asked her.

'Nah! Can't afford to throw them away, even though I wish I could sometimes! For instance, that picture of me in a bathing suit... bloody awful... and fat!' Amirit said with a nervous laughter, waving a large picture of her posing somewhere in paradise. 'I am shuffling them around; it's a little trick of mine. It gives me a feeling that my Book has been renewed.'

'You're weird!' I replied with a frown. 'And you're not fat, stop it already!'

'I'm making tea, girls. Who wants a cuppa?' Betina asked as the kettle started whistling.

'Here's green tea to Elena's eternal optimism,' Betina said as she placed a cup of tea by Elena's easel, who thanked her with a smile. 'White coffee for our Frenchie, no sugar,' she added as she smelled the brew. 'Gosh, how can you like instant coffee? It's revolting!' Betina wrinkled her nose in disgust holding the mug as far away from her nose as she could, 'And black coffee for you my dear Amirit, as black as your thoughts, with one sugar, to soften your soul!' she laughed.

'I didn't know that you were a poet?!' Amirit replied with a large smile.

'Anything to make you smile, my friend!'

We laughed heartedly. At that very moment, the tiny flat that seemed so bare was filled with merry voices. Despite our cultural differences, we seemed to have found a common ground which had no frontier; friendship.

***

When we arrived at the agency on the Monday morning, Florent took me to the Professional department to meet my new booker. I had made it at last!

'Marion, this is Esmeralda. She will take care of you from now on.'

'It's good to finally meet you, Marion.' Esmeralda smiled warmly as she stood up to greet me. She was a very beautiful dark skinned woman with long wavy black hair. She wore a long violet skirt with a violet wrapover top. Her cleavage diverted the eye away from the wide hips she hid underneath layers of billowing clothes.

'I have seen the pictures of your numerous tests; I am very pleased with them. I think your Book is looking stronger now.' Esmeralda stood up and shook my hand, which made her jewellery rattle. 'I especially love the pictures you did with James.'

My face grew sullen and my stomach churned.

'There is something really strong in your eyes,' Esmeralda added, making me feel worse. 'But I am not going to send you on any new castings just yet. This morning, I am taking you shopping!'

'Shopping?' I raised my eyebrows.

'What you need now is re-styling,' Esmeralda pointed at me up and down with her pencil. 'Jeans are boring and will only make you blend in with the rest of the girls. You need to stand out.'

Esmeralda and I took a taxi to *Le Marais* area where small boutiques huddled along the narrow streets. We walked past cafés, crammed with people having coffees and croissants, men walking hand in hand, Orthodox Jews holding onto their Hasidic hats while running across the road and tourists dawdling, admiring the architecture and the numerous shop displays. I followed Esmeralda into several boutiques and left after a few hours with four heavy bags of brand new clothes.

When Betina came back home from her castings that afternoon, I was wearing a long fitted purple dress made of heavy cotton and an equally purple wrapover top.

Betina burst out laughing. 'Esmeralda has turned you into another Esmeralda!'

'I know, and I feel dreadful! It's almost as if I'm her in disguise!' I replied.

'Are you even aware of how much you spent?' Betina replied.

'No. Esmeralda paid for it all.'

'It's on your tab! Believe me! You should pay a visit to the accounting department some time. You keep on stalling, you've been meaning to sort this out since your card was declined, the longer you leave it the worse it will be – trust me. Don't let Florent fob you off with excuses. They can be very crafty when it comes down to money,' Betina warned me as she popped a blue pill.

'Are you really sure you should be taking so many?' I asked.

'They help me keep my weight down.'

'Betina, you're so thin, I could fax you back to your mother!' I said, laughing nervously.

'I don't think she cares too much about seeing me anyway!'

Betina replied as she sat down on the toilet and peed with the door open. 'I think we should celebrate!'

'What should we celebrate?' I asked.

'You are officially out of the New Faces department and in with the professional models and it looks like Esmeralda didn't pull her punches with her re-styling; she turned you into a fortune teller!' Betina could not stop laughing. She poured some wine into two plastic cups.

'Excuse the cups, I've broken most of the glasses and the rest are in the sink, waiting to be washed!'

'I don't drink...' I said.

'Oh, come on, don't be such a killjoy, just a sip! You've made it. You're one of us now.'

I cringed as I sipped her wine so as not to look ungrateful and poured it into the sink as soon as she looked away.

***

The next morning, the phone rang as the four of us were getting ready for the day.

'Marion? Esmeralda here! Good morning!'

'Morning!'

'Are you ready to go to your castings?'

'Almost,' I replied.

'Do you have a pen to write down your appointments? You and Betina have the same castings today. Oh, by the way, I've got good news for you – the picture Marco Tutti took during the contest was sold to France Telecom. Your beautiful face is going to be on thousands of telephone cards! Isn't that exciting?' Esmeralda announced, delighted. 'And they paid twenty thousand francs for it!'

I was shocked. That was a ridiculous amount of money for a girl of my age. I felt both proud to be worth so much and ashamed to be making as much in one day than my hard working mother made in a year.

'That's amazing! Oh my God, when can I have that money?'

'Clients can take up to three months to pay and the agency will take 20% off that amount,' Esmeralda explained.

After hanging up, I turned to the girls, 'Now that's something worth celebrating!'

'What's that?' Betina mumbled, the toothbrush hindering her speech.

'One of my pictures taken during the Icon modelling contest was sold to France Telecom for twenty thousand francs! I never thought that picture had any potential whatsoever!'

Betina opened her eyes wide and gave a thumbs up as her mouth was foaming with toothpaste.

***

For the first time since moving to Paris, I felt positive and walked with a spring in my step. No more wasted days at pointless castings, I was a professional model now. Around lunchtime, Betina and I ventured to Île Saint-Louis, an island nestled in the heart of the city on the river Seine. We skipped along the banks of the Seine and eventually sat down, dangling our feet above the water. Two lovers were sitting next to us, holding each other and kissing.

'I wish I had someone to love! Paris is such a perfect city for romance, isn't it?' I commented.

Betina was quietly day dreaming off in her own thoughts.

I leaned back on my elbows and thought about my news. 'Twenty thousand francs! It makes my parents' salaries look like pocket money! I don't even know how they will feel about me earning this kind of money.'

'Well my Mum is only too happy that I earn what I do, she's keen to get every last franc,' Betina added cynically. 'Anyway, where are we going next?'

I took the appointment sheet from my bag and unfolded it.

'We're off to Madame Figaro Magazine, close to le Sentier area. It's within walking distance. Come on, let's go.'

'Argh… I've been there a hundred times at least. I think we should skip it, it's useless, they'll never book us,' Betina moaned as she dragged her legs under her and stood up slowly.

'Come on, girl. Don't be so negative. It's not far,' I encouraged her.

We walked through a maze of winding cobbled streets, up to

Boulevard Haussman where the magazine had its offices. For the next hour, we dawdled in front of the numerous boutiques and giggled as we ran past the prostitutes standing outside their doors in rue Saint Denis. We took the escalators up and down in les Halles, bought a Nutella pancake for lunch, took pictures of each other wearing hats we had snatched from the displays, and fashioned saris by wrapping ourselves in fabrics from the counters of the shops in Rue du Sentier. The busy boulevard finally brought us to a halt.

'It's over there,' Betina said, pointing at an imposing Haussmanian building.

We were sent up to the first floor by a bored receptionist and joined the many girls standing in a queue.

'See what I mean?' said Betina, exasperated, as she leaned against the wall. 'I was almost hoping we would miss it by faffing around the way we did!'

Forty minutes later, Betina walked into the casting room where four people were gathered around a square table. An open door separated the editor, the photographer and their assistants from the models lining up in the corridor. We were like cattle waiting to be slaughtered. I watched Betina as she approached the clients.

'Can I see your Book please?' the editor demanded.

She was a tall woman with short blonde hair, and she looked at Betina over her glasses. 'Is this your natural hair colour?'

Betina nodded.

She flipped through the portfolio in a flash. Her face was inscrutable; she had no wrinkles at all. Either she had an excellent surgeon or she was totally void of emotions. She took four cards out of Betina's portfolio and thanked her.

Bettina rolled her eyes at me as she walked out. As I neared the table, I heard the blonde woman bitching, 'I've never been a big fan of red heads.'

She then took my Book and looked at my pictures. 'Can you give...? What's her name...?' she closed the Book and read my name on the cover, 'Can you give Marion the *Pain de Sucre* bathing suit?' she ordered the stylist, a small brunette with a sexy mole on her upper lip.

'Next!' She pushed my Book to the side of the table where the photographer was slouching, powerless. The Iron Lady was visibly in charge.

In the meantime, the stylist took me behind a screen to try on a blue bikini. The editor was busy looking at another model's Book when she caught sight of me. She paused.

'Let's see what we have here,' she waved me to come closer. 'Turn round!' she ordered, looking over her glasses and motioning with her hand. 'She's too big.'

A verdict without appeal. She readjusted her glasses closer to her face. I stood motionless, frozen by the comment.

'Thanks, you can get dressed. Next!'

The editor resumed flipping through the other model's Book and the other model continued to smile.

I picked up my Book from where it had been discarded at the far end of the table. I thanked them but no one replied. I don't think they were even listing to me. I found Betina leaning against the wall further down the corridor, waiting for me.

'These people are useless, I mean, did you see how many composites they had? They must have seen all of Paris!' she whispered. 'I'm not going back, ever, waste of my time!'

'Well, if they take four composites from each girl, it piles up pretty quickly! I don't get it, why did they take so many cards if they're not interested?' I suddenly felt tired and weary. 'Shall we skip the rest of the castings for today and just go home?'

Betina's eyes lit up, 'Great idea!'

I noticed her pop another pill, but chose to ignore it.

***

As we walked into our flat the phone was ringing. Elena and Amirit were not back yet. I picked up the receiver.

'Marion? Esmeralda here! Have you done all your castings?'

I hesitated. 'Yes, I have!' I lied.

'Good girl! I have a client who requested you for a three day job. It's in Mallorca. Ten thousand francs a day. It's for a German catalogue. I am not too crazy about German catalogues – it's good money, but it's a bad career move. But since you've had so many expenses, I think you should do the job to repay your debt to the agency. You may have to leave tomorrow evening. I am still waiting for the confirmation though.'

I was speechless. The bad news had annihilated the good. I was trying to fathom how I could possibly be in debt despite the contract money and the France Telecom job. Esmeralda's words came out in a squall. I hung up.

'She said I owe the agency money!' I turned to Betina. I felt as if I had been slapped in the face.

'Happens all the time. The only way to keep on top of it is to ask for a statement when you go to the agency.'

Betina locked herself in the bathroom while I desperately tried to work out the sums. After fifteen minutes of frantic calculations I gently knocked on the door. Betina had never bolted the bathroom door before.

'I really have to pay a visit to the accounting department. They're taking me for a ride,' I said. Betina did not reply. 'Is everything alright in there?' I could hear a faint cry. I knocked. 'Betina, please open the door, you're making me nervous!'

Betina unlocked the door. Her eyes were red from crying. She sat down on the sofa bed and covered her face with her hands.

'I think I'm pregnant!' she mumbled.

'You think you're what?' I knew it probably wasn't the best response but I was shocked. I put my arm around her and we sat on the edge of the bath.

'I slept with a guy a few weeks ago and I haven't had my period since.'

'You know you have to take a pregnancy test to be sure.'

'I'm too ashamed!' Betina sobbed.

'What the pharmacist thinks shouldn't matter?'

Bettina did not look up. Her face was still buried in her hands.

'Do you want *me* to go and buy it for you?' I asked.

'Would you?' Bettina looked up.

Her mascara had run down her cheeks.

'Who is the guy? Do you still see him?'

'Please don't lecture me! Are you going to help me or not?' she snapped.

I grabbed my handbag and went for the door.

'I'll be right back.'

'I'm sorry... I didn't mean to...'

'No worries, I'll see you soon,' I smiled and closed the door softly.

I walked to the nearest pharmacy and rummaged through every shelf for a pregnancy test, feeling the gaze of the shopkeeper over my shoulder. I hoped he wouldn't ask any questions. *It's not for me, I swear!* I decided to pick up a double pack, just to be on the safe side, and placed it on the counter. The pharmacist looked at the blue box with contempt and tutted as he took the money.

When I returned to the flat, Betina was smoking on the balcony.

'I didn't know you smoked?' I exclaimed.

'Only when I'm nervous. Don't worry about the baby, I wouldn't keep it anyway,' she said casually. She had calmed down while I'd been out.

I handed the tests to Betina. She threw her cigarette away and went into the bathroom. I waited anxiously. After what seemed like hours, Betina reappeared.

'It says *Not Pregnant*,' she said in a calm voice, and she disposed of the test in the bin.

We did not speak for the rest of the evening and went to bed early where we both stared at the ceiling, listening to our own anxieties, and eventually fell asleep.

CHAPTER 9

Marion, Mallorca, October 1996

'Marion, you're confirmed. Three days in Mallorca!' Esmeralda exclaimed down the phone the following morning. 'Your plane leaves at seven tonight from Charles de Gaulle airport, I'll fax you the details shortly, OK sweetie?'

'OK, that's great, thanks!' I replied. Elena looked at me in a questioning manner. 'I'm booked for a job! My first actual job!' I shrieked.

Elena smiled and congratulated me in her own subtle way by nodding.

Amirit was busy packing her bags as she was about to go to Munich for a German catalogue and Betina was getting ready for her castings in the bathroom, but I heard her call out, 'Well done!'

I was relieved to hear her voice again. Silence was suffocating.

'Yes, I'm leaving later on today,' I said. 'Although I am a bit nervous because I don't know exactly when I should leave to be on time at the airport. I've never travelled abroad on my own, which freaks me out a little.'

'Where's your subway map, I'll show you the way,' Betina said as she sat down next to me. 'You have to be there one hour before at least. The train will take about forty five minutes to get to the airport from the subway station Châtelet – Les Halles, so I would say that you should leave around 4 p.m. to be on the safe side. Make sure you take the direct train to Charles de Gaulle airport, the RER train,' she explained.

'What are you up to today?' I asked softly, wrapping my arm around her shoulder.

'I have a couple of castings,' Betina looked down.

I hugged her. Even though we hadn't known each other long, I felt very close to her already and it would be strange to leave this new home, even for a few nights but that's just how modelling is – everyone is always going off on assignments.

'Promise me you'll take good care of yourself!'

'Yes, Mum!' Betina replied. 'I am sorry about last night, I was way out of line, I shouldn't have put you through…'

'Don't worry about it, that's what friends are for,' I smiled.

***

I had the day ahead to get ready for my job so I decided not to go to the few castings Esmeralda had given me. I jumped in the shower, shaved my legs and underarms, washed my hair and tweezed my eyebrows. I packed two bathing suits, a few summery dresses as I assumed the weather was warmer there, my toiletries, a book to read and my passport. Then I unpacked everything and selected completely different clothes. I stood in front of my open suitcase for a moment, with my hands on my hips, and decided that after my job, I was going to go shopping. Now that I was a professional model I needed a whole new wardrobe.

Rue de la Sourdière led to Rue du Faubourg Saint-Honoré, a street that boasted a myriad of shops with luxury brands, with no price tags on display. Watches, jewellery, shoes, dresses, cashmere, and many more taunted me. I pushed the door of the Givenchy boutique. A subtle bell rang but the clerks did not pay me any attention. They could probably sense I could not afford anything. In a fit of pique I tried not to let it show that it was cripplingly expensive, and left the shop.

I returned home empty-handed, zipped up my suitcase, put my shoes and my black mac on and walked out. I hoped that soon enough, I would no longer feel threatened by the elegant women walking down Rue Faubourg Saint-Honoré, hiding behind ostentatious sunglasses and casually rummaging through their expensive handbags for their Mini Cooper car keys, because I was about to become one of them.

Châtelet – Les Halles was the station to avoid at all costs. It was big, dirty and overcrowded. Corridors sprawled in all directions, as did the lines of people queuing to pay for their tickets, and the whole place smelled of fast food mixed with cigarettes and urine; it made me queasy. I held my suitcase tight and walked as confidently as I could towards the ticket dispenser. I queued for ten minutes and looked for the right platform for about another twenty. By the time I had made it to the airport, I was already tired and my legs were swollen from being on my feet so long. I queued for the toilets, I queued at the Iberia check-in, I queued to board the plane and finally aboard, I squeezed my bag in the overhead locker, squeezed my book into the seat-pocket in front of me, and squeezed myself into my seat. Planes were not designed to carry people of my height. People of any size, really.

I slept through most of the flight but woke with a jerk as the wheels hit the ground. I squeezed my book out of the pocket in front of me, squeezed myself out of my seat, squeezed my bag out of the compartment above my head and walked out. Some people stayed on board, but I took no notice of them.

I presented my passport to the Spanish Customs and jumped in a cab. I extracted a folded piece of paper from my pocket with the address of my hotel on it and handed it to the driver who started the engine. The driver smoked a cigarette without a filter and the smell was so bad that I found myself starting to wretch. I was a model, I could not puke in a cab – that would not be appropriate. I rummaged through my bag and removed my flip-flops from their plastic sachet, then held the empty sachet under my chin and took a deep breath.

I will not throw up I… I have thrown up.

The taxi driver looked at me in the rear-view mirror.

'Hay un problema?'

Yep, I have a problema; it's sitting in my lap and may end up in yours if you don't stop smoking, I thought.

My Spanish wasn't good enough to be ironic and luckily the driver finished his cigarette and threw it out of the window.

We had been driving for twenty minutes with my bag of sick in my lap the whole time when I noticed the road sign indicating the distances to Madrid and Barcelona. It prompted me to try and ask the driver where we were.

'Donde estamos?'

The driver looked at me in disbelief. 'Alicante!' Even a word with no 'r' sounded like a rumble in his mouth.

Alicante! How the hell did I...

I suddenly remembered the people who had stayed on board. It dawned on me that Alicante was just a stopover. My brain went into overdrive, my pulse accelerated, and my hands became moist and clammy.

'Can you turn around please?' I asked the driver who did not seem to understand. I looked for the words in Spanish but could not get my head straight. I resorted to hand gestures, 'Airport! Airport! Aeropuerto!'

It was close to 11 p.m. when the taxi dropped me off at the airport. Back to square one. I disposed of my soiled bag in the nearest bin and ran inside the airport. The place was completely deserted. I paused, panting. A Customs officer with a moustache was still in his booth. I ran towards him.

'Please sir, could you take me to the Iberia counter?'

'Cerrado.'

The officer's moustache moved as he spoke.

'Euh... the Iberia office? Manager?' I asked desperately.

The Customs Officer stepped out of his booth and said, 'Vien!'

He looked like a cartoon character with his protruding gut and skinny legs. I followed him as he walked with his legs apart, hoping that we had understood each other. *So much for all the years of Spanish in school.* He took me to the Iberia office where thankfully the manager was still working, even though it was so late at night.

'Excuse me, do you speak English?' I did not know where to start.

'I do,' he replied.

I sighed with relief. 'I'm afraid I was supposed to stay on board my flight to Mallorca but got off here when the plane landed. It wasn't clear. It wasn't written on the ticket.' I was out of breath. My hands were shaking as I presented him my ticket.

'You're right, it's not written,' he admitted after reading the ticket. 'I'm sure the flight attendants did mention it though,' he added as he put the ticket down on his desk and looked at me.

'Well, if they did, I didn't hear anything. Either because I was sleeping or because my Spanish is too lousy,' I exclaimed.

'I can put you on the first flight out to Mallorca tomorrow morning…' he offered.

'The thing is, I am supposed to work in Mallorca tomorrow morning and I wouldn't want to get into trouble,' I said, sadly.

'Why don't you call your employer or whoever you're working with and explain the situation?'

He pushed the phone towards me. It was late, but I had no choice. I called the hotel receptionist, who transferred me to the photographer's room. It rang many times before Hans picked up the receiver.

'Hans? This is Marion Durant, the model you're working with tomorrow for *Quelle*,' I said tentatively.

'Hallo Marion, what's going on?' Hans said in a sleepy thick German accent.

'I am really sorry to bother you at this time but I've missed my connection. I'm in Alicante and I will take the first flight in the morning. I am so sorry!' I apologised, creasing my eyes in anticipation.

'Oh that's too bad, but don't worry, we'll start with the other girl and you will work in the afternoon,' Hans replied.

I was relieved, things were looking up. 'Thank you so much! See you tomorrow, Hans!' I said hanging up.

'Thanks for letting me use your phone – very kind of you,' I said to the manager who was fumbling in his drawer.

'Here's a hotel voucher. It's not a five start hotel but it'll do for one night, right?'

'I can't thank you enough!' I replied with a smile.

'Take a taxi, get some rest OK?'

I shook his hand and jumped in the last taxi. As the driver approached the town centre, I rested my head on the back seat and looked out of the window. There was not much traffic at this time. A car was driving next to mine, at the same speed. I focused and realised that the moustachioed Customs Officer was driving side by side with my taxi. He was smiling. I smiled back. After a few minutes, however, I started to feel as though I was being followed. I looked at him again. He was still grinning. I pulled my head back and directed my gaze in front of me, hoping it was a coincidence and that he would soon veer away.

When my taxi pulled over in front of the hotel, I quickly looked round and checked the officer wasn't around. I walked into the reception area towards the desk. My heart almost stopped when the custom officer grabbed my arm.

'Get off me!' I screamed.

The officer looked startled and mumbled something inaudible.

The doorman hurried towards me. The front desk manager's attention was suddenly drawn to me.

'Is everything OK, Miss?' he asked. 'Is this man bothering you?'

I nodded.

'He's a customs officer from the airport. He's stalking me.'

The front desk manager invited me to sit down while the doorman escorted the officer out. I was shaking like a leaf. 'I can't believe he's been following me! This is *crazy!*'

'It's all right. He's gone now. I'll show you to your room.'

Once in my bedroom, I bolted the door, just in case the Customs Officer decided to come knocking on my door. For the first time since I had started modelling, I had a bedroom to myself and I wanted to make the most of it. I walked into the bathroom and ran a bath where I emptied the whole bottle of bubble bath. Feeling grown-up and bold, I opened the mini bar and drank a small bottle of rum. It tasted awful at first, but when the burning sensation went down, I gave in to the soothing warmth and closed my eyes, just for a moment.

When my alarm o'clock went off at 4.30 a.m., I was still dressed, but the water of my bath had become cold and the bubbles were long gone. My stomach churned and my head pounded. I washed my face, brushed my teeth and ran down to reception to order a cab.

This time I managed to get the right cab and the right plane to the right destination. I was so tired I could feel the inside of my eyeballs pulsing. Only the excitement of my first confirmed job kept me going. *Am I going to know what to do?* I wondered. Modelling seemed like a foreign language that I wasn't sure I would ever master. So far it had all felt more like a distant promise, an illusion rather than reality. It seemed so easy and yet I was worried I wouldn't live up to the client's expectations; after all, I had very little experience. Now was the time to deliver and be worth the money the client was paying me. Would I be welcomed with special attention or brushed aside with a sneer for being late and too foolish to take the right plane in the first place?

When I finally made it to the hotel in Mallorca, a note was waiting for me at reception:

'I hope you've had a good flight. Please be in room 404 at 2 pm for make-up and hair. Matthias.'

At 2 p.m. sharp, I knocked on Matthias' door. A tall man with bleached blonde hair opened it. He wore white linen trousers and a matching long sleeved white linen shirt. A tattoo was visible on the side of his neck which was either a lizard or a snake, though I couldn't be sure.

'Hello there! Come on in!' Matthias said. 'Have a seat there please.' He had arranged all his make-up and hair products in a perfect line. 'I'll start with your hair and then move on to your make-up.' He started by spraying water on her hair. 'So...'

Here we go! Explanation time! I thought.

'What happened last night? Missed your flight?'

Matthias was up for some gossip. I explained my journey to him in minute detail, which delighted him and passed the time.

'You're here now, so relax!'

Once ready, I met with the rest of the team by the van outside the hotel. Hans was chatting with the client, a blonde lady whose dress sense made her look deceptively younger than her age which I took to be about fifty years old. Her fake-tanned legs flashed from under her white skirt. She wore an interesting combination of Birkenstock sandals and big gold jewellery. Hans was tall and dark haired with blue eyes and looked about the same age. A tiny earring shone on his left ear. They looked like a pair of overgrown teenagers; I was certainly meeting some interesting characters in this industry. Matthias was busy smoking and chatting with a blonde model when I walked up to him to apologise once more.

'Don't worry, you're here now, so we'll catch up this afternoon. When the stylist comes out, we hit the road,' Hans said.

***

"The road" took us to a salt mine. It was a big, open mine with nothing but brightness, heat and salt.

The other model was reading in the back of the van. She leaned forward while the stylist prepared our clothes and the photographer's assistant setup the cameras.

'Hi! I'm Heidi, by the way,' she said offering me her hand.

'Marion.'

'Are you French?'

'Yes, I am. How long have you been on this job?' I asked.

'Five days, and counting!'

'Five days is a long time!'

'It's good money, you mean!' Heidi smiled, showing a perfect set of teeth. 'Summer season is almost over. I've been working my ass off. I'm completing on a flat in Munich in two weeks. I'm pretty excited!'

'I'm happy for you,' I replied half-heartedly.

'Yeah, you know… I've been working for five years now. German clients are pretty faithful if you work hard and if you sell. They pay well and there's no funny business. It's not very interesting to wear these old ladies' clothes, but you can make a shit-load of money. That's what I'm here for anyway – the cash!' Heidi went back to her book.

That got me thinking. I started dreaming about my perfect flat or house, somewhere sunny, by the beach with my handsome husband and beautiful kids. *Hang on a second. Stop dreaming, Matthias is coming for you.*

'Marrrrrion, you're up darling, Let me take those curlers out of your hair and check your make-up.'

He added powder, blush and gloss to my face.

'Amanda is waiting for you at the back of the van with your first outfit.'

Another blonde lady wearing beige shorts, an orange tank top and Birkenstocks shoes waved me into the van.

'Hallo Marion! I'm Amanda. Can you please put these on?'

Amanda handed me a turtleneck, stockings, a woollen skirt and matching jacket, plus a long coat. I broke into a sweat just by looking at it. Amanda put a few safety pins between her teeth and started pinning each layer of clothes behind my back. The shapeless clothes were fitted within a few seconds. I stepped down from the van while Amanda opened her jewellery box. It was filled with cheap junk. Amanda handed me a pair of gold earrings, a watch and a white leather handbag.

'You're ready. Hans is waiting for us. Come this way.'

Amanda led me up a salt mound. It was so dazzlingly bright that I could hardly open my eyes. Everyone else had sunglasses on. Hans was sitting behind his camera, waiting for me to start moving, but I was at a standstill unable to think of what to do in heels and warm winter clothes, on top of a salt mound in the sweltering heat. My heels began to slowly sink into the salt, which made me terribly unstable. The sun's rays were so strong that I started seeing halos wherever I looked. I felt dizzy and dreaded passing out on my first shoot.

'Move, move, move!' Hans screamed from a distance, gesticulating with his arms up in the air.

There was an awkward silence. I tried to turn sideways, to swing my bag, to smile without grinning too much.

'Open your eyez!' Hans screamed. 'And move, move, move!'

What do you think I'm doing? I'm moving! I mumbled to no one in particular.

Hans pulled away from his camera, tilted his cap forward and paced towards me.

'Try to pretend walk…' he started to explain.

'Pretend walk?' I said, not understanding.

Hans tried to pretend walk but couldn't.

'Oh well, I can't do it but basically, you have to walk, but stay on the same spot. OK? We are late because of you, so now move, move, move!'

I nodded, unconvinced. Hans impatiently rushed back to his camera. I was mortified. I tried to pull myself together. I put one foot in front of the other and went back to my position. I did the same thing over and over again, as best I could. After much pretend walking and German shouting, Hans took his cap off and sent Amanda over to have a word with me.

'Marion, go back to the van and wait there please,' Amanda said, with a concerned look on her face.

'Please... I can try again. I've never done this before! Can't you give me more time to find my bearings?'

At that stage, I knew there was no point trying to have a discussion. I went back to the van and waited there all afternoon. I had never felt so lonely in my whole life. Heidi stood on her salt mine pretend walking, with her eyes wide open and smiling with her beautiful white teeth. At the end of the day, Heidi climbed on board the van and sighed.

'You must be exhausted. I'm so sorry you had to do the whole job by yourself.' I was embarrassed.

'That's OK, because I'm getting your pay!' Heidi laughed when she saw my face grow pale. 'I'm joking of course!'

I wasn't so sure.

Soon enough the rest of the team climbed into the van. They chatted, giggled and spoke German the whole way back; I felt outnumbered. They pretended I wasn't there. I was the odd one out, the loser.

I went to my hotel room and slumped on my bed. There, I tried to reassess the day and pray that tomorrow's job would go smoothly, then the phone rang.

'Marion? Esmeralda here.'

I was so happy to hear her voice. 'Hi! How are you? Thanks for calling. My day was horrible...'

'That's exactly why I'm calling.' Her voice sounded as cold and sharp as an axe falling on the back of my neck. 'The photographer called to say that he does not need you anymore.'

'Why not?' I was taken aback.

'I've changed your flight back to tomorrow morning at ten o'clock.' Esmeralda sounded disappointed.

I stormed out of my bedroom and headed towards Hans' room. I knocked on his door, took a step back and waited. My heart was pounding. I could hear someone giggle. I knocked again. Hans opened the door, dishevelled. He was only wearing a towel around his waist, showing his thick torso. Pearls of sweat were running down from his forehead.

'Hallo there!' Hans said with a crooked smile.

'Hans, my agent said you did not need me anymore, but I feel you haven't given me a fair chance. This is my first job, after all.'

I knew I was in a muddle. From where I was standing, I spotted out a pair of orange legs sticking out of his bed. I could have recognised those legs in a line-up of millions. The client and Hans were having mad sex while I was getting my ass kicked out of Mallorca. I was so angry that I started to stutter.

'I don't have the time to train babies. Good luck and goodbye.'

Hans slammed the door on me. I could feel the pricks of tears welling up while I heard the couple resume their giggling. Back in my room, I called Betina to get some sympathy, certain she would understand. The phone rang but she didn't answer. I removed my make-up, feeling like a clown removing his funny face to reveal the sad one underneath. I called room service and ordered a soup and a salad before changing my mind, cancelling the order, and gulping down the mini bar's stock of Toblerones. I might have been a model, but I still had a pulse and I couldn't tolerate the idea of having salad as a comfort food.

CHAPTER 10

Marion, Bettina Disappears, Paris, October 1996

When I went back to Rue de la Sourdière following my disastrous Spanish excursion, Betina's stuff was gone. Her bed was made up with fresh sheets, waiting for a new warm body. I opened the bathroom door; her stuff wasn't there either. There was no note to be found anywhere. I rushed to the bin, hoping that the pregnancy test would still be in it, beginning to wonder if my friend was ever really there, but the bin was empty. Betina and her secret had vanished into thin air.

I picked up the phone and dialled the agency's number.

'Icon Models, good afternoon,' Esmeralda answered.

'Esmeralda, this is Marion.'

'Hello Marion, are you back? Are you all right? Why are you out of breath?'

'Where is Betina? All her stuff is gone?' I asked in a panic.

'She's in London. We decided it was time she tried a different market, where her edgy looks will go down a bit better.'

I had to sit down. Esmeralda's voice was echoing in my head.

'She didn't even say goodbye,' I said faintly. 'I was only gone for a couple of days. Couldn't this wait?'

'Well, to be honest with you, I don't think it was a good idea putting you two together. Betina was a bad influence – she never went to her castings and therefore rarely got booked for jobs. She was getting a little bit too comfortable, so we decided to give her a bit of a push.' Esmeralda explained.

But what she really meant was that they had given her slightly more than a push; they had *pushed* her right out of the country.

'Is there anything else you wanted, I'm in the middle of—'

'Esmeralda, I am sorry to ask again but do you think I could get an advance on my money. I can't use my card and I ran out of cash,' I begged her.

'I'm sorry Marion, but we had to pay for your photo tests and the flat. We've advanced quite a lot of money and can't keep on doing so. We're not a bank. Surely your parents could help you a little in the meantime?'

I was crushed and felt like crying. I thought about Betina. Would I ever see her again? I felt very lonely without her, broke and lonely – what a great combination. There wasn't much I could do about Betina, but I resolved to have a face-to-face confrontation with the main accountant to clarify my financial situation once and for all. I had been kept in the dark for too long. The contest money was 250,000 francs, the France Telecom deal was 20,000 francs, I was living in a tiny shared studio, sleeping in a bunk bed and I seemed to be in debt. Something was terribly wrong.

Later that day, I walked up to the accounting department in no mood to be reckoned with, only to find myself up against locked door, its blinking keypad was a slap in the face. I took a few steps back and peered over the glass wall to see whether Florent was at his desk. He was reading, with his back to a wall of new models' composite cards with their pictures and measurements.

'How can I get into accounting?' I asked.

'You don't *get* to accounting, you make an appointment with accounting,' Florent replied haughtily, engrossed in his paperwork.

I paced briskly towards Florent; my face had become flushed. Florent did not look up as I stood next to him, fuming with anger. I leaned forward and placed my hands on top of the papers he was reading.

'Are you out of your mind?' he hissed.

'I'm only asking for one minute of the accountant's time,' I kept my composure.

'As I said…' Florent interjected, removing his trapped papers.

'I need the accountant to clarify how Icon have STOLEN my money!' I made sure I stressed the word 'stolen'.

There was a sudden lull in the room. A few models strained their ears and looked in our direction. Florent stood up.

'Fine! Keep your voice down, I'll see what I can do,' he said as he walked towards the locked door. He punched in the code and showed me into accounting for an impromptu appointment with Madeleine.

'Madeleine, I am sorry to barge in on you this way but Marion has a few questions regarding her payroll,' Florent told the accountant who looked at him with a poker face.

I sat down in the empty chair in front of her. My face had recovered its natural colour. The accountant stared at me with bleary eyes and picked up the her phone. Poker-face dialled her boss, tapping the desk with the tip of a long red nail.

'Sorry to bother you, Robert,' she said smoothly into the receiver. 'I have a slight problem… yes… Durant. Could you come over?'

Madeleine hung up and resumed her work, totally ignoring me. I wriggled on my seat and looked around while waiting, rehearsing all my questions in my head.

A bald man with spectacles appeared, armed with a file of spreadsheets.

'Hello, I have your file here and can clear this up for you. The money agreed in your contract as the winner of the Icon contest is paid in instalments. For the first three months, you'll be paid ten thousand per month, the following three, you'll get fifteen and so on until it reaches two hundred thousand francs. But your monthly expenses will be deducted from the amount before you are paid. I can see you've got quite a few.'

'But I thought it amounted to two hundred and fifty?' I asked faintly, totally lost.

'That's correct! You'll be paid the final fifty thousand francs once the first year is complete… just in case you should decide not to honour the full year's contract,' he explained, sweating slightly as he spoke. 'We guarantee you that amount whether you work or not, but it is in our best interest that you get bookings for at least the equivalent amount of time so you might break even on the total amount. Any money you earn on top of that is yours, but until that is the case, you'll only get the money stipulated in your contract.'

I was speechless and yet it was now so clear to me that I was stuck in a downward spiral from which it would be very hard to get out, considering the ever-growing expenses.

I gazed at the spreadsheet. The numbers swam before my eyes.

Flat: FF1,000 per month

Composites: FF500

Courier: FF350

Photo Test: FF1000 per test.

Number of tests: 10

I realised that once the FF250,000 had been hacked into by the agency fee, the taxes, assorted charges and miscellaneous untraceable expenses such as couriers and composites – there was hardly any money left. Everything had gone full circle, the money was back with the people who had given it to me in the first place. I was dumbstruck, even a loan-shark would have been fairer. At last I understood the game.

'Could I please have an allowance until my next pay roll?' I asked as I slouched on my seat.

'I am afraid we cannot do that,' the accountant said firmly. 'It would only deepen your debt.'

***

As I walked out of the building towards the tube station, I dragged my feet into a small shop where I bought a phone card to call my parents. I realised that I had been handed a card with the black and white picture of me taken by Marco Tutti during the Icon Modelling contest the previous year. A few weeks prior to finding out that I was broke and nowhere close to becoming a good working model, I would have shared my moment of fame with the shopkeeper, but I chose to keep it to myself.

As I inserted the card into the slot, the picture of my face disappeared, swallowed by the machine and the screen displayed ten francs. My father picked up the phone.

'Dad? It's me! Could you please call me back?' I pleaded.

'Where are you Pup?' My father had picked up on my sad voice.

'In a phone booth,' my voice quavered as tears welled up.

My father called me back immediately.

'What's wrong?' he asked, worried.

'I… I thought I was getting a certain amount of money with the contract I signed with Icon,' I sniffled. 'But they'll only give me more if I work for over two hundred thousand francs, plus the expenses. The first instalments are so low; I can barely make it through the week.'

'Hold on a second, I don't understand. How is that possible?' My father interrupted.

'Apparently, the instalments are cancelled out by the various expenses such as photo tests and the models' flat. The money I earn needs to add up to the amount stipulated in the contract, before I start getting extra money.'

'So, if I get this right, only once you've broken even, you can start taking home extras? Is that right?'

'That's right, but they charge me for so many things that I doubt I'll ever see a cent!' I sobbed. 'This is my second instalment… I am bound to have debts from day one, debts that I will never be able to pay off!'

'It sounds like a total scam! They certainly did not explain it that clearly when you won your contract! What a bunch of crooks!'

'I am stuck in a one year contract which has only just begun. I can't… I don't *want* to give up so soon.'

'Listen Pup, do you need money?'

I did not reply. My father continued, 'I'll tell you what. I'll go to the bank in the morning. Hopefully that will sort you out for a while.' He paused. 'I don't like the sound of it, Pup. Come back here if you feel the need, OK?'

I felt a lot better as we said goodbye and, with the remainder of the money on the phone card, I dialled the London office of Icon Models.

'Icon Models, good morning!' answered a jaded voice. I couldn't hear the voice clearly because of the buzz in the background. I pressed my finger tight into my other ear.

'Hi there! I'm trying to get in touch with Betina Christensen. I used to be her roommate in Paris. Would you—'

The line was suddenly cut – I had run out of credit. I banged my hand on the machine in anger.

'Stupid machine!' I yelled.

'Are you all right in there?' An old lady asked as she strolled by with her zimmer-frame.

I stormed out of the booth. The door swung closed with a slam which startled the old lady. I threw the useless card into the nearest bin and scampered away.

Back on the tube, I sat absent-mindedly on my journey home, looking at the commercials covering the walls; the model wearing a red dress on the poster sneered at me. I tried not to let it get to me and directed my gaze at the empty seat in front of me.

CHAPTER 11

Betina, London, October 1996

It was still dark outside when Betina woke up in the basement flat Icon had put her up in. She gently stepped down the wooden ladder of the bunk bed in order not to wake her roommate and tiptoed towards the door, careful not to trip on the threads of the worn out carpet. There was a pungent stuffy smell pervading the bedroom. The windows had been painted closed, confining the stale air within.

The bathroom light switch triggered the fan. The dull whirring sound drilled into Betina's skull every morning, but there was nothing she could do about it. While she waited for the shower to warm up, she leaned over the basin to inspect her face in the mirror. The intense heat and stuffiness in her bedroom had dehydrated her, puffed up her eyes, and given her that drunken look she had too often observed on her mother. She hadn't removed her make-up in the hope it would dry out the pimples on her face that had emerged after spending too long on a diet which had been based on cereals. She wiped the cotton bud soaked with make-up remover over her face, slowly revealing a grey complexion. Her skin had cracked in certain areas, her lips were dried out and her hair looked dull.

After fiddling with the blemishes burgeoning on her tired face, she stared sullenly into the mirror. She sighed and examined her hands. Inflamed cuticles had peeled off on her bitten away fingernails. She ran the water in the sink, put soap into her hands and frantically rubbed them with a brush until she bled.

'Shit, Shit, Shit,' she mumbled as she thrust her reddened fingertips to her mouth. She felt the metallic taste sting her tongue and closed her eyes in pain. In the meantime, the hot water running into the shower had steamed up the bathroom. She stepped into the bathtub, pulled the plastic shower curtain and stood under the burning water for several long minutes.

When she came out, she wrapped herself in her towel and wiped the condensation off the mirror with her pyjama top and stared at herself once more in the dry stripe of the mirror. Her skin was red and scorched and her hair was in a huge knot of tangles. She warred with it, harshly pulling out a large lump of hair with the brush. She fumbled into her beauty case and extracted her scissors. She combed her hair forward in front of her eyes, grabbed it firmly with one hand and cut an askew fringe to frame her sad green eyes with the other hand. Once she was finished with her awkward alterations, she let her arms hang limply by her sides and dropped the scissors on the dewy floor.

After painting her cauterised fingernails with bright red nail polish she stepped out of the bathroom, walked to the small windowless kitchen and flicked on the light switch. The neon strip light blinked and buzzed as if a fly had been caught inside it. The paint was chipped, mould was growing on the seal between the tiles and a residue of frying oil stained the stove and the hood above it.

Betina grabbed a bowl and a spoon amongst the stack of dirty china crowding the sink and washed them with the mildewed sponge. She shovelled the soggy cereal in her mouth without much appetite and chucked her bowl into the sink. It had gone full circle.

Betina slouched into the brown velvet couch which had seen much better days and scanned the map to find out where her various castings would be. Above her head, a waltz of footsteps of passers-by was visible through a small barred window as they strutted by towards Maida Vale tube station. She loathed the flat. She felt like she had been buried alive in a rotten shoe box. She had only been there for a couple of weeks and there was a constant flow of teenage models coming in and out. None of them knew how to look after themselves or a home. The carpet and sofa were covered in coffee and food stains, the bed linen and towels were threadbare and the stench was unbearable. There were dubious brown traces on the toilet walls and the mould was spreading along the ceilings. This was not how she imagined life as a professional model, but the agency had promised her that this would jump-start her career.

Betina grabbed her coat and closed the front door behind her. She walked past the large trim houses with bay windows, flowers beds and steeply pitched roofs. They all seemed to have been built at different times. Most of the houses were owned by just one family, hers seemed to be the only one which displayed a multitude of doorbells. Above the models' flat, lived Icon's owner, Carole; the wrinkly version of Jerry Hall. She lived in comfort, entertained her guests in the garden while her employees were crammed underground in the damp. Betina could hear Carole's footsteps as she watched her favourite TV programmes and if she listened hard enough, her laughter. It wasn't fair.

She inhaled deeply to fill her lungs with welcome fresh air after the stench of the flat, wrapped her scarf around her neck, and walked towards the old red phone box on the other side of the road which was covered with pictures of naked women. While Betina fed the machine with coins, a woman on all fours caught her eye. She was looking at her over her shoulder with a concupiscent gaze and Bettina wondered what that poor woman's life was like. She punched in the thirteen digit phone number for Icon's models flat in Paris.

'Hullo?' answered an unknown voice.

'Hi! Is Marion there please?' Betina asked.

'Hullo? Hullo?,' the voice said before the line went dead.

Betina looked at the receiver in dismay and put it back gently. She leaned back against the booth and thought about Marion. Every time she tried to call, she didn't get through. For some strange reason, a different person answered every time. She had sent a letter to Icon Paris, and had waited for an answer but the hope to find her friend was growing dimmer with each attempt.

Betina walked to the tube station and hopped on the Bakerloo line towards Elephant and Castle. The tube wobbled its way through the tunnels, slowed down, stopped, and few unintelligible words were muttered over the tannoy by the driver. The train jerked, screeched and halted for a few minutes. Betina rolled her eyes to the ceiling and looked around. People were scattered all over the carriage, reading or sleeping, but overall remaining phlegmatic. A man wearing a shabby business suit swayed from side to side in front of her and was clearly unsteady on his feet as he gripped onto the pole in the mid-section of the train. Betina caught a whiff of his alcohol breath and decided to shuffle down a few seats.

***

Thirty minutes later, Betina was in Holborn, walking down Kingsway, a large road studded with office blocks and impersonal cafés. As she waited for the red light to cross the road, she noticed a man with a weather-beaten puce face sitting on a canvas stool by a flower display, hailing the newspaper's headlines. She sympathised with the man who stood there, as she knew how it felt to slog her guts out day after day. Come rain or shine, hail or snow, whether it was a bank holiday or a week day, he was always in the same spot, calling out the news.

Icon London was in a quiet street sandwiched between two large buildings. As she arrived, Betina could see from the street, the ground floor window and behind it the five bookers sitting around one big table.

Several models who were sitting on the pavement smoking, gave Betina cold blank looks as she walked into the agency. Pointedly ignoring them, Betina crept behind her agent Hendrick and kissed him on the cheek stealthily. Startled, he greeted her with an uneasy smile.

'*Komme med mig,*' he ordered Betina in Danish as he stood up from his chair.

He was a fairly good-looking tall man with a high-waisted pair of jeans and a beige V-neck jumper. He had long curly black hair, an aquiline nose and a dark complexion which belied his Scandinavian heritage, the sole indication of which were his light blue eyes. He sat down on the leather couch with Betina at the rear of the agency and stared into her eyes.

'Please don't do that again,' he commanded, as he nervously tapped his fingers on the table. The nail of his little finger made a louder noise as it was longer than the others.

'Don't do what?' Betina asked gingerly, with her head askew.

She had that gullible look about her that irritated him. And then there was that voice, the bird-brained voice which grated on him whenever she addressed him.

'No displays of affection between us in public. I've told you before. You could cost me my job,' he grimaced as he looked around suspiciously. 'Let's keep our business private. I work here and I don't want anyone gossiping,' he whispered a little more softly.

Betina looked down sadly.

'I'm sorry, I don't meant to… but I love you.'

Hendrick's legs fidgeted, his lips twitched.

'Don't be daft!' He cleared his throat and changed the subject to avoid any further talk on the subject. 'On another note, I've got your pills. Come over to my place after your castings, OK?' He lowered his voice and searched her eyes. 'Right, go to your castings, now.' He stood up and turned around. 'And I'll see you back at mine around seven, all right?'

Betina nodded.

***

Later that evening, Hendrick analysed Betina as she undressed in front of him. Her breasts seemed disproportionately small for her height, as if they belonged to her younger sister. She was self-conscious about it and held her arm across her chest as she approached the bed where he lay. She was completely shaved and her legs were so spindly that her thighs did not meet at the top, creating a small gap. Even though her legs were slim, there was something awkward about them. Without her clothes, he felt as if he wasn't looking at a model but a random student in a changing room. Her auburn hair rested on her shoulders and framed her striking features and overpowering green eyes. As if it was their first intimate encounter, she jumped onto the bed, crawled on top of him, unzipped his jeans, and pulled them down. With a skittish look she unbuttoned his shirt and playfully threw her jaw at his neck. He tittered and threw her off him like a feather. There was something about her that ripped into him with desire. He held her hands down on the mattress while he gently bit her lips and made love to her. She slowly rocked back and forth and closed her eyes surrendering to the swaying.

'That was amazing!' he said as they lay panting, naked on the bed, with the sheets and pillows strewn on the carpet. She flipped on her side and caressed his hairless chest with a contented look. She could have stayed there forever, but he pushed her hand aside, sat up, stretched his limbs, and with a groan he stood up. He slipped his underwear on and disappeared into the bathroom.

'There you go!' he exclaimed as he threw a small plastic bottle at her filled with blue pills. 'I had to change dealers; Tim was becoming a bit too unreliable.' He pulled his pants up and buckled his belt. 'I found a guy who does home delivery.' He pulled his jumper over his head and ran his hand through his hair. 'Much better than waiting around in dodgy places.'

Hendrick sat back down on the bed and took a small plastic bag out of his bedside table drawer. He shook the sachet, opened it and extracted some powder out with the nail of his little finger. He brought it to his nostril and snorted the coke before offering it to Betina, who rolled over, pinched her left nostril and sniffed the powder with the other one.

'I've got to attend an event with the agency later tonight. You can stay here if you want. Order some Chinese or something.' He leaned over to her and kissed her on her forehead. 'Get some rest before tomorrow's surgery.'

He gave her a paternal smile, and left the room. As he closed the front door, Betina got out of bed and went to the bathroom. The beige limestone floor felt cold on her bare feet. She hopped onto the white fluffy bath mat with one foot and dragged it towards the lacquered basin with the other. A pale and tired face stared back at her from the ornate mirror. *It's probably for the best that I'm staying in tonight, I look terrible!* she thought. She then poured precious scented oils into the warm water, and lit up the two La Durée candles. She waved her hand in front of the Bang and Olufsen stereo which opened automatically. She selected Massive Attack's album *Protection*.

With her body immersed in water, entranced by the singer's voice, she felt as if she had gone back to her mother's womb. His flat felt so much homier than her models' den where she felt she more rotten each day.

She held her breath and let herself slowly sink under the water. A feeling of wellbeing ran through her, relaxing all her muscles, cutting her off from all sounds. After a few seconds, she started feeling slightly dizzy, so she popped her head out of the water and gasped for air. Still in a daze, she stepped out of the bathtub and dressed herself in Hendrick's bathrobe. Feeling a little steadier, she grabbed one of the shirts from the chair by the bathtub that Hendrick liked. She brought it to her nose and inhaled his Acqua di Gio aftershave; it was redolent with fresh notes of bergamot, neroli and green tangerine. She closed her eyes and kept it on her face for a moment. As she opened her eyes again, she noticed her bottle of pills.

Placing the shirt back on the chair, she took the small container. It was time for a tablet. She pushed the lid of the small bottle open with her thumb and poured a couple of blue pills out into her hand and threw them into her mouth. She leaned over the basin and drank some tap water and wiped her mouth with her sleeve as she looked into the mirror. There were two fine lines around her mouth that were not apparent before; she assumed that it must be because of the weight-loss. She looked and felt old.

***

'Hi, Mum,' she said as her mother picked up her call. She wasn't sure Hendrick would approve of her using his phone, but it was always cheaper than him taking her out for dinner that night.

'Who's this?' shouted the voice on the other end of the line.

'It's me Mor, Betina.'

'Oh, hi! Actually, I am glad you called. I wanted to ask you if you could send me a bit of money, you know, for your sister's school fees and all.'

'Have you already spent the money I sent you last week?' Betina asked with concern, while she rubbed her left hand on her robe. She could feel her heart beating faster and her breath shortening.

'Well you know, I don't work, life is expensive...'

Her mother coughed and Betina heard the wheezing coming out of her lungs but decided to ignore it. Over the past few months Betina had developed a defence mechanism whereby she stopped listening to her mother's complaints. She blocked them out as if turning down the volume on a radio. She put the receiver to one side allowing her mother to list her latest worries into thin air and looked for the Chinese restaurant leaflet in the kitchen drawer.

'How's Mia?' She asked as she put the receiver back on her ear.

'Oh you know, she's fine. She's sleeping.'

'She always seems to be sleeping when I call. Alright Mor, I've got to go,' Betina said as she fiddled with the phone cord, feeling guilty that she was distancing herself emotionally more and more as the months went by.

'Will you send the money? Can I count on you?' her mother asked with a hoarse voice.

'Yes, I will.'

Betina hung up, and sat on the kitchen stool, sensing the emotional vacuum compressing her stomach once more. She was so alone. What felt like some robotic force moved her hand back towards the phone and she dialled the restaurant's number.

CHAPTER 12

Marion, Paul Newhouse Comes to Town, Paris, November 1996

Paul Newhouse had an immaculate set of white teeth, a perfect tan, manicured hands and a solid build. He was the epitome of the all-American male; he was a Chevrolet in a land of Peugeots. He sat behind a large wooden desk, flipping through the girls' Books surrounded by a harem of bookers. They bustled around him while he sat upright in his chair, elbows on the desk, fingers intertwined.

The greasy-haired booker Gus acted as the new girls' passionate spokesman as he pitched them in a well-articulated speech, gesticulating wildly. Gus commanded the room; no one dared to speak up or laugh louder than him, even at his jokes. Meanwhile, the New Faces were waiting in the booking area, as their destiny was being decided behind the large window panes.

Girls smoked nervously and waited. Amirit and I chatted while Elena sat in silence holding her bag against her chest. Icon was at a standstill.

'Why is it so important to go to New York?' I asked Amirit.

'As Frank Sinatra sang, '*If you can make it there, you can make it anywhere*'. It's a very competitive market, but you can seriously make it big there!' Amirit explained. 'Vogue Paris is good for your career but Vogue US is even better. Everything is better in New York – more money, more prestige, more campaigns… It's the place to be!'

'They're coming out!' whispered someone down the line. All the attention shifted towards Gus. This felt like the contest all over again.

'Elena, Marion, Amirit, Karine, Elodie, Anna and Kate, please come through,' Gus called.

All seven of us stood up and made our way towards the main office while the remaining girls looked at each other in a questioning manner.

Amirit shook Paul's hand while he remained seated. He flipped through her Book again and looked up at her a few times, showing no emotion. Amirit shifted her weight onto one leg and then the other, trying to stand in the most flattering manner.

Gus introduced her, 'Amirit has been with us for three months now and has had a very promising start. She's very commercial and has been booked for many editorials. The magazines should soon come out. Her Book is already quite strong for a beginner. My only concern is that she's put on weight.'

'I'm sure she can lose it fast. Can't you Amirit?' Paul addressed Amirit as he picked up on her distraught face.

'Sure,' Amirit replied ruefully.

'Right, who's next?' Paul asked, talking across Gus just as he was about to open his mouth. Amirit took her portfolio and stomped angrily out of the office. Gus waved at Elena to take a step forward.

'Elena is Russian, she has a very unusual look, very Eastern; high cheek bones and beautiful skin. Chanel really liked her the other day. Unfortunately they chose someone else in the end, but I believe she has great potential for a beauty campaign, such as Olay or Maybelline, even L'Oreal.'

'Can you turn around for me please?' Paul asked Elena turning his fingers. Elena slowly turned around while Paul whispered something to Gus. 'Thank you, Elena,' Paul concluded.

'Marion, please step forward,' Gus said with a smile. My heart started racing. 'Marion is French. She is last year's contest winner, and reminds us of Andie McDowell. She has just graduated from high school and is now quite eager to work and travel. She does not have a full Book, no tear sheets from magazines but a couple of very strong pictures taken by top photographers such as Marco Tutti,' Gus said as Paul nodded. Paul looked at my portfolio and thanked me.

Once reunited with my flatmates, I sighed with relief.

'Hard to say whether he liked me or not,' I confessed.

'I guess I'm going to have to take twice as many pills from now on if I want to be on board,' Amirit said pensively.

Gus came out of the meeting, and called on seven other girls.

'Don't be silly, you take too many already!' I nudged her.

'Gus literally said I was fat!' Amirit bent down to get her bag. 'The fat one is now off, see you!' Amirit walked briskly away.

As I was about to follow Amirit, Gus called my name. He guided me gently in a corner of the room in order to be discreet.

'What would you say about going to New York after Christmas?' he asked softly with a large smile.

'That would be great!'

My face beamed with joy.

'Paul Newhouse really liked you and truly believes you could do well in New York!'

I felt like I had won another contest. New York was the toughest and most sought-after and competitive market there was, but I was determined to make it there.

'Are Amirit and Elena coming along?'

'They will, they will,' he glanced around him, 'Amirit needs to lose a few pounds first and Elena... Well, Elena is not quite ready to go yet. Getting her a visa isn't exactly easy,' Gus replied. 'Don't worry about them, you'll do well over there.'

CHAPTER 13

Elena, Paris, November 1996

Elena was wrapped in warm clothes, dreaming over her steaming cup of tea and enjoying the heat of the café when Monique made her move. Monique thoughtlessly parked her red Fiat in the bus lane and left the hazard warning lights on, before storming in and making a beeline for Elena.

Monique had long thinning salt and pepper hair tied up in a no-nonsense pony tail. Wearing high waisted tight blue jeans, a worn-out leather belt, a fur coat, and a Hermès silk scarf around her neck, she was no longer the fashionista she once was. She tried to ignore the bags under her eyes and the rough sagging skin of her face, but unhealthy living had taken its toll on her once model-like looks. For someone in the fashion industry, she lacked finesse and carried her whole office in her bumbag packed with dog-eared pieces of paper while everybody else had embraced the digital era. She believed there was nothing more reliable than paper. Computers always crashed or misbehaved.

***

There was a time when Monique was better organised and a bit more polished but the many years of drinking had taken its toll on her health. It had started as a social thing when she wore her seven-league boots and shorts, sitting astride motorbikes and sipped beers by campfires with her hippy friends. Her long legs got her noticed by a young movie director who introduced her to his showbiz circles.

Her drinking habits had worsened as she started mixing with people in the entertainment industry and managed a small up-and-coming model agency. Over time, long drinks had turned into long drinking hours; the occasional cocktail had become fully-fledged alcoholism.

Her former-big-shot-movie director husband had stopped tolerating her excesses and spent more and more time in their countryside mansion away from Monique and her best friend, the bottom of a whiskey bottle. He did not want to grow old with the sad projection of the wife she had become.

Despite her life being in total disarray, she was eventually offered a director position at Number One Agency Model agency and with time, she had become closer to the owner, Mr Carillon. Mr Carillon had made billions from his private investment company and had set up Number One Agency on the same floor as a side business –not the most obvious choice of diversification, but it did ensure a steady supply of pretty young girls.

Monique would have gladly used her charms on him, if only she had any left. She was well aware of his motives: he demanded that Monique organise dinner dates for his network of investors with all of Monique's young recruits. Desperate for cash, she started to build a network of businessmen in want of fresh blood – Lord knows they paid better than the magazines and were more reliable. Number One Agency regularly stocked up with young, willing models whose fate depended on how fast they went in or out of Mr Carillon's favour. Whatever his motives were, one couldn't see what business a billionaire saw in a tiny modelling agency, if not to handpick a girl of his choosing.

He had been more careful lately as his wife Virginie had started hinting at his suspected treacherous escapades. He knew that his marriage was hanging by a thread and that should his wife catch him red-handed he could face the devastating financial effects of divorce. He had hired a private investigator to follow her trail and make sure he could beat her to it should he find any trace of betrayal. Lately, his wife, also a major shareholder in his firm, had been meeting a few investment bankers; Mr Carillon feared she may have been sharing trading secrets with his competitors. He wasn't *paranoid*, he was just being *cautious*, as he always told his lawyer.

***

'I am not very well parked, but hopefully I'll get to my car before the cops do!' she said as she sat down, catching her breath and wheezing like someone who'd had a life of far too much booze and cigarettes. Elena smiled shyly as Monique introduced herself.

'Elena, Icon models did not want to keep you on their books, because they did not manage to make you work as much as they'd had hoped, so they have asked me if I could take care of your career from now on.'

Elena listened to Monique's husky words and paid close attention to her lip movements, not to miss a word, as they curled around her uneven teeth. She wasn't sure what to make of Monique and her proposal, but Elena knew one thing; she could not go back to Kholui and disappoint her parents but she was running out of options. The prospect of working with her mother on the market or teaching in their small town would never be enough now she had tasted Parisian life.

'I run the woman's department, and I think you would fit perfectly in the more commercial look that I represent and believe in,' Monique continued. 'If you're happy with this, I would need you to meet with Mr Carillon. I need his approval before we can go any further.'

'OK...' replied Elena with a faint voice.

The conversation was rendered difficult by Elena's shyness, but Monique wrapped the meeting up in a few minutes, and ran back to her Fiat. She started her small red car, stepped on the gas and drove away at full throttle.

***

On Rue Duvivier, in the seventh district close to the Eiffel Tower, Elena crossed the cobble-stoned courtyard and pushed the heavy wooden door of her building. She walked up the five flights of stairs leading to the tiny flat she now rented in the building loft. Yves Saint Laurent hired her weekly for fittings and she had to stand there for hours, trying on fabulous dresses while talented seamstresses touched up their masterpieces. By modelling standards the salary was peanuts, but she had hoped that it would give her just enough for a tiny studio where she could paint in peace and be alone with her thoughts, but she was struggling to pay the rent.

Her cheeks were slightly pink from climbing up to her one bedroom apartment. The mantelpiece displayed her father's lacquered boxes and family pictures and one look at that and she felt she was home. She kicked off her shoes with a smile, switched on her Apple mac and put on some Radiohead. Tom York's lamenting voice filled the room as Elena checked her emails and did a quick Internet search on Monique. She discovered that Monique had been in the industry for at least thirty years and championed beauty at all ages. Fashion had always been about youth, but Monique brought it to the next level and focused on women's true inner beauty. Elena sat back and looked through the pictures on Number One Agency's website. Monique's website conveyed the impression of a boutique agency. Elena hoped that being represented by a smaller agency would give her a better chance, things were getting desperate.

Over the music she heard steps in the corridor outside her flat. The footsteps stopped and an envelope was pushed under her door. She held her breath, lowered the volume and waited for the person to walk away before picking up the letter. She opened it and scanned the words on the sheet – another demand from her landlady. She had been getting phone calls and letters from her recently, requesting the past month's rent. The landlady had gone quiet for a while, only to hit harder by sending a bailiff with a legal warning. She knew she would not be legally able to kick her out during the winter period, but it gave her very little time to gather the money she owed her. She slumped on her chair and with a wilting movement of the hand she dropped the letter on the floor.

***

Later that week, Elena sat with her hands on the pristine white tablecloth, contemplating the piece of art displayed in her gold rimmed plate. Dressed in a simple blue dress that perfectly matched her eyes, she had pulled her hair back in a pony tail, thus enhancing her graceful poise. She had come along way from food rations, and for the first time, she was nibbling a trio of fish tartare arranged as a *millefeuille*. Crostinis and mint leaves were delicately laid out on the plate with subtle dashes of balsamic and blackberry dressing. Mr Carillon sat opposite her, eying her greedily. His toad-like face grinned widely. His large body was wrapped in an elegant grey suit. As her graceful hands wavered over the delicacy, he eyed his prey.

'Don't use the normal knife, use the fish one,' he said as he caressed her hand with his index finger.

Elena looked down and smiled timidly. She had never been to a Michelin-starred restaurant before. Every glass, plate and napkin was impeccable; the food was sophisticated and unknown to her palate and all the waiters wore tuxedos. An exquisite arrangement of pastel roses was placed in the centre of the table, and faint candle-light flickered. Although Elena's French had improved, conversation was minimal due to the considerable language barrier not to mention the age gap. Elena tried to make a good impression and shared her passion for painting and explained, as best she could, that she had inherited it from her father. But overall, Mr Carillon enjoyed her silence and peacefulness.

After the meal, Mr Carillon guided Elena to his Rolls Royce and opened the passenger door. He sat behind the wheel and peered at Elena's legs as her dress moved up slightly as she sat down. Uncomfortable with his insistent gaze, she tugged at the hem of her dress and looked away coyly, unsure of how to get out of the situation. Her innocence was arousing and resistance always stirred his deepest impulses. His last conquest had kept him at arms' length for almost a year but, sure enough, she had eventually given in. For a man who was used to getting what he wanted, this was a real novelty. But after a few weeks of rapture, he had grown weary of dating the same person over and over. Sex with a very young person was only formidable the first time, when things were new and awkward, but after a while he grew bored with the courting, with the lack of desire in the young women's eyes and their thin, inexperienced bodies.

However, he felt there was something special about this one. She did not speak much but came across as a young lady with a strong personality. No one else before her had made him wait, change his plans or turned him down. She had a mind of her own and he was determined to tame it.

As they drove over the Pont de l'Alma towards Elena's flat at Rue Duvivier, Mr Carillon tried one last manoeuvre.

'You know, I was thinking…' he began.

Elena turned her head towards him, causing her white pearls to sway gently. She reminded him of Jan Vermeer's portrait of the *Girl with a Pearl Earring*. She had the same imploring eyes; her lips were lightly parted and revealed a perfect set of white teeth. She stirred mixed feelings inside him as he could sense her innocence as much as her experience, her inner joy as much as her utter loss, her longing as much as her strong ethics. God she was killing him. He paused, looked ahead and turned his head towards her once more.

'I was thinking that, if you wished, I could help you.'

'Help me?' Elena asked, with her eyes scanning his.

'Well, you mentioned at dinner that you enjoyed drawing, painting and had once dreamed of becoming an art teacher. What about having your own studio and tools to make that dream come true and become the artist you've always longed to be?'

He was making eyes at her. She could feel the lust devouring him.

Elena smiled and shook her head slowly, 'I can't'. She replied. 'I can't pay for rent, so I can't pay for more bigger apartment,' she replied in bad English. 'But thank you… for your helping.'

Mr Carillon resumed looking at the road. His face grew inscrutable. He clenched the wheel harder and ground his teeth. With his cold executive voice, he continued, 'You're not really enjoying modelling, are you?' He slid his hands up and down on the wheel, causing the car to swerve a little. 'You may have booked Yves Saint Laurent, but I can't see how it can be exciting to stand there all day while being fiddled with. I bet you'd rather be painting,' he said with a cunning smile.

Elena scrutinised his facial expression while fiddling with the strap of her handbag. She could sense the tension between them and knew what he was trying to imply.

'I sorry! I don't understand,' she said clumsily as she looked down.

'The least I can do is help you, I wouldn't want one of my girls to be let down or bored. But of course, you consider the offer I am about to make,' he continued. Elena's hands became moist and her throat constricted mildly. 'I own a flat overlooking the River Seine, on Île Saint-Louis. It has large windows and lots of light for an artist like you. You could move in and paint at your leisure… for free.' He paused. She noticed a twitch in his eye. 'Once a week, I would visit you to check on your progress… and keep you *company*,' he stressed the last word, pregnant with sexual innuendo.

Elena's brain suddenly triggered her inner alarm system; her eyelids fluttered nervously, her heart beat wildly, and pain burst through her chest. 'And when the painting is finished, I would come and buy it from you. You would make good money, potentially get your name out as a fully-fledged artist and be kind to me in return… It's a win-win situation.' He looked at her with luscious eyes.

'Can I think about it please?' Elena asked in as calm a voice as she could muster as his car stopped in front of her entrance door.

Silence.

'Don't think too long,' he replied in earnest.

Elena walked out of the car, punched in the digital code with her shaking fingers, pushed the building door open and disappeared. Mr Carillon smirked, put his car into first gear and drove off and the cool whirring engine of his large car hummed away in the night.

PART THREE

NEW YORK

CHAPTER 14

Marion, The New York Models' Flat, New York, November 1996

The hundreds of weary travellers dawdled along the US customs queue, shuffling their bags and themselves along the grey worn out carpet. I unfolded the green non-US immigration form I was given on board and read the questions one more time. Had I participated in one of the great wars? Was I smuggling or using drugs? Had I ever been in jail? Had I participated in Nazi atrocities? I put it down and wondered whether these questions were seriously expected to be answered? I would need to be close to a hundred years old to qualify for half of the first question and even Pablo Escobar thought he was a businessman, not a smuggler. America was a paranoid place and as far as they were concerned they were only ever going to allow the good guys in. Old Glory had its pride of place in every corner of the airport. I approached the stern Customs Officer who took my passport. He was a well-built black man, the kind of guy I did not want to discuss my green form with. His face was as welcoming as a shop with a 'closed' sign on its door. He looked my passport and me up and down in turn.

'Is it your first time in the US?' he asked as he flipped through my passport.

'Yes,' I replied while I looked at my watch. It was one a.m. Paris time.

'What's the purpose of your visit?' He said automatically, barely moving his face.

Blank. *Shit. What should I say?* I thought. 'Pleasure!' I blurted out. My blood froze in my veins.

'How long will you stay in the US? Do you have a return ticket?' He had made his point clear.

'Three months,' I answered in a constricted voice. I handed him my return ticket.

'Have a good stay.' He closed my passport and slammed it on the desk.

I crossed the yellow line. I was officially in America. I took a deep breath and made my way towards the baggage reclaim. I wound my watch forward to seven a.m. and thought about my parents who were probably thinking about me. *I'll call them later once I manage to buy a phone card.* I remembered how excited my father was when I had told him that I was moving to New York. He had never been to America and probably never would, but he held fond memories of the jazz bands in local bars in Paris, where he grew up shortly after World War II. At the same time he also dreaded America's hegemony and feared their policies. He both envied and resented the New World, but I was too young to ponder on political issues. I looked up to the New World, their trends, their music and their drive.

***

The Customs Officer's cool apathy was nothing compared to the excruciating cold that awaited me outside. New York was experiencing unprecedented low winter temperatures. As I stepped out of the airport, the biting cold seized my nostrils and bitterly burnt my face. I felt as though the oxygen had frozen into minuscule stalactites inside my nose. Despite my warm jacket and leather boots, my body threatened to become a giant icicle if I did not get moving quickly.

'Taxi?' hailed a tall man wrapped up in a thick parka and a trapper hat.

I nodded. My chattering teeth prevented me from emitting anything more than a grunt as I followed the trapper whose job – or penance, depending on the weather conditions – was to escort people to the next cab on line. I tried to climb through the dirty snow that had been shovelled onto each side of the road. I made a hesitant first step into the icy mound of snow, followed by a second one, simultaneously dragging my heavy suitcase and balancing my other bag on my shoulder. In a final spurt of effort, I pulled everything over the accumulated snow and came skidding down against a yellow taxi.

'Sorry! I'm so sorry!' I apologised as I bent down towards the passenger seat window. The Indian driver wore a tall red turban that touched the car roof, preventing him from turning his head towards me.

'That's fine, get in! It's cold out!' the driver exclaimed.

'No kidding!' I said as I heaved my suitcase into the boot. *I guess you're not going to help me put my stuff in the boot.*

'Where would you like to go?' the driver asked in a sing-song voice, once I was sitting in the back seat.

'206 East 15th Street and 3rd Avenue, please,' I replied as the car drove off with a screech.

The taxi's dead suspension shook me around as it skidded its way out of the airport towards the Big Apple. As we crossed the Queensboro Bridge and approached the city, tall buildings sprung up out of the ground like mushrooms. The taxi sped through the crowded streets and was regularly sent up in the air by the various potholes and lumps of asphalt. The bumpy roads were like the face of an old woman, worn with fatigue and wrinkles and I was beginning to understand one of the side benefits of wearing a turban.

'There you are Miss. Forty-five dollars please,' the driver said as the race came to a halt.

I had hardly shut the boot when the taxi sputtered off, trailing heaving fumes behind. I stood there for a moment with my luggage, dumfounded. The buildings seemed to meet at the top as they sprawled upward towards the sky, enclosing me in a prison of concrete and noise. I felt giddy with so many towers swirling around and above me.

A metal number 206 was screwed into a wooden door, however, the number 6 had decided to break loose and reinvent itself as a 9. I dragged my luggage up the stairs and pressed the bell for Flat 2. Somebody buzzed me in and left the door ajar as I made it to the landing of the second floor. I carefully pushed the door open and was met by a pale looking girl who stood there, looking at me as if I was an alien. Her hair and skin were very pale and she wore white pyjamas. She looked as if all life had been sucked out of her.

'Hello! I'm Marion, I'm also with Icon Models and I'm going to be staying with you guys,' I spoke with a hesitant voice.

Emotionless, the phantom girl pulled the door wide open to let me in.

'Hullo,' she said faintly.

I walked through a corridor that led onto a large living area with high ceilings. Daylight from the narrow space between our building and the neighbouring one was glimmering through a film of dirt on the three large windowpanes and a rank smell of cigarettes which pervaded the whole place. As with all model flats, furniture was kept to a bare minimum: wide brown sofas framed a battered mahogany coffee table in the middle of the room, which was crowded with empty glasses and bottles. I looked around. There was nothing else, no plants or paintings on the once-white yellow walls.

A broad staircase off to the right led to an exposed mezzanine floor. I followed the pale girl as she shuffled straight on, past the living room, back to the bedroom she shared with two Eastern-looking girls and stood by their door uncertain what to make of it all. I could sense from the girls' uninviting faces that I would have to look for my bedroom myself. How different this would be to living with Betina, Elena and Amirit.

I turned around and spotted what looked remotely like a kitchen opposite the Eastern girls' bedroom. It seemed as if the builders had forgotten about it then tried to cram it into the utility room as an after-thought. It was a small windowless room, tucked under the attic, with a fridge, a sink and a couple of shelves, bowed with the weight of cans and stacked plates. Between the girls' bedroom and the kitchen, there was a rather large bathroom with chequered floors and mouldy walls. I turn around as I heard footsteps. A dishevelled blonde girl with never-ending legs strutted towards me, breasts pushed out. Her dressing gown trailed behind her, revealing a white cotton baby doll nightdress. I caught a glimpse of the nipples under the thin material, blushed and looked away. I was starting to believe that it was quite normal in the modelling industry to flash one's boobs. 'Hi! I'm Kate,' she said as she offered a limp hand.

'Marion.'

'Are you French?' Kate asked as she tied up her robe.

'Is it that obvious?' I asked.

'It *sounds* obvious! I'm Canadian, from Toronto, the Anglo-Saxon part of Canada, ' Kate said as she poured some cereal into a semi-clean bowl. 'How long are you staying?'

She bent down to find some milk in the fridge, took a carton out and smelled it. She wiggled her nose and pulled back, then decided against binning it and put it back in the fridge door. She selected another bottle randomly, repeated the same action and poured the milk into the bowl.

'As long as possible, I guess,' I said. 'If I can find my bedroom, that is!'

Kate looked for a clean spoon in the drawer and soon gave up. She rinsed one that she had found amongst the pile of dirty plates and dug into her cereals.

'There'ch a free bed in che Russians' room, ch'ere,' Kate said with her mouth full, pointing with her spoon.

I had been dreading living in another model flat since I had left the girls in Paris, and these girls seemed so cold and unapproachable.

I turned towards the bedroom. There were two bunk beds; the pale girl was perched on the top bed on the left, dangling her feet while listening to the monotonous rambling of her blonde comrade in front of her. A third girl with short black hair sat on the bed below her, absent-mindedly smoking a cigarette. She inhaled the smoke, squeezed her lips together, above which was nested a perfectly round black mole, put the cigarette down on the rim of the ashtray, then held up a small mirror and started tweezing her eyebrows. The cigarette consumed itself until the ash fell into the ashtray, and the cigarette rolled onto the sheets. Engrossed in themselves, none of the girls noticed smoke grow thicker. I suddenly heard a shriek: the three Russian girls were frantically pounding the bed with their pillows, in an attempt to smother the incipient flames. Kate set her bowl aside, filled a jug with water and took long strides towards the burning bed. The water splashed everywhere. The brunette stepped back, and looked at Kate, panting and wet.

'You're welcome!' Kate said aloud as she walked out, leaving the three Russian girls to their bickering. Kate rolled her eyes and resumed eating her breakfast.

'I guess that woke me up alright!' Kate smiled.

'Very impressive!' I commented.

The girls coughed and opened the windows in order to ventilate the room. The brunette took her belongings away from the burnt sheets and moved them onto the available bed. What should have been my bed was now officially unavailable.

This is madness, I thought. I suddenly felt pangs of angst in my stomach. 'Was this my only option?' I asked Kate.

'Well, I guess you could either stay in my bed...' Kate smirked, and then looked up, pensive. 'Or stay in the attic.'

'The attic?'

'See that wooden ladder behind you? That goes up to the attic.'

I grabbed the narrow wooden ladder and shook it to check its stability; it was wonky but, given the options, I decided it was worth a try. I climbed carefully, with my feet sideways. Once I reached the top, I stretched my arms forwards and hoisted myself up. As I removed my foot from the last rung, the ladder wobbled, tipped back, and finally toppled over onto the ground.

I went on all fours to avoid feeling giddy and looked down.

'Kate?' I called sheepishly, 'Er... The ladder fell... could you pick it up and hold it upright for me please?'

Kate popped her head out of the kitchen underneath the attic, 'That doesn't look safe at all!' she said as she lifted up the ladder and propped it against the wall.

I took light hesitant steps back down.

'I have to call the agency. I cannot be risking my neck every time I climb up the attic or enter a room filled with pyromaniacs.' I was agitated and paced back and forth. 'I didn't sign up for this shit!'

'Well, I suppose you could call the agency, only it's Sunday. The agency is closed and you need a phone card to make a phone call. The agency has blocked the home phone', Kate replied.

'This is absolutely crazy!' I almost choked with anger; the veins of my neck had swollen. I sat down on the floor and buried my head in my hands.

'Take it easy. You can sleep on the sofa tonight and sort things out with the agency tomorrow,' Kate tried to sound reassuring.

Alerted by the noise, a dark-haired girl in her pyjamas came down from the mezzanine at the other end of the living room and stepped into the kitchen.

'What's that racket all about?' she asked.

'Morning Helen!' Kate said with a smile. 'You've just missed an interesting series of events: a fire, a ladder accident… This is Marion, by the way. She's our freshman from Paris.'

'I see! I hope you're not hurt at least?' Helen asked as she put her long jet-black hair up in a messy bun.

'I'm fine, thanks… just annoyed, I'm tired, jetlagged, and…' I was looking for the words. 'There doesn't seem to be a bed for me. I never fit in anywhere. I mean, how can the agency ask me to fly the whole way here to camp on the ground?'

'Are you new in the industry?' Helen asked.

'I started a couple of months ago now,' I replied.

'Aw… I see, that's why!'

'What do you mean?'

'You're just a number you know. We all are. You'd better get used to it!' Helen laughed.

'Sad but true,' Kate added. 'I've been doing this for five years now and it's not getting any better. The agency will tell you that if you're not happy, you can find your own place, which is virtually impossible if you don't have a visa.'

'Or you'd end up paying twice the price. You're better off here, trust me,' Helen explained.

***

That evening, after exploring the buzzing downtown neighbourhood all day, I lay wide awake on the sofa, with my legs twisted on the right side and my left hand under my head. I sat up, puffed up my pillow, and tucked my duvet under my body so the cold draft would not sneak in. I couldn't get away from the pungent burning smell coming from the sheets. I sat up again, cross my legs, wrapped my duvet around me and looked at the looming, dark emptiness of the flat. Perched on the sofa, with messy hair and tired eyes, everything seemed to swirl around me. I felt like a homeless person who had found a squat to crash in for the night. I dreamt that night that I was in a canoe, adrift in the middle of the ocean towards an unknown destination.

When day finally broke, I awoke back in the reality of the sofa in the models' flat. I heard Kate and Helen giggling upstairs in their bedroom up on the mezzanine. The Russians did not stir; they were probably fast asleep. I was buried deep into my duvet when I eventually heard footsteps.

'Good morning!' said Kate in a singing voice as she glided past me. 'How did you sleep?'

'I feel battered!'

'Good! Welcome to New York!' she said before disappearing in the kitchen.

I put my jumper on and joined Kate in the narrow room. We both stood there and ate Kate's cereal with somebody else's milk.

'Make sure you wrap up warm before you go out. It's freezing cold out there!' Kate advised. 'It has probably killed most hobos, there aren't many out there anymore.'

'You mean Giuliani has pushed them down the Hudson River!' Helen joined in the conversation, unexpectedly. Both Kate and I started laughing.

'Morning, sleepy-head!' Kate replied.

'How long have you both been here?' I asked.

'Five months,' Helen replied.

'Six, but sleeping together the past three,' Kate added with her now recognisable smirk.

I looked at both of them with a start but Kate and Helen went on with their morning routine.

CHAPTER 15

Marion, The New York Agency, New York, November 1996

Wrapped up in my long black Moncler Down jacket, I stepped onto the street on my way to the agency. A cold wind seized my face; I lifted my hood and zipped up my coat. I held onto the railing and carefully walked down the frozen steps. During the night, a thick white blanket of snow had covered the entire town. Snowflakes swirled around me as my feet sank in the crunching snow. Black garbage bags were piled up on top of the older ones trapped in the snow. Some of them had been dumped in the road, narrowing its width by half and bringing traffic to a standstill. On Third Avenue angry drivers swerved into the middle lanes, blaring cabbies honked away, cars skidded, wheels spun; the whole town was battling with nature. Dressed in black woollen coats with their collars up, dark pants and walking shoes, New Yorkers struggled to find their balance, coffee cups balanced in one hand and briefcases in the other. Unflinching, they all made their way to the subway station at Union Square. It was another normal day in Manhattan.

I was plunged underground with a briefcase-touting army of New Yorkers. As I hurried down the frost bitten steps, my soles suddenly slipped and sent me flying into the people in front of me. They turned their heads for a moment and continued their journey casually, leaving me where I had landed. People coming down the stairs stepped around me and carried on.

'You should sue 'em!' a tall man in his forties commented as he walked past me.

139

'Sue who? The snow?' I asked, with a raised brow.

'The street sweepers! The City! They should keep the streets clean!' The man continued his descent. I was dumbfounded. I stretched my arm and inched my fingers towards the railing and pulled myself up. I held a firm grip of the banister and walked down the stairs sideways, my feet firmly flat on the ground as if I was wearing skis.

The metal carriages screeched to a halt and disgorged passengers. People on the platforms huddled together forming a featureless mass. They stood silent and remote. With a deafening screech another train drove past in the opposite direction, at full speed.

The commuters stared blankly ahead while they were being transported uptown, disappearing behind newspapers and sipping coffee out of thermos flasks, or eating bagels they had just bought at nearby delis. New Yorkers brought their breakfast to work, caught up with their unfinished books in the crowd, continued their night's sleep on the subway and carried their work shoes in their backpacks. White tags covered the windows. Signs. Slang. Secrets. Insults. Love messages. The pulse of the city beat in the subway. Rustling newspapers. Rocking carriages. Blasting music. Rattling empty bottles. Snores. Smells. Elbows. Braking. Screech. Jerk. Halt.

I surfaced at last at Park Avenue South and quickly scanned the neighbourhood. I could not see the street names or building numbers as scaffolding and shop signs largely obscured them. I walked in one direction, then the other, braving the gusty winds, and trying in earnest to protect my face from the snow. There it was – a tall grey building with a revolving door. Two window cleaners were abseiling down the walls on ropes. They pushed their feet against the concrete and swung from one corner to the next with ease, like city monkeys.

I stepped through the revolving doors and noticed an unmanned security desk on the left.

Icon Agency, fifth floor, said the board above it. I jumped into a lift and caught sight of myself in its mirrors. My make-up had run, my curly hair looked frizzier than usual, I looked tense and miserable, on top of which my feet were terribly wet and cold. I wiped my smeared mascara with my right hand and shook my hair down to give it more body. Hopeless. I would have to make a stunning first impression despite the raccoon circles underneath my eyes and my wild mane.

The doors opened. Two black-clad flinty-faced businesswomen clutching folders to their chests stepped in hurriedly. I looked up at the red number above the women's heads – ten. The lift was rocketing towards the higher floors and there was nothing I could do to stop it other than trigger the alarm. Short of options, I gave a cursory glance to the selection of buttons panel and noticed it started with the tenth floor.

'*Have I read it wrong*?' I wondered as I frantically pressed on the number ten. 'Do you know how to get to the fifth floor, by any chance?' I dared asking the two stern women.

'Go back down and select a different elevator,' the tallest lady replied with a look that could break glass.

That's not very helpful! I thought but nodded anyhow, 'I see!'

The women resumed their conversation, and kept a suspicious eye on me. Trying not to make things worse, I kept my finger pressed on the "G" button the whole way up.

Once back on the ground floor I approached the security guard. 'Good morning, sir,' I started. His chalky-white beard moved as he chewed a sandwich dripping with ketchup. I pursed my lips, 'Would you happen to know how to get to the fifth floor please?'

'Sure thin'! Take the elevator on the left,' he said with a drawl, and wiped his mouth with the back of his hand. 'But I need you to fill in the register for me, doll!'

He stood up slowly. The chair squeaked as it released him. He put his chunky hands on the visitors' book and opened it. He sucked his index and flipped through the large pages, then pointed at an empty spot with his greasy finger.

'Right there. Your name, please,' he said with his head cocked to one side, peering at me.

I could feel his gaze while I was signed in.

'Are you a maw-del?' he asked.

I wavered between being pleased he had called me a model and being disappointed that he had hesitated and asked. My lips twitched into a faint smile.

'You asked for the fifth floor, so I figured...' he said.

Never mind, I thought.

Back in the lift, I turned towards the door, to avoid the mirrors. The guard beeped me up to the fifth floor with his badge and waved. My smile vanished as the doors shut.

I made it to a reception area with polished wooden floors and modern red seats which were occupied by a few long-legged creatures nervously twitching with their portfolios on their laps. I approached a pretty young receptionist wearing a black dress with a plunging neckline, revealing two small apple-shaped breasts. Her blonde hair was held up in a bun by a long chopstick.

'Good morning, I'm Marion Durant. I have an appointment withDavid.'

'Please take a seat. He'll be right with you,' the receptionist replied fiddling with her chopstick. She picked up the receiver; her long hairpin took advantage of the situation to break free from her hair and roll off under the desk.

As in Paris, glass panes separated the waiting area from the booking area. I could make out silhouettes moving behind the frosted parts of the windows like shadow puppets. I turned around and made my way towards the seats. I slowed down as I realised that none were available. The other girls were swivelling on their chairs, glancing occasionally at the glass windows in expectation. Most girls had long straight hair and wore leggings with knee-high boots. I took my jacket off as it was dripping with melted snow. I carefully folded it around my arm and placed it on the floor with my bag. I couldn't have felt less glamorous if I tried, and I marvelled at how the other girls managed to look completely unaffected by the extreme weather.

The glass wall suddenly opened and out came a tall dark-haired man rolling the sleeves of his white shirt and flashing his many large silver rings. His skinny bowed legs were squeezed into tight jeans; he ambled towards the waiting area clicking his pointy cowboy boots on the wooden floor. Most girls uncrossed their legs and flicked their hair, ready to stand in case he was going to stop in front of them. The booker suddenly paused, hunkered down and picked up the chopstick which had ended its course in the middle of the room. He handed it back to the receptionist and smiled in a conspiratorial way.

'Marion! Welcome! I'm David,' he said in French as he clicked along, past the other girls, his arms wide open. 'Viens! Suis moi!'

He invited me into the booking area. I felt welcome upon hearing my native language.

'Everyone, this is Marion, the winner of this year's contest. Marion, this is everyone,' David said as he introduced me to the other four bookers sitting behind their desks.

'Hi, Marion,' they casually replied in chorus and resumed their work.

Most agents were busy playing lieutenants with their appointed models, planning and scheming, mapping their itineraries with military precision, going through their castings or pictures, and organising their daily schedules. One blonde girl sat on her booker's desk dangling her red stilettos off the edge. Her yellow mini-skirt flashed far more skin than reasonable. Despite the snowstorm, she was dressed for summer. Two other girls were curled up against the wall, smoking cigarettes and chatting. Others were idly leaning on the counter while copies and cards were being printed off. The walls were covered by rows of composites; hundreds of faces were looking over the bookers' shoulders, hoping they would find them the right jobs to either propel them into stardom, or simply pay their rent.

'How are you today? Have you adjusted well?' David asked. 'Have you met the other girls at the apartment?'

'I sure have, yes. Talking of which, I was wondering how I could get a new duvet?' I asked.

'What's wrong with yours? Didn't you have one on your bed?' David asked, fiddling with his rings.

'Well… the thing is… the duvet was burnt.'

'Burnt?' David asked, taken aback.

'It caught fire because… a cigarette,' I tried to explain. 'It was an accident.'

David shook his head and tutted, 'I'm ready to bet it was Irina. She's the only smoker anyway. I'll have a word with her. There are extra duvets and pillows in the cupboard underneath the staircase.'

'I'll check, thanks. Is it OK if I stay in the attic?'

'I didn't even know there was an attic!' He replied. I had no further questions. I realised I'd have to figure out the ladder issue on my own. 'Soooo… where were we? Let me see your Book first,' David said as he started sifting through my portfolio. 'You don't have any tears, just tests?'

'Tears?' I was unsure what he meant.

'Editorials. Magazine sheets you tear out and put in your book to showcase your work. You know… to get more work,' David explained impatiently. He sat back and started biting his nails. 'I guess we will have to organise a few *go-and-sees* with the various magazines and maybe more photo tests, as these ones are not very strong,' he added as he flipped through the book with one hand and bit the nails of the other one. 'I'm going to contact Macy's and a few other department stores to get you making some cash.'

'Kate told me I needed a visa to work,' I said.

'We're working on it, but we'll advance you the money in the interim; it'll be deducted from your monthly contract allowance.' David replied with a shifty look. 'Right! Let's measure you now,' he said as he sprung to his feet. I tagged along. '90-62-90'. Broad shoulders,' he commented as he petted my shoulders. 'Do you still swim?' I nodded. 'You'll have to stop.' He then looked up at my face. 'What's wrong with your eyes? They are red.'

'Are they? I did not sleep very well last night.'

'And your hair?' He was studying me intensely. 'Is it naturally so… frizzy?' he asked.

'Curly. It's naturally *curly*, but because of the horrible weather…'

'You have hair on your forearms!' David exclaimed as if the building was on fire. I blushed and pulled my sleeves down as best I could.

'First thing's first, I am booking you an appointment for hair removal,' David said as he went back to his desk. He dismissed me with a wave, 'Give me a few minutes. I need to make a few phone calls to organise today's appointments.'

I looked around me, smiled shyly at the other girls, and spent over a quarter of an hour browsing through the rows of composite cards on the wall. None of the girls smiled in their pictures; they all looked as if they had been brought in against their will. Wasn't there anything to be happy about being a model? Was fashion big fat attitude? While these questions went through my mind, David's boot clicking brought me back to reality.

'Right, I have ten appointments for you today, mostly *go-and-sees*; not for actual jobs, just meetings with photographers' agents and department stores. We have to try and see as many people as possible this week. They're all within walking distance; it shouldn't take you too long. But before that, here's the address of the beauty salon. The lady there takes care of most top models, so you're in good hands. She's expecting you now.'

David handed me a piece of paper.

Ten appointments. I was gutted; I'd be pounding the nearly frozen pavement all day long.

'I have selected a couple of strong pictures for your composite: a close-up of your face and a body shot from behind. Zion will print a few cards for you. Give him a couple of minutes and you're good to go!' David said with a smile.

It was lunchtime by the time I was out of the building. The ten awaiting appointments did not promise an early night. The snowstorm had grown fiercer and I zipped up my hood with my frozen hands in a vain attempt to protect my face from the biting cold. As I staggered along the pavement, I felt faint; my stomach was rumbling and my limbs were shivering with cold. My thick jacket had not had time to dry at the agency making me cold and wet. I walked past a few restaurants that I couldn't afford before seeking shelter in a deli around the corner. The shop was badly lit and filthy-looking men in suits were biting into their bagels most with a copy of the Financial Times stuck under their arm. Two men stood behind the counter taking orders and cash from customers. Hundreds of fingers had handled the gum, nuts and candy stacked by the till. I queued by the throbbing fridges which looked as though they were about to break down at any moment and noticed a stack of fading maps on the counter. I took a deep breath and, before I knew it, I was next in line. I quickly scanned the different bagels on display and ordered the cinnamon raisin bagel and a warm coffee with milk.

'What would you like on your bagel, Miss?'

I had a second look at the various fillings and noticed the eggs frying on the hot stove. Impatient customers started stomping their feet; while the shop owner took other orders.

'Cream cheese please,' I ordered. 'Oh, and a city map please.'

I stood outside in the cold and tried to unfold the map but it flapped around in the wind. I rushed into the subway station, leaned the unfolded map on the wall and pencilled out the various locations of my appointments. I gulped down my bagel and my coffee in record time. Next to me, a huddled up elderly man was biting into a stale sandwich. I stopped chewing for a second and wondered how different I was from that despondent homeless man. I barely had a decent place to sleep, no money, I was lonely and frozen to the bone. At least I wouldn't be stuck out in the cold at night.

The entrance to the salon was falling apart and looked like a drug den. I came to a halt in front of a rusted grille and buzzer. A large woman opened the door and peered over the safety chain with a face like a prune. She shut the door, unlocked the chain and ushered me in.

'Sit, please!' she ordered.

I sat down on the white fake leather sofa, looking up at her in dread. A few dog-eared magazines were displayed on a glass table. I heard her spray some disinfectant, drag some furniture and shut the curtains.

'Come!'

I followed her into a small white room filled with old metal tools and prayed that David had told Mrs Evil that I had come in for hair removal, not an abortion. I nervously sat on the side of the old salon bed before being pushed back. She talcum powdered my forearms and spread on thick sticky wax all over and before I could say a word. She quickly pressed thin strips of cotton in the wax and pulled them off with a frank jerk. There was no warning and tears silently rolled down my cheeks.

'Take pants off!' she ordered in a bad Russian English accent, as if what I'd just endured wasn't enough.

I muttered, 'but that's all I came for!'

'Let me see hair. Down there!' she instructed.

I reluctantly unbuttoned my trousers, which the Russian lady whipped off. She grabbed my leg and pulled me towards her so that my bottom reached the end of the table and repeated the same waxing procedure. I felt as if I was being plucked like a chicken. I was absolutely certain that no top-model had ever set foot in there.

After hours of braving the cold, swapping walking shoes for stilettos, warm layers for alluring clothing, and plenty of portfolio flipping, I went back to the apartment feeling as tired and weary as a fisherman who comes home empty-handed after a long day out at sea. I tried to dry my coat and shoes by the heater and sat down on the couch, staring blankly in front of me. I put my feet up on the coffee table and wriggled my toes back to life. Soon after, Kate stumbled in with grocery bags and slammed the door. It sounded as if the storm had invited itself in.

'Hello there! How was your day?' I asked. 'Do you need some help with those?' I offered, hoping the answer wouldn't force me up out of my comfortable position.

'I'm fine thanks!' Kate replied, panting. 'Had a few interesting castings.' Kate dropped her bags on the floor and sat on the couch opposite me to catch her breath. 'I have been working on a new face and I think it's working!'

'A new face?' I could still find the energy to be surprised. Kate took off her jacket but kept her woollen hat and mittens on. She joined her hands together and blew hot air while rubbing her hands. She adjusted her hat, turned her body sideways, and stretched her left leg forward.

'Watch!' Kate said as she lowered her face, sucked in her cheeks and twitched her nose. '*That* face!' Kate said once she released her cheeks and nose into their original shapes.

I guffawed. 'Don't be ridiculous! That's so unnatural!'

'Who said fashion was about being natural?' Kate rubbed her hands and got up. 'Want some tea?'

'Sure! Good idea! I'm too exhausted to even get up.'

'Why don't you take a shower and warm up?' Kate shouted from the kitchen.

'I'm good thanks. Later.' I shut my eyes for a few seconds.

Kate came back with two mugs and a big bowl.

'I've made some dinner, would you like some? It's pea and sweetcorn salad?'

'Try it, eat it, or make your own, you French snob!'

'I'm not being a snob, I have just never seen peas in a salad before!'

'It's good for you. Dig in.'

'Thanks a lot for looking after me,' I replied slowly. Kate had been a good companion in New York and I had badly needed one to help me survive.

***

Irina came home an hour later with one of the blonde girls. Two older well-dressed men fell in behind them and waited in the corridor. The girls giggled as they made way towards their rooms to dress up for dinner. Bemused, Kate and I followed their comings and goings.

'What the hell are they doing with these old men?' I whispered to Kate with goggled eyes.

'Getting free meals and eventually a visa, who knows!' Kate replied, suspiciously.

'They are older than their fathers! Yuck, disgusting,' I tutted.

'I have lived in this flat for months and have never spoken to them, I'm not even sure they speak English.'

'What are the two Russians' names?'

'Yelena is the girl we just saw, and the one that looks like a ghost is Katerina. I don't know if they work or not, but they seem to go out a lot and often bring older guys back to the welcoming ambience of our mouldy flat.'

'I'm sure that the agency would not keep them on if they weren't working.'

'Don't be so sure…'

Half an hour later, Irina and Yelena came out of their bedroom both wearing tight black dresses and holding mink coats. Their childish desire to resemble one another by wearing matching outfits made them look even younger, and the men older by the same token. Curls of smoke surrounded Irina's made-up face. She wiggled her hips towards the two men, ignoring us as she strutted past.

At bedtime, I checked the stability of the ladder again and climbed up to the attic. The room was dark and cold. I managed to make out a single bed and a lamp on the side table. I fumbled to find the switch and scanned the room through the dull glow of the lamp. The slanted ceiling did not allow for much furniture, apart from the bed and side-table, there was only a small wonky cupboard with an empty vase on top of it.

More than anything, the place needed serious dusting. Every time I touched something, I sneezed. Other than that and that a colony of spiders would have to be forced into immigration it would have been almost habitable. I came back down and Kate showed me a narrow cupboard under the staircase where the bedding was kept. I flung my duvet up through the hatch and hoisted my suitcase up with Kate's help. I thought about taking a shower but the idea of crash landing on the floor put me off. I made my bed and stared at the bleak room once more before switching off the light.

After a few minutes, my whole body started shivering uncontrollably; the dampness of the attic had crept inside my bed. Steamy breath came out of my mouth and nostrils and it felt as if I was going numb. I kicked my duvet back and fetched my hat, mittens and my woollen jumper. Back in my bed, I tucked my duvet as high up as possible, snuggled into the foetus position, rubbed my feet against each other, and waited for the shaking to stop.

Once my temperature stabilised, my bladder decided to play tricks on me. I tossed and turned, tried to ignore the irrepressible urge but eventually opened my eyes and looked around for ideas.

'The vase!' I thought. I groped in the dark for the vase, placed it on the floor and pulled off my pyjamas trousers. As it was too narrow to sit on, I squatted higher up. Instead of coming out in a single spurt as it normally would, the urine I had held for too long was now squirting out, down my legs and in all directions.

'Oh no!' I exclaimed. I stayed in the most awkward position a bit longer, at a loss. I mopped my mess with a towel and climbed down the ladder with my soiled vase, praying I would not meet anyone on the way to the bathroom.

***

The next morning, unable to face yet more cereal, I ventured into a coffee shop on Union Square for breakfast. At that time the place was packed so I went for the stool by the bar. I grabbed a newspaper from the counter and ordered scrambled eggs on toast and a large coffee with milk. The place had a retro feel to it with its yellow walls, high stools, booths and metallic tables. Broken cups were gathered into a mosaic on the concrete wall behind me. The cups had made it from broken to beautiful. I wondered if I was going the other way.

A handsome dark-haired man in his mid thirties sat on the stool next to mine smile at me. He wore dark blue jeans and a smart black shirt. *Paul Smith shoes*, I noticed.

'Don't believe anything that's written in that paper,' he said.

'Why is that?' I asked, taken aback.

'It's either bad news or gossip. Ignorance is much safer and happier!' he smiled and turned towards the waiter.

'Same as usual?'

The handsome stranger nodded.

'Do you often come here?' I asked, even to me the words sounded unbelievably corny.

'More often than you do!'

'How can you be so sure?'

'Because I manage the place and I have never seen you before!' He held out his hand, 'I'm John, nice to meet you.'

I shook his hand and introduced myself.

'Where are you from?'

'I'm French.'

'I gathered that, but where from?'

'Avignon, in the south of France.'

'Très joli!' he replied.

'You speak French?'

'Just enough for you to ask. But no, I don't,' he added. 'Do you live around here?'

'Literally around the corner – on 15th Street.'

'The models' flat?'

'How come you know so much?' I was starting to smarten up.

'Because I don't read the paper, I only gather information for myself.'

I looked confused.

'Only pulling your leg. My flat is just across Icon's. Beautiful French girl in this neighbourhood, it's a pretty easy guess.'

'Am I that obvious?'

John stood up, 'Not really, I used to be a model myself so I had an unfair advantage. Marion, it was very nice to meet you. I've got to get crackin' but make sure you have a good day, and if you're bored or hungry, more likely, you know where to find me,' John said with a charming smile.

I left the café with a smile and put my earphones in and pressed the play as I headed toward Macy's department store.

***

'Karen will see you now,' the receptionist said as she leaned over her desk. 'Through those doors to your right; it's the first office on the right.'

'Thank you,' I replied as I gathered my belongings.

I gave a gentle knock on the door.

'Come on in!' said a voice.

It was a large office with two white shiny desks. A brunette with black Prada glasses smiled and greeted me. She pushed the pile of papers and magazines on the side and took my portfolio. I sat down and waited patiently.

'Have you been here long?' Karen asked.

'I have just arrived; this is my second day.'

'Nasty weather out there, you poor thing!'

'That's alright, I've got a pretty good jacket,' I was trying to stay positive.

'That's the spirit! I like that,' Karen smiled. 'Thank you for coming, very nice Book, I'll stay in touch. Who's your booker?'

'David.'

'See you very soon Marion.'

I stood up, shook Karen's hand and walked out, very conscious of my gait.

***

My next casting was for L'Oreal and it brought me to the lobby of a very tall building which was crammed with models. I handed my passport to the security guard, took a seat and sifted through the magazines on the coffee table, hoping that one day I too would be on those laminated pages displaying that jaded, *I'm-too-cool-to-smile* face all the models had, instead of my *I'm-too-cold-and-tired-to-smile* look.

'Hi Frenchie,' Kate said as she approached me and sat down next to me. 'Nice to see you! I didn't realise you'd be here. Do you have a lot of appointments today?'

'A few, not too many,' I huffed.

'Are you going to the agency's event tonight?'

'Oh yes, David did mention something earlier on… I don't know if I will.'

'You have to come!' Kate winked. 'Top photographer Paolo Piviano will be there. It's his birthday. Let's say that it's a much more fun way to do castings and in the worst case scenario, we'll have fun and a free meal, trust me!' Kate opened a magazine and started flicking through it.

The security guard called us in. We lined up as if we were on a catwalk and made our way towards the elevator. Packed like sardines, the ride up went on forever. We entered a brightly lit studio where a photo session was taking place. Flashes crackled in the background. A team of art directors, hairdressers and colour specialists were bustling about around a large rectangular table where boxes of hair dye were displayed along with wide sheets of paper where they were matching colour samples with headshots of the models used in their on-going campaign.

'Who's first?' an elegantly dressed man with spiky hair asked.

Like a cog in a machine, I made a few steps forward. Mr Spiky Hair ran his fingers through my hair, brushed it and felt it. An assistant took a Polaroid. I was thanked and I gave way to the next model on line. I took the lift as if in a daze and left the building. Kate caught up with me.

'Where are you going? Wait for me!' Kate was out of breath.

'I'm off to my next *thanks-but-no-thanks* appointment!'

I was walking at a quick pace.

'Don't be like that. This is how it works… it doesn't mean they won't book you! There are lots of girls, they can't sit down and have tea with all of them… think about it, it's best they keep it short and sweet so that you don't get your hopes up and… the greater the surprise is if they do choose you in the end!'

Kate wrapped her hand around my shoulders in a sisterly way and I was glad she was with me.

CHAPTER 16

Morten, New York, November 1996

Morten was standing shirtless by the make-up table, while the make-up artist, an older man with a scarf around his neck, gleefully massaged oil into his golden skin. Morten had been given dark eye make-up that intensified his stare. His square jaw tightened as the make-up artist powdered his face. He thought about his ascending career and how, just a couple of months ago, he was in a country most Americans haven't even heard of, struggling to make ends meet and now here he was, making it.

His Swedish agent, Bjorn, may have looked unimpressive when he had first approached him, but he definitely knew what he was doing and had bet on the right horse so far. Morten had effortlessly gone from small campaigns to bigger campaigns. Everywhere he went eyes turned: women lusted after him and men pined with envy. His icy eyes showed no emotion and yet revealed something feisty burning inside his soul. He seemed blank and vacant yet oozed with passion and desire. Aloof, feline and elusive, there was something animal-like about him that held everyone in awe. His controversial sex appeal was enhanced by the mystery surrounding him.

Within two months, he had travelled business class, drank the best champagne and accessed free drugs, lots of them. His New York agency laid it all out for him. He felt the cocaine rush inside him licked his teeth, and twitched his nose. That stuff was good. He was on a rollercoaster and did not want it to stop.

Mark, another male model was undergoing the same treatment, but he remained seated. A female hairdresser worked some wax through his long brown hair while he stared coolly at his reflection in the mirror, now and then looking from side to side. His muscles gleamed with oil.

Rumour had it that he had been dating top photographer Tao Wang and but no one had ever been able to confirm it. *Rumour and sex sell*, he thought. Who could blame him for trying hard and for wanting to make something of his life? Who cared about the means, what mattered to him was the end. Today, he was posing for the Versace campaign, which he hoped would propel him into stardom, away from his native Germany where he believed he had no future. Mark's folks may have been lousy parents, but they had given him the gift of beauty, and he was prepared to use and abuse it.

Marta, the new flavour of the month, had her own make-up artist and hairdresser. She sat alone on her swivelling chair while the last touch-ups were being done.

She was about to shoot the Versace campaign with one of the most famous photographers in the world, Marco Tutti. Success was around the corner, she could feel it. She ate it, she breathed it, *she* was success. She felt she deserved it after all those years of struggle, of never-ending castings, of striding along the streets, of rejection. She had endured as much as humanly possible and now it was now rightfully her turn to shine.

Marco Tutti hardly turned around when Morten, Mark and Marta entered the studio. He was absorbed in conversation with the art director and going through the storyline which hung above a small light box.

The light boxes blinded Marta and whirred as they recharged for the next shot. The wind machine blew her long eggshell dress, flashing her beautiful tanned legs. She bent one knee, then the other, swaying her hips slowly and sensuously.

One strap slid down her shoulder and revealed her small plump breast. She held it up while Marco exulted with joy. She looked like the she-wolf from the myth of Romulus and Remus as she leaned towards Mark and Morten and caressed their hair. They clung tighter to her thighs and looked up with an imploring gaze, which delighted Marco. She was in a trance and the flashes filled her with glory.

***

When Morten got back to the spacious but sparse models' flat on Christopher Street, his brother Charli was sitting on the carpet with two pale male models snorting cocaine off the coffee table. Dark rings had formed around all of their tired eyes; they did not slept much but most designers had gone for that heroin chic look lately. Being high was cool, being tired or late was equally cool. Morten did not have to try hard; he was naturally *in*. Charli had followed Morten the whole way from Stockholm to try and become a photographer but he spent most days feasting on drugs.

Dead bottles and empty glasses were strewn over the wooden floor. A stench of old cigarettes seized Morten as he walked through the door.

'It stinks in here,' Morten said as he opened the windows, threw his jacket on a chair, and grabbed a beer bottle that someone had left on the table.

'Have the hair of the dog that bit you,' Morten said to himself, draining the bottle in one gulp, trying to overcome his hangover from the previous evening's party. He had gone straight to the photo shoot from the party at nine in the morning without a wink of sleep. He gathered a few bottles and ashtrays and went to the kitchen to get a bin bag.

As he walked by the guestroom, he noticed two naked girls on the mattress on the floor. They were lying flat on their stomachs with hair and legs entangled, fast asleep. The room was in a state of complete chaos. The floor was covered with clothes and cigarette butts in half-finished drinks.

Morten saw a smeared CD case on the table and a picked up credit card next to it. He tapped the card out onto the CD case and gathered the remainder of the cocaine into a thin line. He searched his pockets for a banknote but could not find one. He fumbled in one of the girls' jackets and found a dry cleaner's receipt, it would do. He rolled the receipt up, and snorted the CD clean. After rubbing his nose, he wiped the CD with his finger and ran it on his gums and resumed tidying up the living room.

'Who are the chicks in the bedroom?' Morten asked.

'I'm not sure. I think they were with Anders last night. He went home a couple of hours ago,' Charli answered.

'Looks like he had some fun. Lucky bastard.' Morten said, laughing whole-heartedly, his pupils dilating. The large grin on his face and his messy blonde hair made him look like a henchman from an action film.

'What do we have here, a bra?' Morten asked as he rolled up his sleeves, no longer interested in cleaning. 'What's this stuff anyway?'

'Titi's latest delivery, pure blow,' Charli replied. 'And it's good!' he added with a wicked smile and wide opened eyes.

Charli handed Morten a credit card, and unable to fight temptation, Morten set about the pile of cocaine and crunched little boulders into mist. He coaxed two white lines from the snowy mound with the card. He placed Charli's rolled one dollar bill under his nose, leaned over and vacuumed the dust into one nostril and then the other.

'Nice one!' Morten exclaimed as he sat back in anticipation with pleasure.

He was filled with sudden warmth as the drugs whistled through his head and a metallic taste tingled down his throat. He moistened his finger, mopped the remaining particles from the table and rubbed his finger against his teeth.

'Right!' Morten said as he stood up sniffing and rubbing his nose. He walked casually towards the fridge and extracted two beers. He pressed each bottle against his belt buckle, whizzing the caps away from the neck.

'How was the shoot?' Charli asked Morten as he swallowed his first swig.

'It was pretty easy actually. Both Mark and I were lying on the floor grabbing this chick's legs. All we had to do was look at her,' Morten began. 'The photographer, Marco Tutti, took a few shots of us separately afterwards.'

As he slumped on the sofa, the phone rang. Charli picked it up.

'It's for you, bro. The agency.'

'Hullo!' Morten said as he slouched back on the sofa, one arm behind his head and his legs propped on the coffee table.

'Good news Morten, Marco Tutti has confirmed you for the Bjorn Borg underwear campaign! He would like to see you again though, as the client is in town. How soon can you go today?' his agent said.

'I have just left the studio. Do I really need to go back now? It's six p.m.! Is it good money at least?' Morten asked.

'It's $30,000 but it could be much more if it's used worldwide. He's asked to see you at his flat, he often meets with his clients in the penthouse.'

'OK then, cool! Where should I meet them? Hold on a sec, let me find something to write on.'

Morten sprang up on his feet and looked everywhere for a piece of paper. He started by searching in his jacket, then the drawers of the table in the entrance when he remembered the dry cleaner's receipt. He fetched it in the bedroom where the girls were still sleeping, unfolded it and wrote down Marco Tutti's home address.

'I'll get ready and get there as soon as possible,' Morten told his agent and hung up.

'Right, guys. Got to go!' Morten told his friends.

'You'd better throw some clean clothes on; you don't exactly smell like roses!' Charli teased.

Morten sprinted to the bathroom, washed his face, and ran his fingers through his hair. He sniffed his armpits, removed his shirt and threw it in the laundry basket. His jeans and on-show Calvin Kleins would be fine even though he had put them on for the party about that time yesterday. He rushed to his bedroom, opened his cupboard, tried a couple of t-shirts, threw them on the floor, and went back to the bathroom. He took his old shirt from the night before out of the basket and put it back on. He brushed his teeth and walked back to the living room, grabbed a military jacket and gave a twirl.

'You're ready? You haven't changed, have you?' Charli told him.

'Nah! I couldn't find anything decent,' Morten replied in earnest.

'Well I guess you've decided that dirty is decent!'

'Who cares? Anyway, I'm off! See you guys!' Morten gathered his portfolio and his jacket and walked out of the door.

Two minutes later, someone rang the buzzer.

'Charli, it's me, Morten. I forgot my subway pass, man. Can you throw it from the window? It must be on the table by the door.'

Charli opened the window and looked down. Morten looked up, smiling. Charli dropped the bus pass, but the wind caught it. It fluttered away and eventually landed on the road. Morten waited for a few cars to drive past, stepped down on the road and swiftly picked up the pass. As he walked back onto the pavement, he waved at his brother to come down and shouted, 'Want to come along? I don't think he would mind. I think he's into men. The more, the merrier!' Morten guffawed, displaying two full sets of teeth.

Morten and Charli walked up the carpeted stairs to the second floor to Marco's apartment. The concierge at the reception desk noticed that the boys twitched and stank of alcohol, but there was nothing unusual or alarming about them, so he let them up.

With one hand on the wrought iron balustrade, Charli hoisted his long body up the stairs. It wasn't easy to drag six feet five inches of well-stacked flesh and bones one step at a time and he was quickly out of breath. *Too much coke*, he thought as he huffed and puffed. He paused and readjusted the black-rimmed glasses on his nose. His mouth felt dry. His left arm felt stiff and uncomfortable. he shook it, moistened his lips and started up the stairs, again.

Morten was restless and jogging cheerfully in front of his brother.

'Come on bra, hurry up! What's up with you?'

Morten rapped on the large door with the golden handle and took a step back. He looked back in angst for his brother.

'Hurry up!' Morten called out for his brother.

'I'm here!' Charli whispered as he appeared at the turn of stairs. His face had become crimson.

Marco opened the door with a jerk, smiling. He was wearing a white silk bathrobe and sleepers. His smile faded as he caught sight of Charli.

'Hello, Morten!' Marco started. 'I was expecting you to come alone!' he added with a pout.

'Oh well, this is my brother Charli...' Morten stammered, not expecting that Marco would be so under-dressed.

'Well, hi Charli! This is a business meeting, the client should be here soon... I would appreciate some privacy if you don't mind,' Marco said.

Charli nodded. 'I guess I'll meet you back to the flat then!' he said in a faint voice. '*Farval bror.*'

Morten's coke-filled mind processed that something was wrong. He turned to face Marco who was smiling, with his robe slightly undone. Morten's throat constricted, his mouth suddenly felt very dry, as if he had swallowed a handful of sand. His hands became moist and he felt pangs in his chest. He'd heard about this shit from Mark but could this really be happening to him?

Morten made a few steps, which seemed to take forever and startled as the door slammed behind him. Marco sat down on the green velvet sofa in a spacious living room and smirked as he patted the space next to him on the couch. Morten reluctantly sat down. Pictures of the campaign were strewn all over the coffee table, amongst art books.

'This campaign could be a real career boost, you know,' Marco insinuated as he handpicked a few pictures. The belt around his robe loosened slightly, revealing his shrivelled penis and pendulous testicles. Morten pretended not to have noticed and focused on the pictures. 'But of course, it depends on *me*, really, whether I choose a picture of you... or not.' Marco added as he took Morten's hand and directed it towards the slit in his robe.

Morten felt like screaming with all his might but no sound came out. What could he do? He felt trapped in a body that would not cooperate. He started breathing with difficulty and sweat collected on his temples. His stomach churned until it eventually ached. He felt as if his heart had missed a few beats and pumped all his blood to his face.

When Morten left Marco's flat, time stopped. He felt as if the whole world around him had been muted. He could hear himself breathe, his heartbeat pounded like a drum, and his feet hardly touched the ground. He did not exist anymore, he was just a shell. He had left his soul behind that door. He flew down the stairs, past the concierge, burst the main doors open and took a loud breath once on the street. He got caught up in a sea of people. He managed to make it to the curb where he threw up spasmodically. No one noticed him. No one noticed his shame.

He wiped his mouth with so much vigour that his lower lip split and started bleeding. He ran as fast as his legs allowed him to and wobbled down the stairs into the subway station. As he sat with his elbows on his lap, holding his head, he noticed some vomit on his shoes and the bottom of his trousers. *No one can know this*, he repeated to himself, shaking his head in disbelief. He was going to calm down, he thought. He *had* to keep a straight face in front of his brother, he promised himself. Hopefully he would forget about it the following day. So he hoped.

As he walked back to the flat in a daze, he noticed an ambulance parked in front of the building. He jogged over and saw two paramedics dragging a stretcher out of the building. The onlookers crowded around the ambulance which was obstructing the scene.

'Do you know what happened?' he asked a man standing in front of him.

'I'm not sure,' he replied, pursing his lip.

Morten ran up the stairs and barged into the apartment with an interrogatory look. His two flatmates, James and Craig stood up from the couch as Morten walked in.

'Morten…' James started his sentence and walked towards him, rubbing his moist hands on the side of his trousers. He put his hand on Morten's shoulder and it dawned on Morten that the body on the stretcher was Charli's.

He heaved and coughed. His whole body started to shiver uncontrollably.

'Was that Charli? What's happened to him?' Morten could hardly breathe.

'It's his heart… He had a heart failure,' James said. His face was worn; he muttered words that Morten did not hear. The words '*heart failure*' swam around in his head and his head started spinning, stars swirled around him. He collapsed on the floor.

When he came to, he asked his friends which hospital Charli had been taken to and ran downstairs to hail a cab in the street.

'Where are you heading?' the driver asked.

'Downtown Hospital, please.'

Morten held his fists tight on his lap as the cab drove off in a hurry. *'Please, please, please...'* He prayed with his both hands clasped in front of his mouth.

Fifteen minutes later, he threw a couple of crumpled up bank notes at the driver and hurried towards the hospital entrance.

'My brother Charli Enqvist was brought in an hour ago or so, for heart failure...' Morten told the nurse behind the reception desk.

'You said the name of the patient was?' She asked coolly as she stared at her screen.

'Charli Enqvist, E-N-Q-V-I-S-T,' Morten replied while tapping his fingers nervously on the counter.

The nurse's eyes scanned the screen and suddenly paused. She raised her eyes towards Morten and reached out for the receiver.

'I'll call a doctor. He'll be right with you, sir. Please take a seat,' she said with a nod and pointed at the waiting area.

A few minutes later, a tall doctor in a white overcoat presented himself to Morten.

'Mr. Enqvist, I'm Doctor Willow. I'm afraid I am the bearer of bad news. We could not save your brother. He died twenty minutes ago.' Doctor Willow said with a grave face. 'I'm truly sorry.'

The patch of guilt was now festering inside Morten's chest. It was his fault they were here in New York living this ridiculous life. It was his fault they did so much coke, his fault he wasn't there. His lips trembled as the pain welled up. In an attempt to keep his composure he asked, 'What do I do now?'

'The nurse will have you fill in a form and help you decide with what to do with the body.' The doctor said. 'Once again, I'm truly sorry, we did everything we could, but it seemed that his heart was too small for his size and eventually gave in.'

CHAPTER 17

Marion, Fast-living in The Big Apple, New York, December 1996

I eventually got a few odd jobs in New York. They were enough to eat and pay my rent, but not much else. On one job for *Vanity Fair*, I had to pose for a painter. It involved patience and balance – sitting on a piano with one foot on a chair and the other, shoeless on the ground until the sole of my foot cramped. What could have been great editorial ended up as a picture the size of a stamp in a corner of a magazine amongst countless other scribbles. Some Japanese clients who had probably read my measurements backward and had planned very skinny clothes started off well, with a head and shoulder massage but ended up with cropped shots and a great deal of yelping from the client.

In between shoots I spent more and more time at the coffee shop with John. I needed a place where I felt anchored and it seemed to be there. John was funny and his jokes made everything so much brighter. He knew the industry and sympathised with my colourful stories. No one models forever and he had a good life running the deli. His true aim, however, was to become a journalist. When I went to his flat he told me all about it. He dissected my every word, twang, body language and told me how he'd write about it.

I wasn't quite sure how relevant John's job at the deli was to the pursuit of his dream but '*everyone needs to make a living*', as he often said. He was right, having dreams was a luxury not everyone could afford and I wondered how much longer I could hang onto mine. Nothing ever happened between us. I knew it would blow everything if anything did happen. There was a tacit agreement between us not to move the relationship forward. I was probably too young for him anyway, too easy a prey, and he was my rock. You don't sleep with your rock. The good news was that the little bell that had died away the previous year seemed to want to chime again.

'You mean you're horny!' laughed Kate.

'That is not what I mean. I am just saying that when I am with him, I feel alive...'

'Oh that's horny, but poetically put!'

Kate and I were in a cab on our way to a party. She was smoothing foundation over her pale skin, lingering on a thin blue vein on her cheek. She was dabbing and dabbing to cover it up. She lifted up her pocket mirror and sighed.

'Paper bag-over-head-time,' Kate said. 'I can't hide that little bugger.'

'A Saks bag may fit your dress better,' I replied.

We laughed. Kate's laughter was gleeful.

The agency often called us during the week to invite us to various events which kept us busy and entertained us while we pined for work. We took their offers gladly. There was nothing wrong with a free meal. Anything that kept us away from the smelly damp flat was a godsend. Mostly the parties were fairly tame, but the previous week had been Leonardo DiCaprio's birthday. My heart beat faster when I got the invitation, I had made myself pretty for him, I deluded myself into believing I could become his Cinderella. Leo showed up late, well after midnight, and I was probably back to looking like a pumpkin by then. He didn't even notice me, but at least New York allowed me to be part of something bigger. Being small in New York meant being big somewhere else. Or so the agency made it clear, especially when they got rid of girls and sent them away to strange countries they had never heard of.

Kate and I did not feel big in that sense of the word. We were just two normal girls whose belts occasionally had to be loosened after two months on an American diet. We were on our way to the birthday party of top photographer Paolo Piviano, who I am certain was at least ten years older than he said he was. We were just another bunch of small time models crowding the bottom of the fashion food chain around which predators hovered, while supermodels swam in clearer waters, hawking a complex and glamorous lifestyle.

'Here we are,' said Kate as she tugged on her skirt and undid a button of her shirt.

A dishevelled girl opened the door with a wide smile and a 'Hi!'. It did not matter much who we were, she just let us onto a mezzanine gallery that circled in a large pit of a room filled with a drunken crowd. Like two bewildered spectators, we leaned over the balcony and tried to spot a familiar face or two before diving into the lake of men in tuxedos and thin, beautiful women. The guests swarmed around champagne buckets, filling themselves with bubbles and laughter, then broke up and formed other combinations of people and drinks. They looked like knots tightening and loosening to the rhythm of the music. Lulu, the famous transvestite was there, swaying his hips. He strutted from one tray to the next, snatching flutes filled with champagne as he walked by.

Suddenly my view was eclipsed by a field of golden sequins.

'Hi!' said a very pretty girl with straight red hair.

It took me a few seconds to recognise Amirit.

'Wow, you look so different with straight hair! What are you doing here?'

'Same as you! Partying!' Amirit replied, shimmying.

'I meant in New York! How long have you been here?'

'Paolo flew me in for a beauty campaign a couple of days ago! I've been staying at his place!' she said, tossing her head to the beat. 'Things are looking up you know!'

As Amirit took my hand and led me down the stairs, I noticed how gaunt she had become. Her tight dress revealed her protruding hips; even her feet were bony and veiny and aged. Her hand felt cold and skinny. She snatched two drinks from a table and handed me one.

'They were calling for us!' Amirit said with a wink.

It was a cocktail; the fruit juice masked the strong liquor. I took a few sips and cringed. A dizziness started tingling in my head. The strange sensation ran down my legs and numbed my limbs, giving each movement a clumsy echo. We waded through the mass of people, looking for Paolo, but he was nowhere to be found. A tall girl was dancing on the table for an older man in a chalk-striped suit. Lumpish with desire, he sat there yearning and leering at her not-so-natural breasts, arousal clear through his suit trousers.

When we came to a corridor, I turned around and noticed that Kate was no longer with us. The walls weren't straight anymore and seemed to close in on us, threatening to squash us like pancakes. The paintings and pictures hanging on the wall now loomed out of their frames. My legs wobbled as I walked giddily in Amirit's steps. She dragged me around like a rag doll through the maze of the apartment. Amirit opened the doors of the all the rooms along the corridor where more guests buzzed about. I was at a loss; I wasn't sure what we were looking for anymore.

'Where… Where… are we going?' I asked Amirit in a faint voice.

Amirit opened the door at the very end of the hallway. She took a step back, froze, and let go of my hand. We stood limply in front of an enormous orgy scene. Naked bodies were entangled in sordid positions, men and women were engaged in multifarious group sex before our disbelieving eyes. Chest of drawers, tables, bed, couch, carpet, walls all supported nude couples and debauchery. There was shuffling, panting, mumbling, slapping, gulping, licking, swallowing, and much more than we could bear. Sounds and colours intermingled as if I were looking through a giant dissonant kaleidoscope. Amirit turned around like a robot and scampered off. I wanted to follow her but I did not know which Amirit to follow. My distorted vision had tripled, my pulse thumped in my skull, and I suddenly felt very nauseous. Panic-stricken, I managed to take a step, then another, and eventually made it to a sofa to sober up. Whatever had been dropped into my glass had impaired my depth and time perception. I wasn't sure how long I had sat there when Kate's voice became clearer and clearer. She was kneeling in front of me, calling my name.

'Are you alright?' she asked with a quizzical brow.

'Hi…' I replied, faintly.

'My God, you're so pale, are you alright?'

'I had… I had a sip of that drink Amirit gave me and it made me feel so… weird!'

'Pull yourself together, Paolo is over there, you need to meet him!' she whispered.

'I don't think I can...'

Kate took my hand and helped me up towards a small gathering of people. David, my booker, was one of them.

'Hey, Cherie! Ça va?' David said as he put his arm around my shoulders. 'Paolo, this is Marion, our latest contest winner. Isn't she beautiful?' David's mouth seemed so wide and toothy.

What I perceived as a small dark-haired man with a very pointy nose grinned while David went on speaking highly of me. His huge, ripe face was studded with two tiny black piercing eyes that made me feel uncomfortable. Dressed in black, with his long snout, and his small claw-like hands, he resembled a crow. As he shook my hand, chills ran through my spine. In my delirium, the vulture spread his wings and flew out of the room, dragging me in his grip.

'She bears a striking resemblance to Andie MacDowell!' Paolo commented with a shrill voice. My whole body was swaying like reeds caught in the wind. I was nodding and smiling incessantly, trying to appear composed whilst I subtly held on to Kate for support. I scanned the room for Amirit, but I could only make out a heavily bundled throng.

'I can't see anything!' I whispered to Kate as we shuffled off to get some fresh air.

I slowly regained the feeling in my legs and I managed to hoist myself in and out of the cab without tripping over the curb. Things were normal again: the railing felt like metal, the steps like stone, the door like wood and the flat like a models' flat. I was even relieved to smell Irina's cigarette smoke. Things were getting back on track. I was regaining my senses.

That night I dreamed of naked bodies inviting me to their bed. Undressed women crept towards me and caressed me; their teeth were sharpened and their eyes strangely red. As one came squawking towards me, the image became clearer – a feathered Paolo was aiming to peck at my neck. I woke up with a start and sat up in my bed sweating. I switched on my bedside lamp and looked around. Hot air steamed out of my mouth as I panted heavily. I grabbed the bottle of water next to my bed and gulped it down. I was alone, I was safe, and it was just a nightmare. I repeated these words to myself a few times like a prayer for comfort. I thought about my parents. I thought about how much I wanted to go back home. I wished I could wake up in the bedroom I had grown up in and realise that this was all just a bad dream. I didn't call my parents much; the time difference didn't help but mainly, I didn't want to worry them. I knew that it wouldn't take much for my mother to insist I should ditch it all and go back to my studies.

I pulled the duvet on top of my head and cried. I let it all out: the anxiety, the frustration, and the waste of my time New York was turning out to be.

My alarm clock woke me up at 7 a.m. the next morning. I felt like a porcupine turned inside out with a cotton-wool mouth and a vast headache. I lay recumbent for what seemed like hours before I eventually made it down the ladder to the bathroom. In the mirror, my eyes were puffy from crying and lack of sleep. I decided to skip my castings that morning and sleep it off. The phone rang a few times, but I ignored it. I grumbled and turned around in my bed.

Three hours later, I finally made it back downstairs. I put the kettle on and I leaned against the kitchen sink, pensive. The whistle of the boiling water made me come round. Every movement I made was slow and awkward; I dropped the spoon on the floor and spilled half of my cup of tea on my pyjamas. A few seconds later the pain shot through me. I let out a shriek and went back upstairs to get changed.

Once dressed in jeans and a warm grey woollen cardigan, I punched the bleeping answering machine. David had left me three messages, asking me to call him back urgently.

I picked up the receiver and dialled the agency's number:

'Icon Models, good afternoon!' the voice said.

Good afternoon? I thought. *How late is it?* 'What time is it?' I asked.

'I'm sorry, you were saying?' the voice asked.

'Oh… Erm… sorry, is David around please?'

'Sure! Hold on please.' The voice said, 'May I ask who's calling?'

'Marion, Marion Durant,' I replied.

David picked up the phone, out of breath. 'Cherie, where are you?'

'At the flat…' I confessed.

'Have you done all your castings already?'

'I haven't done any. I feel like shit. Somebody put something in my drink last night…' I started.

'Listen, Paolo absolutely adored you! He wants to do a photo test shoot with you tomorrow for a trial perfume campaign for Armani.'

My blood froze as I heard Paolo's name. I felt deflated by David's news; I had to sit down as my legs started shaking. My eyes twitched from fatigue, I could envision Paolo sneering over his shoulder.

'If the pictures are good, he will present them to Armani. Your luck's come in, Cherie!' David was excited and spoke fast. 'Go to your castings and call me back later OK? Got to go, well done!'

I put the receiver down, held my mug in one hand and my head with the other, trying to shake myself out of it: he had been part man, part raven, it was just a nightmare, it was just a nightmare… Armani.

CHAPTER 18

Amirit, 8.45 a.m. the Same Day,
New York, December 1996

Amirit was fidgety. She frantically rummaged through her bag, then tipped its contents onto the table: lipstick, hand cream, subway card, wallet, book, receipts... She ran her fingers through the items and flung them on the floor with rage. She stamped her feet and threw her bag across the room. The phone rang. She panted and watched it buzz loudly. She threw her hair back and picked up the receiver.

'What?' she barked.

'Amirit, where on earth are you? You were supposed to be at the studio at eight!' David said.

'I can't find my pills OK? Cancel it! I don't want to do it anymore.'

'Alright, now you listen to me! I'll get you your pills but first you have to make your way to the studio,' David said calmly over the phone. 'You're not shooting one of your stupid German catalogues, you're shooting a story for *Vogue*! You're not a superstar yet, so don't act like one!'

Amirit slammed the receiver and grumbled 'You stupid French prick!'

The tinted mirror in the elevator reflected the image of a bleached blonde troubled girl: her face was a mess, her pupils dilated and dry patches encroached down her neck. She scratched them frantically, until they threatened to bleed, gulped down the small bottle of vodka she kept in her leather jacket, and spluttered in a coughing fit. She wiped her mouth and wobbled out of the elevator. The concierge peered over his glasses as she staggered past him and tutted.

'Fucking shoes!' she mumbled as she twisted her ankle. She removed her stilettos and carried them in her hands. Standing by the curb in her red mini-skirt with ladders in her stockings, she pranced around, waving at cabs. Eventually one stopped and she dived in.

She nervously tapped a cigarette on a silver case and brought the cigarette to her lips with shaking hands. She inhaled sharply and puffed the smoke out as the streets unfolded in front of her eyes. Her nail polish was flaking off and dirt made a black line underneath the fingertips. The driver glanced at her in his front mirror.

'Are you feeling all right Ma'am?'

'Fuck you!'

The car screeched to a halt and ejected a cursing Amirit. She put her shoes back on, flipped her hair back, lit up another cigarette and started walking while people jumped aside, avoiding her like the plague.

***

Amirit barged into the studio. It was 10.35 a.m. All eyes turned to her.

'Where the hell have you been?' whispered the stylist.

'To Hell and back!' Amirit shot at her as she walked to the hair and make-up studio, taking everyone aback. Roy and Charles, the hair and make-up artists sat up in the black leather sofas, wondering what to do next. They followed her in order to get her ready for the shoot, but Pru, the art director held her hand up to catch their attention.

'This girl is totally shit-faced! I'm not sure we'll get much out of her today. I'm calling David. Jesus how many times?' she said as she snapped her fingers at her assistant. A tiny brunette dressed in black strutted towards her Pru and handed her the phone.

Pru was tall, her black hair was cut in a perfect bob and wore a piece of the latest Versace Winter collection. Her long manicured hands held an elegant silver cigarette holder. As David took the call, Pru turned her back to the rest of the team and spoke firmly.

'Amirit has arrived. I don't know who's done her hair but she looks like a cheap whore. Roy is going to do his best to fix that for today but it will take a bloody *magician* to do her face!' she raised her voice towards the end of the sentence. 'We'll try the shoot, but if we cannot make anything out of her, you can be sure we'll never take one of your girls again. Send me a professional for God's sake, not a junkie!' She hung up, turned to the others and added, 'that'll set his record straight!'

Amirit sat in her chair swinging her legs back and forth. She was smoking her fifteenth cigarette of the day and did not look at Roy and Charles as they walked in. They did not mind the attitude; it wasn't anything new to them. There was an attitude that came with being a supermodel which everyone took as being all part of their stardom and there was the not-so-super models' attitude which could nip any aspiring model's career in the bud and end any future prospects for good, either way, the boys had a job to do. Roy wet Amirit's hair and flattened it against her scalp. The water dripped off her but she did not budge. He towel-dried it and applied a thick product on her hair, that same silken hair that once rippled under the wind like a field of wheat – now parched for want of care and water. Roy asked her if he could cut the ends. She nodded in assent and continued smoking. Once cut, the damp hair was combed over her head, the wet claggy ends formed a smooth wedge that touched the back of her shirt. He twirled her hair in locks around his finger and dried them with a diffuser. The firm grip of Roy's hands, the wariness and visible reproach in his coal-black eyes reminded Amirit of her father. She could imagine his caustic rebuke, his brow wrinkled with worry and the sour taste of disappointment at watching his cherubic child wither away. Roy could tell that Amirit's dark shadows beneath her ghostly translucent blue eyes carried the tell-tale signs of drug abuse. He felt sorry for her but went on with his job without a word.

Months ago, David gave her a few pills 'to help you shed a few pounds.' What started as a mild kick had totally enslaved her. Amirit naively imagined it was regular medicine to help her lose weight. But as her dependence grew, she came to realise that would she had been taking were amphetamines, or by their street name, speed. When David ran out of speed, cocaine was offered and even crystal meth. Drugs had been introduced like a Trojan horse and an army of demons had been released into her internal system, ravaging her once clean body. Within a few weeks, she had become a shadow of herself.

Her chest hurt as if a cord had been wrapped tight around her lungs. She realised she was having a panic attack and started rocking back and forth, humming mournfully. Charles and Roy stared at each other. Roy knew the drill and beckoned Charles to get some help.

By the time Pru and the photographer came back, Amirit was convulsing on the floor. Snot trickled down her nose and tears marked her cheeks.

'Call 911!' Pru ordered. 'I knew she was trouble!' she told the photographer. 'It's OK, you're going to be OK!' She told Amirit, softly. She took a magazine and fanned her face. She caressed her damp hair with the other hand and made soft hushing sounds while Charles and Roy held her hands and feet. 'She's totally drenched! Get me a wet towel and some water. She needs to be rehydrated.' Pru gently poured some water on Amirit's lips, she seemed to come round then spat it out and screamed. People gathered around her startled and looked at each other in dismay. The studio staff had seen it all before. The receptionist barged into the studio, her forehead burrowed with worry.

'The ambulance is on its way!' she said.

***

Amirit lay in her hospital bed, breathing to the rhythm of the bleeping machines, a drip in each arm. She fluttered her eyes open and recognised her father as her vision became clearer.

'Dad...' she sighed.

Her father always looked impeccable with his worsted jacket and felt hat. He held his pinstripe Trilby in his right hand and touched her wrist with the other. His eyes were riveted to her, and his naked forehead was wrinkled with concern.

'Shhhh... stay still, you need to get some rest,' he said. 'You're very tired.'

'I am so sorry Daddy!' her voice was shaky as she was struggled to hold back her tears.

'I am getting you out of this mess. We're going home.'

Her plain-speaking burly father did not scold her as she thought he would, which meant the situation must have been seriously bad.

'I can't, I have signed a five year contract with Icon,' she mumbled.

'We've already taking care of it. Don't worry about it now, OK?' He ran his hand on her cheek and kissed her forehead.

CHAPTER 19

Marion, New York, December 1996

It was the day after Amirit's collapse at the Vogue photo shoot. I arrived at Pier 59 studios at three in the afternoon. It was a large concrete building with wooden staircases with big pipes running along the ceiling. Black and white framed pictures of naked women in trees hung along the wall. Assistants bustled about as models sauntered back and forth holding coffee cups and cigarettes. A florist was arranging the weekly bouquet and the receptionist looked up and greeted me. She guided me to a large studio filled with wind machines and cranes. Music was playing softly in the background.

I jumped as Paolo sprung out like a rat from behind the towering machines. His small body twitched with malice, or so it seemed to me. He was dressed as he had been at the party; top-to-toe in black. I was expecting cockroaches to crawl out of his turtle neck and physically recoiled at the sight of him.

'Ciao Marion! Nice to see you again, Darling,' Paolo said. 'Please follow me.'

I flinched as he put his arm around my waist and gripped my arm like a vice. His clothes emanated a rank smell. I walked stiffly towards a grey curtain, holding my breath. Two tall men looked up as Paolo pushed the curtain aside.

'Boys, this is Marion. Dave, we're going to keep her curly hair as it is. Tony, I want ashen eye make-up and red lips,' Paolo ordered. 'Marion, can I get you something to drink?'

'I'm fine, thanks.'

I wanted him gone and luckily, Paolo vanished as fast as he had appeared.

'Do you want to come and sit here, darling?' Tony asked as he dragged the chair back for me to sit.

I nodded and sat down, as if hypnotised. He slathered a layer of foundation and powder over my face. Then, he selected a brush and smeared as much black as possible around my eyes. As he applied eye pencil above my eyelashes, and in the inner rim of my lower eyelid, my eyes started watering. I pushed his hand back gently as a pencil-induced tear trickled down my cheek. I apologised, wiped my tear with the tissue he handed me and riveted my eyes onto the ceiling once more. Small veins had burst and formed a thin web in my eyes. My hands tightened in a fist and my legs started shook from exasperation. He applied some red on my lips, some blush on my cheeks, and declared me ready at last. I looked into the mirror in amazement; it had aged me in a good way. At eighteen, I was starting to feel sultry and womanly.

Dave rolled his long black hair into a knot and grabbed his spray bottle. He sprayed water on me while Tony watched tensely. I grabbed the *Vogue* on the table in front of me.

'You're spraying water on her face! Be careful, Dave. I spent hours doing her eyes. Don't fuck it up now!'

To cut the tension and avoid a tantrum, I started some small talk. 'Do you know who this is?' I asked pointing at the blonde model on the Versace campaign Kate had shown me earlier.

'Oh My *God*, you don't know Morten?' Tony exclaimed in awe, holding up one hand in a traffic-cop gesture. 'You have to catch up with your homework, girlfriend!'

'He's everywhere, any campaign or magazine, you name it. Rummage through the pile of magazines over there, I am sure you can find other stuff he's done,' Dave said, pointing at the right corner of the make-up table.

While Dave was dowsing my hair, Tony frantically flipped through the magazines, as if looking for treasure. Dave worked foam into my hair, set his jaw in firm determination and switched on his blow drier.

'*There he is*! Oh my God, he's so *hot*!' Tony pointed triumphantly at the Versace campaign where a tall brunette in an haute couture white dress stood proudly as two bare-chested male models clawed around her legs. She was staring into the camera with her hair floating around her shoulders like a Greek Goddess. The blonde male model resembled Mick Jagger, only younger and fairer. His ice blue eyes were underlined by black make-up, which only served to intensify his stare all the more. There was something ethereal about him and I was under his spell. The other male model had long black hair with brown eyes and a powerful body. Marta was surrounded by good and evil, only the tables had been turned – the devil had blonde hair.

*** *

Paolo crept up behind me as I tried the dresses on that the stylist had selected. For a moment, I had forgotten about him. He had pushed through the curtain, unnoticed and was watching me change. Ill-at-ease, I grabbed a garment to hide behind.

'You're definitely the kind of girl who looks better naked than dressed!' he exclaimed with a lecherous smile, while simultaneously picking a scab on his elbow. I felt my blood drain out of me as his lewd eyes ogled me. 'I was thinking that she'd look great in that simple black dress,' the stylist told Paolo, ignoring his comment.

'Let's start with the black dress then.'

His eyes were darting poisonous arrows at me.

I reluctantly followed him to the centre of the set where he propped me up like a mannequin.

'Stand still on the mark on the ground,' he commanded as he tightly held my arms with his unpleasantly firm hands.

I then watched him scurry along like a mangy dog as he vanished behind the props. A current of anticipation crackled through the dense air. I stood there, wringing my hands, feeling terribly isolated, as if I had been taken to a warehouse to be gunned down. I was startled by a loud bang. Spotlights suddenly flooded the studio with a blinding light. I held my hand up in front of my scrunched up eyes. Paolo's silhouette came back in focus and stood behind his camera.

He activated the wind machine which lifted the hem of my dress. I swayed to the rhythmic click of the camera. I let the wind catch my hair, I looked down, and then up with despondent eyes. As the wind dried my lips, I wet the lower one softly and released a wet plump lip. I heard Paolo exult with a few sickening grunts. He walked towards me with his arms wide open ready to embrace me.

'Let's see a bit more flesh!' he said with a salacious smile as he started unbuttoning my dress, without asking. 'I love goose bumps on a woman's body, it turns me on.'

My whole body shuddered under his touch. I felt as if I had been dipped into a bucket of ice-cold water; my breath grew shorter and my limbs became paralysed with awe. I fluttered my eyes shut and tried to focus on the fact I was in an Armani campaign.

I tried to convince myself, that it wasn't me standing there, that it was someone else; a puppet held up by invisible hands. The puppet kept a blank stare while the small man dug his hands inside the dress and caressed one of my breasts. He tiptoed and licked and kissed it, then eventually scuttled back towards his camera to take pictures of me, this marionette with broken joints that I had become. There was smile on the wooden face which felt not like my own, and red smeared lips. Panicking, I looked around and searched for Tony and Dave, but there was only Paolo and myself. I was myself again. My mind was spinning faster and faster and I started coughing; eventually instinct took over and I ran back to the make-up room holding my dress tight to my chest. I slumped onto the chair, aghast, heaving loudly. My whole body wanted to spurt out its disgust.

'What's wrong with you?' Dave asked.

I held my breath and looked around. My eyes were twitching and my mouth was wide open, dribbling trickles of saliva.

'Please let me out of here', I mumbled.

I fumbled around for my belongings, took off the dress, hastily threw my own clothes back on, and stumbled out of the room.

Once out of the studio, I ran with a bewildered look on my face, pushing past everyone on the busy avenue. I tried to hail a taxi with my hand but none of the ones that passed were lit up. I was panting and leaned against a wall to catch my breath as the cars zoomed past.

I held my arms up in frustration, looking frantically from left to right. Then I rocked my body back and forth, my feet ready to spring for a race. Ready, steady, run for your life!

I walked across snowy Manhattan all the way back to the models' flat. Kate was the only one I could think of turning to at this point in time. I held my hood tight as the sharp wintry wind bit my face and beat my legs.

Kate had left me a note on the coffee table, asking me to meet her at a party on Christopher Street. My boots were damp and my feet felt numb from running for half an hour in the cold and wet weather. I removed them and checked that I could still wriggle my toes. I changed into dry clothes, took off the thick make-up from the shoot, and left the flat without a word. I plodded along 15th Street and noticed the Christmas decorations; the shop windows lit up with delicate tinsel and fairy lights. A Santa clone with a dirty outfit rang his rusty bell with one hand and shook a bucket with the other.

I strutted past the corner deli on Christopher Street and looked for number 20. I noticed some lights on in lower ground apartment. White reindeers sat on the windowsill and colourful lights flickered by the fireplace. After a short moment of hesitation, I pressed the buzzer 4 and leaned on the door to shelter from the fresh flakes floating down from the sky.

'Yeah?' A voice asked.

'It's Marion!'

Silence.

'I'm with Kate.'

I was about to turn around when somebody let me in. The door was ajar and I could hear music and cheers in the background. I hesitated; I wasn't sure I was feeling up to meet people, I just needed to talk to Kate. As I slowly pushed the door, a stunning blonde guy jerked the door open all the way.

'Hi!' An unknown foreign voice said. 'Are you here for the party?'

Even though I had never met Morten in person, I recognised him instantly. He was wearing a khaki army jacket and light blue jeans. He had a winning smile and dancing eyes that made me feel slightly light-headed. I was suddenly filled with an astonishing sensation I had not expected to feel, especially after what had happened earlier. At that point, it seemed that all my emotions had been enhanced by my ordeal. I removed my woollen hat and arched my neck like a swan. Morten was dazzling with light and energy; his hair floated around his perfectly structured face and intense eyes. He was a pixie escaped from the woods, a happy goblin inviting me inside his den to play.

'Come in, you look frozen!' He said.

As I hawed a few inaudible words, Morten wrapped his warm hand around mine and pulled me indoors. I followed him inside where there was a small gathering of people chatting and drinking beers.

'Marion!' Kate exclaimed. Kate came closer and helped me take off my damp down jacket. 'You are freezing! Let me make you some tea!'

'I'll take care of it, Kate,' Morten said as his flirtatious eyes locked onto mine.

'Are you OK?' Kate asked me. 'You look a bit upset!'

'I'm mainly cold… I'll tell you later,' I replied as I looked down and decided to avoid the subject. I would probably need to vent, but not now, not there. 'I didn't know you were friends with Morten?' I whispered as I watched him amble towards the kitchen.

'I've met him at a few parties here and there,' Kate explained as she sipped a glass of wine. She turned around to make sure Morten wasn't coming back and lowered her voice, 'He's had a rough time lately. His brother died a couple of months ago, he pretends he's OK, but I'm concerned about his health.'

'His health?' I enquired.

'He does way too much coke, even for a model,' Kate explained.

Morten walked back from the kitchen smiling at me. He had rolled his sleeves and handed me a smoking hot mug of tea.

'There you go, this should do the trick!' Morten said as his hands enveloped mine once more around the cup.

A sensation of warmth and peace ran through me. Small butterflies spread their wings and tingling the inner wall of my stomach. I watched him as he made way towards the sofa and set both his feet on the coffee table, wedging his beer bottle between his legs. I stood there idly for a while, looking around, blowing on my tea, while Morten stared at me ardently. I suddenly felt extremely self-conscious and fidgety. His gaze somehow always strayed back towards me. I tried to avoid it but I could feel it. I carefully stepped towards the couch where Morten was, and sat down next to him. I grabbed a magazine and rested my cup on top of it. For lack of words, I stirred the spoon and watched the swirls inside my mug. I removed my boots and socks and set them next to the fireplace. I curled up on the couch and rubbed my feet.

'It's funny, your feet are small and square; your small toes are all the same length!' Morten said.

'I know, I don't like my feet,' I crossed my legs and nestled my cup in my hands.

'There's nothing wrong with your feet, beside the fact that they are small and square!' he laughed and stared at me.

His laughter was deep and guttural, almost like a roar. I smiled coyly and pressed the hot drink to my lips, enduring his insistent gaze while I drank.

'I like your hair... it's very...' he started as he ran his fingertips through my curls.

Curly, I thought.

'...very thick and healthy.'

He took clumps of hair in his hand. A part of me hoped he would stop touching me, but another part felt like purring, literally. My eyes shut surreptitiously as I let my whole body relax. I did not dare look at him. I stared blankly in front of me. It seemed as though everyone else had vanished into oblivion and it was just us two in the room, rocked by the crackling of the burning wood and the regular stroking.

A tiny teardrop pearled in the corner of my eye and ran down my cheek. My lips parted and words came uncontrollably out of my mouth.

'I had an awful experience today.' My lower lip trembled slightly and I nervously chafed my hands on my jeans. Morten's fingers suddenly stopped touching my hair. 'I did a campaign test with a photographer and he... well, he...'

Morten took his hand away and sat up, staring at me in expectation. Words that had seemed to be stuck in my throat suddenly came out in

185

a spurt. I gesticulated, 'He…he touched me. He touched my breast and kissed me… and the worst part is that I didn't do anything to stop him. I was paralysed with fear or surprise, whichever, I'm not sure. It was awful.' I paused and looked down. 'Everyone had gone, I was alone with that vile…' My lip quivered again. I stumbled for words. 'That disgusting midget of a man.'

Morten put his arm around me and pulled me gently towards him. I rested my head on his shoulder while he stroked it with his free hand, whispering, 'I know, I know…'

When the guests started leaving, Morten and I were still cuddled up in the sofa.

'What are you two lovebirds up to?' Kate asked with a conniving smile as she closed the door after the last leavers.

Morten and I looked at each other for an answer.

'I think we'll go and grab something to eat! I'm starving!' Morten roared as he sprung up to his feet.

'I'll see you back at the flat, Marion!' Kate smiled. 'Seems like your day picked up.'

Morten and I walked side by side to the coffee shop, at times bumping into each other as our shoes slipped on the icy pavements.

'I'll have the mashed potatoes and green salad. Does it still come with cheese and ham?' I asked the waitress.

'It does!' she replied and turned to Morten, 'What about you, sir?'

'I'll have the hamburger with fries, please.'

He closed the menu and handed it to the waitress who squeezed it under her arm.

'And anything to drink for either of you?' she asked, holding her notebook and pen, ready to write.

'Diet Coke for me, please,' I said.

'Same.'

The waitress scribbled on her pad and walked away.

'Not the healthiest meal, but I'm hungover today and fancy something greasy,' Morten explained, wide-eyed.

'I have to be careful, I have put on weight since I got here, I think.'

'You look pretty damn good to me!' Morten said with a beaming smile.

I blushed slightly and looked away. There was a silence between us. The café was buzzing around us, oblivious to our moment.

A thick white blanket of snow covered the streets as we walked back to my apartment. We trudged through the inclement weather with our bodies set against the wind. Within a few minutes, we were standing in front of number 206.

'Can I see you again?' I asked him. I had never been forward like this but something had prompted me to ask that question.

'Sure... I'll meet you here tomorrow afternoon, let's say four o'clock? Central Park is really pretty at that time,' Morten offered.

I nodded and smiled. My whole body shivered and my teeth started shattering. Morten held me in his arms for a few seconds and eventually pulled my chin up with his hand. He pressed his lips on mine in the most tender and sensuous kiss. His blue eyes flickered as he looked into mine and invited me to guess their desire.

As I watched him stride away, he lifted his collar and tilted his cap. He dug his hands in his pockets and disappeared around the corner.

The next day, we strolled along the lake, looking at the skyscrapers in the distance, their white flanks lost in the clouds. Silence was all around except for the rustle of the few remaining tree leaves and the chirping of a lonely bird. The faint glimmer of sunrays licked the frost that had built up linking both sides of the narrow river. As we leaned against the stones, Morten remained quiet for a while.

'This place strangely reminds me of home,' he started, in a daze. 'There is a beautiful park where my brother Charli and I used to lie in the cool shade of poplars and weeping willows with our mother. We'd have a picnic among the bright flowers.' He heaved and sighed. 'He's gone now,' he added and looked up, his reddened eyes glistened sadly. My brother died from heart failure two months ago. I guess that our way of life wasn't the healthiest so there is no wonder his heart failed him.'

'I don't know what to say.'

I looked at him tenderly and put my hand on his shoulder.

'There is nothing to say. Except that I wasn't there when he died and I am having trouble coming to terms with that.'

He stood straight again, and faced me. He drew me closer and caressed my cheek softly with the back of his hand. His piercing eyes locked into mine, his lips parted, releasing hot air and he kissed me passionately. My knees gave in and my whole body became limp as he squeezed me against him. I felt protected, stuck in a timeless place from which I did not want to escape.

We agreed to meet again the next day for lunch. I watched him stride away and just as he had done the day before, he lifted his collar and tilted his cap, dug his hands in his pockets and disappeared around the corner.

***

Later that evening, Kate and I were gossiping and watching the Jerry Springer show, when the doorbell rang.

'Who could that be?' I exclaimed, springing from the sofa. She was too absorbed in the show to even look at me.

'Are you seriously into this lowbrow shit?'

Clearly she had no intention of getting up.

'I'm not dressed!'

No response.

'Fine, I'll get the door!' I ran to the front door to buzz the person in and waited. A few seconds later, a skinny girl arrived on the landing with a suitcase that looked heavier than she did. She wore black leggings that sagged under her knees and a thick tattered sheepskin jacket slightly worn out around the elbows. Her hair was rather short and black. She came towards me with a smile.

'Marion!' She said as she opened her arms wide and hugged me. As she realised my embarrassment, she stepped back and added, 'It's me, Betina!'

I felt as if I had been electrocuted; an acute pain shot through my limbs and lingered in my chest.

'Oh my Gosh, Betina. I hadn't recognised you. You have lost so much weight! Where have you been?'

'I have tried to call you a few times without avail,' she confessed.

Memories of Betina flooded into my brain. The person standing before me was only the shadow of the girl I had once known. After looking at her for a while, I realised that all that was left of Betina was the freckled face that she used to hide behind layers of foundation. The red hair that had been her trademark was died black, and the healthy country girl had become all skin and bones.

Betina dropped her suitcase on the living room floor and removed her jacket.

'Hi! I'm Betina,' she told Kate as she shook her hand softly.

'Kate. Nice to meet you!'

Betina flopped into the sofa, turned towards me and said, 'Haven't you noticed anything?'

'Well, Betina, I have indeed. Your hair is darker and you're… skinnier, definitely skinnier!'

'I meant the boobs! Haven't you noticed? I had them done in the end,' she smirked proudly while both Kate and I stared in disbelief. 'When I went to London, I dated my booker Hendrick – he's half Danish, half American – and he really took me under his wing. He suggested I had them done. He also suggested I try the American market, so here I am!'

I looked at her, agape. *What has happened to her?* I thought. I wanted to ask her about the pregnancy test, as something in me doubted that it had been negative but instead I embraced her. I had missed her terribly and felt sorry that I had failed to track her down. She now appeared in front of me as a walking stick with boobs that weren't even real. I hadn't seen her in three months, but in that time she had aged terribly; she didn't look at all like a sixteen-year-old should. I was enraged and wanted to punch whoever this Hendrick was. Once more, the agency had disposed of her and sent her far away. But to what avail? Here she was, as fragile as ever and I was powerless.

'Do you know where my room is?' Betina asked.

'I guess you're staying in my room, now that Helen has left,' Kate said.

'I didn't know she had left! I thought she was away for a job!' I exclaimed.

'It started as a job and ended up in staying in Toronto. She felt like staying home with her folks for a while.'

'I don't blame her,' I mumbled.

***

The next day Betina and I strode along the streets, trying to make up for lost time but she just wasn't the same: her face was unhappy and dour, and she was a bagful of obsessive compulsive disorders which ranged from washing her hands thirty to forty times a day, to opening and closing the fridge door many times in a row, to checking the front door again and again before leaving the apartment, even if it meant running back up the three flights of stairs. I grew more and more worried about her. The special connection we once shared seemed to have been severed by whatever drugs she had been taking.

As we walked down into the subway station, a young girl was curled up at the bottom of the stairs, constantly shuffling the cardboard shrouding her. Betina stopped, as if she had recognised her. Despite the low temperatures, I could smell the pungent reek of the young homeless girl who was burbling to herself. She smelled of urine and sweat and worse, she smelled of decay. I beckoned Betina to follow me, as the sore sight made me uneasy. She clasped to the railing and continued walking down with a hunch, as if she had been punched in the stomach.

'Are you alright?' I asked her. She grunted and kept that dazed stare for a while.

'She looked like my sister,' she said with wide eyes. 'I could have sworn it was my sister.'

'Was it your sister, or was it not?' I asked her with a concerned look.

'It wasn't,' she replied with a nod.

'Betina? Should I be worried?' I asked, as I glanced at the young bum over my shoulder.

Betina slowly lifted her head and looked at me with a troubled expression, 'I've had the same recurrent nightmare lately where army ants march toward Mia as she lies wounded in the desert. I don't know why she's wounded, or what she is doing in the desert but it's been haunting me for weeks.'

'Are you still taking those pills?' I interrupted her, as it dawned on me that her babbling might be the sign of something deeper that was going wrong.

'Once the ants have devoured everything on their path, carrion birds squeak and circle around Mia, waiting for her to die.'

Betina had a crazed look on her face.

'Oh my God, Betina. You're scaring me! Your sister is alright, we can call her if you want. But you need to stop taking whatever you're taking,' I implored her.

'For some strange reason, my mother won't let me speak to Mia and it worries me.'

'What do you mean she won't let you speak to her?'

'Well,' Betina shook her head slowly in a disapproving way. 'Mia is either sleeping or at her friend's or too sick to speak…' She paused. 'There is always a good reason not to speak to her and it's worrying me sick,' Betina explained as she stared blankly in front of her.

The world moved quickly around us; there was no idle time, no room for compassion nor complacency. I felt stuck in the middle of it all, with the rest of the world swirling around me. The other passengers walked mechanically in and out of the subway station, the young homeless girl was stuck in a dark present, but Betina's future looked just as dark especially if she was still on those pills.

CHAPTER 20

Morten, New York, December 1996

Morten woke up in a strange room. It took him a short while to come round, when someone walked past his bed and pulled the curtains open. He recoiled in horror at Marco Tutti's flabby buttocks.

'Good morning!' Marco chanted.

Morten's dizziness renewed. He remembered going to Marco's birthday party in a gallery downtown but wondered how he had winded up in his bed. He rubbed his eyes, hoping to wake up to another reality but Marco's miserly blue-veined penis was as real as could be. Morten grew aware of the teak chest of drawers with its myriad compartments, the expensive golden lamps, the hand-woven rugs, the thick velvety curtains; they all closed in on him, stifling him until he could hardly breathe.

'We didn't sleep together, if that's what you're worried about,' Marco said coolly as he could sense Morten's agitation. Morten struggled to swallow and stared at Marco pleadingly. 'You were totally out of it yesterday. Even a bomb wouldn't have woken you up,' Marco explained.

Morten looked under the sheet and realised he was stark naked. That didn't make any sense. His fingers shook as he held the sheet tightly. He could taste aniseed in his mouth. He licked his lips; he remembered the absinth, and the flashes of rapid-onset hallucinations. He remembered the concoction of booze and cocaine and held his head in his hands in disbelief. He had to keep Marco interested in him as career insurance, but he hadn't anticipated this. The Versace campaign hadn't paid off the way he had thought it would. They paid the big stars a lot of money and only promised fame to the new models. *'It's not a lot of money,'* Bjorn had explained, *'because they assume that following that campaign your career will soar. Take it as free exposure!'*

'I need to go!' Morten stated, suddenly remembering Marion who had been waiting for him. Trying to hide his embarrassment, he sprung from the bed, dragging the sheet along with him. As he looked for his clothes, a brain-crumbling dizziness almost knocked him off his feet. Morten leaned on the chair until the ground stopped moving.

'I have folded them on the chair on your right,' Marco said as he approached the unsteady Morten. 'What's the big rush anyway? Stay for breakfast!' Marco pleaded, but Morten had come round and scurried away, tiptoeing as if he was trying to avoid gooey things crawling in a quagmire of sludge.

Once at the door, Morten stopped and waited for Marco to see him out. In one last attempt, Marco grabbed Morten in a stranglehold and kissed him.

'It's not the first time, you'll be back little boy!'

Morten managed to disengage and unbolt the front door, excusing himself profusely.

***

That day Morten never came. I could have watched him from the window but I was so eager to see him that I stupidly waited for him outside in the cold. I stood on the doorstep for half an hour until the paralysing cold had totally extinguished the ardour in my eyes. After an hour and a half standing outside, my hands started shaking despite the fleece gloves. A burning sensation spread on my cheeks, my nose hurt as it slowly turned into an icicle. I scanned the streets, like a child awaiting the parent who forgot his birthday. I was hoping that Morten would turn up at the corner of the street, apologetic about his delay but soon enough, I had to face the fact that I had been stood up.

The cold breeze licked the tears off my face as I turned around and walked up the stairs.

'That was fast!' Kate chirped as I dragged my semi-frozen body to the kitchen in need of a hot drink.

Kate sat across from me in the sofa as I cupped my tea in my hands. I could feel her insistent daze but my eyes remained riveted on my steamy tea.

'OK, you win, he didn't come!' I said, playing with my spoon.

'And you stayed in the cold all that time? That's a bit silly!' She noticed my uneasiness and took a more reassuring tone of voice. 'Maybe something happened. There may be a reason why he couldn't make it!'

'Yep, like a hangover or another girl,' I replied with a raised brow. I stood up and walked back to the kitchen thinking I may as well channel my anger into cleaning up the place. Kate came after me as I was reading the back of the label of the washing up liquid. 'Removes the strongest stains, bla bla bla… I wish this new improved formula with miracle stain remover would also lift up my spirit, give me a real job and fly me home!'

***

That evening, Kate, Betina and I decided to go out to cheer me up. As we were lining up at the cloakroom of an up and coming club, I noticed a tall blonde guy kissing a girl with long dark hair. Morten turned around and saw me. I felt as if somebody had punched me in the stomach and squeezed the air out of my lungs.

'Hey, Marion! Good to see you! What's up!' Morten asked as he gave me a big hug.

'Who's that?' I pointed at the brunette, with a constricted throat.

'She's a friend!' he replied with a shrug.

'I don't understand!' My eyes searched his for an explanation. 'I thought…' I suddenly felt his icy cold look on me and could not finish my sentence.

'Hey, Marion! I'm not your boyfriend, I don't owe you anything!' he answered coolly.

It felt as if a cold axe had fallen on my neck.

'I suppose you're not,' I mumbled.

As Morten walked away, Kate wrapped her hand around my arm and said, 'I don't know what you see in him. He's a prick!'

I released her hand with a jerk and stepped inside the club.

I sipped my Vodka and Cranberry, sitting at our table, while the brunette writhed around Morten like a snake. She tugged him against her and licked his ear lobe, and looked directly at me in a suggestive way. I was sitting in a room filled with strangers, and I could barely hear Kate over the music. It felt like my blood was being pumped around inside me by steel pistons. I stood up and walked towards them, ready to lunge at her and rip her heart out, but I stopped. Adding my own body to the packed fray, I closed my eyes and I started moving my feet on the plywood. The alcohol made me more attuned to the music and I wriggled rhythmically to the bass line.

I had been lost in my own world, but when I lifted my head up, Morten was dancing alone in front of me, looking straight into my eyes. He reached over and stroked my hair, softly. He ran his fingers down the small of my back and up my neck. Then he grabbed my hair from underneath, tilted my head back and kissed me. His tongue almost suffocated me as he wrapped his other arm around me and tugged me towards him. His embrace was reviving the emotions I had tried so hard to smother the whole day. He was in command again, and I was yielding to his irresistible charms once more.

'Should we get out of here?' Morten asked.

We kissed our way out of the club, into the cab and under his sheets. We lay side by side for a few minutes in the dark while he caressed me. He rolled over me and started torturing me with rhythmic frictions. As he touched my thighs, I came to my senses.

'Do you have a condom?' I muttered.

Morten did not listen. Mad with yearning, he lowered his underwear and pushed mine aside. Before I knew it, he was thrusting erratically inside me, rubbing his torso against mine and biting my nipples. Panic pervaded me, I wanted him to stop, it was too risky. As I pushed him away from me, he pulled out and came on the sheets with a moan. He rested his head on my stomach and panted. I stroked his hair like you would stroke a child's.

Finally, I untangled myself from under him and retreated to the bathroom. I had red marks on my neck and my lips seemed bee-stung. I sat on the toilet and wiped any trace of my misbehaviour.

When I came out of the bathroom, he was all curled up in the foetal position. I crawled back in bed next to him. Lying sideways with my head resting on my arm, I traced the contours of his body softly. He was mountains and valleys, he was rocks and sand, he was wheat and sky. He smelled as welcome as a loaf freshly out of the oven and his skin was as soft as a baby's. He seemed so vulnerable, so lost. I rested my head on his chest and shut my eyes.

However, there was something not quite right that prevented me from being at ease in his arms. I lay there, thinking about the passion I had perceived in his eyes the day we had met. I wondered if, after all, I wasn't just another girl in his bed, another tool filling in the void of his emotional life.

I sat up on the bed, and turned my head to glance at him once more. I felt full of sadness. I had once read a book that stated men fell in love with women who made themselves scarce. I had done exactly the opposite – I had been waiting for him in the cold and I had yielded to his sexual urges on demand. Living in a constant state of uncertainty had caused my stomach to churn and left me sleepless. I longed for him constantly, even when he was lying next to me.

As the first rays of light appeared, I despondently gathered my clothes, which were strewn all over the floor and quietly got dressed. I took a piece of paper and scribbled "*Couldn't sleep, went back home. Marion* x", put my hair up in a bun, and left his apartment.

As I stepped out of his building, I swiftly looked at my hand watch. It was six a.m. Outside, cars were already rushing up and down the streets like angry wasps smoked out of their hives. I stopped by the corner deli and ordered my favourite toasted cinnamon raisin bagel with cream cheese. It was both sweet and sour and delighted my taste buds.

I endeavoured to open the front door as gently as possible not to wake up anyone at such an early hour. I wasn't sure whether Kate and Betina were back or not. The flat was unlit and quiet. I removed my boots and tiptoed to the living room where I threw my jacket and bag on the sofa.

I noticed that the bathroom light was on and the door was ajar. I pushed it gently and scanned the room, clothes were folded on the chair, and Betina's bag was open on the floor. I started to undress, poured some make-up remover onto a cotton wool pad and leant above the washbasin to look into the mirror. From the corner of my eye, I saw a foot sticking out of the bathtub, behind the curtain. My blood froze and my whole body tensed. With a hesitant hand, I grabbed the hem of the curtain and opened it with a jerk. Betina lay at the bottom of the tub with her eyes open and purple lips. Small bubbles pearled all over her face and the water was strangely still.

My whole body retracted and shrunk as I shrieked. 'Betina, no, no, no, Betina, what have you done?'

I reached out to her, plunged my hands in the cold water, clenched them under her arms and pulled her out of the water. The bathtub was lined with hundreds of bottles of shampoo; some of them were buoying around Betina's naked body. I felt as if I had swallowed gravel; my stomach swilled painfully and my hands shook relentlessly. Irina ran into the bathroom and uttered Russian words; she was wide-eyed and the tone in her voice translated the fear in her eyes.

'Call 911!' I shouted at her, even though I knew that it was probably too late.

Betina's skin was translucent with delicate blue veins like ink on parchment, but the story written in here wasn't a happy one. I pressed my fingers on her wrist but could feel no pulse. I pinched her nose and blew in her mouth a few times, then clenched my hands together to press as hard as I could on her chest. I had seen it done so many times on television, but it was not so easy – I couldn't get it to work. Betina's limp body yielded as I squeezed between her silicone breasts but no breath.

When the paramedics arrived with their gear, I was sitting on the cold floor in my underwear, holding Betina in my arms. The Russian girls and Kate formed a guard of honour around us, which opened as the men in blue stepped in. A man kneeled and placed his stethoscope on Betina's chest while the other one, visibly younger, looked at her eyes.

'I'm afraid she's gone,' the older man said with a grave face.

My whole body started convulsing; tears welled up as I howled and sobbed uncontrollably. I sat against the bathtub limply, wailing, with tears streaming down my cheeks. The other girls stood against the wall, in a stupor, with their arms crossed over their chests.

'Did *you* find her?' The man with the grey hair asked me. I nodded as I held my breath. 'Any idea why she may have drowned? Was she depressed or on drugs, drunk maybe?'

I shook my head, 'I don't know!' I whimpered, stroking Betina's hair.

Kate stepped forward.

'We were out with her, at a club, but we didn't come home together. She said she had to meet someone, so I headed home without her.' Kate's brow was furrowed with worry. 'I should have waited for her,' Kate confessed as she looked down.

The young paramedic had another look at Betina's eyeballs; he lifted her eyelids and directed a small flashlight towards her pupils.

'I think it may have been caused by drugs,' he said.

We all looked at each other in confusion. 'Right, let's lift her up on the stretcher and take her out,' the paramedic said with a glum face.

I watched Betina's face disappear as they zipped up the black bag. I noticed the two small erect bulges formed by her breasts, sad reminders of her attempt to enhance herself. My friend was gone along with her secrets buried somewhere deep inside.

We all sat forlornly in the living room, listening to the raindrops lashing against the window. For the first time, the five inhabitants of the Icon models flat were gathered in the same room, sharing the same feelings, ones of sadness and distress. Time had stopped; I noticed the moulding on the ceiling, the intricate puzzle-parquet floor, cracked and dented in places and the small willow standing morosely in its pot next to the fire exit door. The models' flats held fractions many lives; most girls came in and out of each other's lives, were made and then broken, got their hopes up and failed. The cracks in the wall were a reminder of the scars on their souls.

'David was selling her drugs,' Kate said, with her head in her hands.

We all looked at her.

'She confessed to me the other night. She told me that she started heavier drugs in London with her ex-boyfriend. But when we went separate ways last night, it didn't occur to me that she would go and get drugs from some random dealer on the street. I mean, it must be what happened, right?'

'I'm not sure. Do you think David would give her a fix in the middle of the night or try to give her bad crank?' I asked Kate with a quivering voice. 'Even if it wasn't bad, she was taking way too much…'

Kate was visibly contrite.

***

In the days that followed the tension amongst us was palpable; it hung in the air like we were due a storm. It wouldn't have taken much for any of us to break down and cry. Betina's death was a blow to all of us. The agency had to fight off bad press and nosy journalists, but the whole thing was still not a big enough story to make the boldface headlines of the local newspaper and it wasn't long before it was reduced to a footnote in the back pages. The big shots in the industry had made sure the story was killed off before it could do any real damage. Betina's death hadn't set the cat among the pigeons as we hoped it might. There would be other Betinas, in fact there were other Betinas out there right now whose agency got them hooked on life-destroying drugs, and I struggled to make peace with that.

The girls in the flat barely uttered a word; there was no music, no TV, we could hear no sounds other than those of the streets below. The air was thick with prayers and doubts. Alcohol was poured into glasses, empty glasses became ashtrays, loaded ashtrays became book stands, books landed on the ground, raising clouds of ash and dust, ashes becoming dust and somewhere in the thick of all the silence and dust, our wish for our friend to rest in peace.

CHAPTER 21

Marion, Five days after Betina's death,
New York, December 1996

Morten's bewildered roommate opened his door wearing worn out sweat pants and a white t-shirt. He casually let me in and dived back into his bed. Morten was still asleep. I got undressed and lay down next to him. He smiled and wrapped his arm around me.

'Where have you been?' he muttered and dozed off again.

While he kissed my neck, I stared at the cobweb that had been meticulously woven in the left corner of the ceiling. The couple of flies that had had the misfortune to be too blind to see it had surrendered to their fate. Eventually, a fat hairy spider would come strutting about, toy with them a little and behead them for a feast. I could sympathise with those sorry insects, strung up by a contract with no other option. Despite the big names I now worked with, I was barely scraping by. I missed my family and everything was so transient. The ties I had with the people around me only lasted as long as a fleeting embrace. Morten's hug would last as long as he was asleep, he would then loosen his grip and release me. I came in and out of his life like a breeze – a fleeting caress, a soothing hug, a brisk flutter through the curtains, and out again by the window.

When he finally stirred, he looked at me with his ice-blue eyes and smiled.

'Want some breakfast?'

'Sure!'

As Morten sat up on the bed, he unwittingly kicked a bottle of vodka sending it onto the floor, and eventually against the wall with a clinking sound.

'I feel like shit!' he said, rubbing his sallow face and running his hand through his dishevelled blonde hair. He grabbed the smeared CD case that was on the bedside table, gathered the remainder of the cocaine, poised the rolled up dollar bill by his nostril, and snorted it loudly.

'Want some?' he asked.

I hesitated. Drugs didn't scare me anymore. Nothing moved me anymore. I felt totally void of emotions, too much had happened and now I felt utterly numb. Robot-like, I awkwardly manoeuvred the rolled bill and vacuumed the last traces of the white dust. The tang of the coke tickled the back of my nose and ran down my throat. I waited for the big wow effect to hit me but nothing happened. I was left with a metallic aftertaste and nothing else. After Betina's death, it didn't make sense to try drugs, but I felt invulnerable and weary at the same time. I wanted to brave the drugs, look them in the eyes and turn them down with contempt.

'That's my girl!' Morten said in admiration and gave me a long kiss. I suspected he want to get some of the coke back. He rubbed his nose, cleared his throat and walked to the bathroom to clear his phlegm.

As he pissed loudly with the door open, I propped my head up on the pillow and wondered how I could possibly be in love with a blonde cocaine fiend. What was I doing? I had to get myself out of the hole I had crawled into. Things had to change.

***

On my way back home, I paused in front of the large Air France poster. Since I had arrived in New York, there wasn't a day when that sign had not beckoned me. It took me fifteen minutes to book my flight home, knowing I was inexorably maxing out my overdraft. I had no money left on my agency account and nothing left at the bank, but I had to go home, whatever the cost. I put it on a credit card. I could deal with my financial problems later. Right now, I really needed the reassurance and stability of being at home, somewhere comfortable where there was a routine and life carried on as always. There was no reason for me to stay there any longer.

New York had a great energy, it propelled everyone forward as they flocked together down Fifth Avenue, it sent the New Yorkers flying to their big buck jobs, until the day they tripped and got trampled to death by the rest of the herd; then they got squashed like a pancake. I wasn't utterly destroyed yet, but I certainly felt as if I could be falling. Modelling was devouring me, grinding every bone in my body down to a fine powder. I was gradually disintegrating into nothingness. People were literally walking through me. I needed to make it in New York, but New York had no need for me. I was out, and I knew it.

I went to the agency in order to let David know that I was leaving. I had only been in New York for two months and had worked hard but yet, in such a short time, my financial problems had deepened and I couldn't seem to get over Betina's atrocious death. David stood behind his desk, leaning on crutches, with a plaster cast up to his right hip. I hadn't seen him since Betina had passed away. I held him responsible for her death and I couldn't find the strength to even hear his voice over the telephone. I longed to kick his bad leg. I just wanted to give him a bruising jolt, to hurt him for all the harm he had done to Amirit and Betina, but I knew that kicking him would not change anything. If I brought the subject up, he would most certainly avoid it with an innocuous comment. I braced myself to speak up, but David caught me on the hop with a serious tone of voice.

'Marion, I am afraid we have had to do a bit of cleaning up lately and I am sorry but we cannot keep you on.'

I was dumbfounded. Calling in to say I was leaving would have been far less embarrassing. I was broke and I felt broken inside. My composite card was probably in the bin by the time I stepped into the cab.

It was the twenty third of December; I had booked my flight earlier that month to make it home for Christmas. I both longed for and dreaded facing my parents' disappointment. Kate tried to convince me to stay longer, but it was only a matter of time before she moved in with her new boyfriend. I guess that after Betina's death, no one really wanted to spend much time in the flat. I hugged her goodbye and she helped me into the taxi with all my bags. The driver fished around for a cigarette, and didn't ask me if I minded, but I didn't care about anything anymore.

Forty minutes later, I was walking through the miles of carpeted corridors of JFK airport. Small blue flags studded with stars were lined both sides of the boarding gates. I was about to leave the most patriotic country I had ever been to with what seemed to sum up my experience of the nation; a Starbuck's cup of coffee and a cinnamon raisin bagel filled with cream cheese.

PART FOUR

ITALY

CHAPTER 22

Marion, Avignon, Christmas Eve, 1996

I thought my mother would be happy to see me and hug me with tears of joy, declaring she had missed me, and that I hadn't called often enough. She did cry, but because the fashion magic wand had turned her daughter into a toad rather than a princess. The bagels had encroached on my thighs and the numerous sleepless nights had ploughed dark circles underneath my lustreless eyes.

My suitcase had hardly touched the floor that I was already on a strict diet. Eventually, the hours of stomach rumbling paid off, my skin cleared up and my weight dropped within a month.

'How could you put on so much weight?'

Typical of my older brother Patrick to always be so blunt and straight to the point. The years of competitive swimming we had done together still showed. Broad shoulders firmly topped his lean body, his joints were as supple as chewing gum and he still shaved his arms and legs. His job as a commodities trader had taken him to Singapore and had taught him all about willpower and guts. Patrick loved a challenge and he excelled when confronted and taunted. He told me that he stared at his four flat-screen monitors banked above his desk every day while red and green lights bleeped on the screens, with graphs going up and down, zigzagging before his eyes. He witnessed the rise and fall of the world many times a year without batting an eyelash. His instinct was his true north; he mastered his risks and kept calm and cool despite the market's upheavals. As he came to master the black gold curb, whether bullish or bearish, millions of dollars started streaming his way. He was given his own office at a young age and within two years of trading, at the age of twenty four, he had siphoned all the attention away from the other traders. Competitors fought over him, tempting him with shares and bonuses; his own management consequently allotted him a larger portfolio, which he increased exponentially with ease.

He screwed up his sharp blue eyes and reiterated his question, 'How could you put on so much weight in such a short time?'

'I didn't see it coming, OK? Give me a break, or I'll start thinking I was better off in New York, freezing my butt off. You would not believe how cold it was.'

'I am not judging you, I am just telling you that your weight is your commodity, you cannot afford to let yourself balloon up.'

'Oh, come on, it's not that bad!' I exclaimed. 'I went from swimming for two hours a day to having two bagels a day… that's probably why!'

We laughed and Patrick put his arm around my shoulder. Although we both had grown up a lot in the months since last summer and it felt good to be connected again.

'What do you want to do, now?' he asked.

My mother stepped in, 'I should not have let you start this modelling contest in the first place. It's my fault. I should have insisted you started studying; now it's too late.'

She twitched her thin lips and screwed up her eyes in the same fashion as Patrick did.

'Mum, Marion can't even count up to one hundred; forget about sending her to college, it's not for her,' Patrick said with a smirk. I punched him on the shoulder and we fought playfully for a while, wrestling on the sofa. 'But you're still strong; you may still have a potential career in wrestling!' he roared with laughter.

My father who had been quietly watching us, decided to speak up at last.

'How on Earth could the agency let you put on weight without saying a word?'

'Maybe because I always covered it with so many layers, but most likely because they don't care. There are hundreds if not thousands of girls buzzing on their door every day, why would they bother with one?'

'It doesn't make any sense at all. Why would they let down the winner of their contest?' My father insisted, shaking his head.

I leaned back on the sofa, and stared at him sternly. 'Because I am just a number. Because I didn't make them enough money; so they stopped looking at me. Think how many girls they take on a year – how many of them do they really expect to make it?'

**

After a few months back home, I felt much stronger and clear headed. Summer had finally arrived and I spent most of my time swimming and spending time with my family. I received a postcard from Kate telling me she had moved in with her boyfriend as I'd expected she probably would and they were living on Church Street. Patrick had given me enough money to put me back on my feet and I had surrendered to my parents' pressure and applied to University to study English Literature at the end of the summer. My mother envisioned me becoming an English teacher like her, finding a nice husband, living in the suburbs and raising my children under the cloudless skies of the south of France just as she had done.

While I considered it as a comfortable option, the alluring promise of money and success was still lurking in the background, not to mention the excitement of living in a big city. That was when modelling came knocking on my door again. Carla, an Italian booker at Icon Milan was on the phone.

'Marion! It's Carla from Icon. How are you *Amore*?'

'I'm good thanks,' I replied sceptically.

'I spoke to David in New York yesterday; he told me that you were back in Europe. As you know, Icon is a big family and we're all connected. David thought it might be a good idea to try the Italian market. *Amore*, I happen to have a few options for you, and some good clients, here that want to meet you.'

How often had I heard the same old refrain? It was just like David to try and palm me off to his Italian colleagues. How often did they do that to girls, to Betina in particular? But what other option did I have? The same hand that slapped me unconscious always picked me up and stroked me. Unable to make any decision that lasted more than a month, I felt like a weathervane, turning wherever the wind blew. I knew that my mother would be very disappointed. She had finally managed to turn me away from the industry, but the sound of fast and easy money was always terribly tempting. Maybe things would be different in Milan.

It was only the matter of weeks before my university course started in September, but there I was, on the road again, driving to Milan, a city whose secret beauty lay behind a few privileged doors. Milan was intoxicating. It swarmed with cars, mopeds and flocks of people in a hurry. Icon Paris and New York had cut me loose, but it seemed that their Milanese branch, however had not only agreed to keep me on their books, but appeared to be quite positive about me.

The bookers had that Italian easiness about them which alleviated all pressure. The models I encountered during the castings came in all shapes and forms. Any girl with two legs could call herself a model in Milan. There seemed to be neither real selection nor criteria. Most models stayed in a *penzione* or residence. It was a dismal building with a Princess' name on via Luigi Galvani, two steps away from the Central train station, filled with models, prostitutes and transvestites. As usual, they hadn't spent much on the accommodation for Icon models.

In the evening, as I made my way back from Gioia tube station after my castings, I walked past a display of transvestites, freshly ashore from Brazil, masturbating on the pavement for the drivers to see on their way back home. Occasionally a man in a suit with a couple of booster seats in the back of his car would pull over.

It was not rare to meet one of these peculiar neighbours in the lift on the way to my bedroom, which, once again, I had to share with strangers. Overall, the community was colourful and happy. All rites of courtesy were demolished as the bedroom doors remained open, calling for parties and easy bonding. Despite everything I liked it there. It felt freer than New York or Paris. After a few months with my parents eating green beans and ratatouille, I was pleased to spice up my life again.

Mama Teresa, the owner of the Penzione sat on her stool behind the reception desk surrounded by a few rumbustious young men who spent great energy waving their hands, speaking loudly on their mobile phones and riding sputtering mopeds. Despite her thick grey rubbery skin and a voice abraded by years of smoking, Mama Teresa displayed the friendliest smile and had a sincere affection for all of us. She held court at the residence day in and day out, perpetually with a cigarette dangling from her lips. Her hair was sprayed in a spectacular beehive and her generous bosoms were flashed to the residents, whether they wished to see them or not.

***

I had been in Milan for a week when I decided to pay a visit to the accounting department. I was determined to keep an eye on my finances this time, especially now that I wasn't bound to a contract. I sat on the red lip-shaped sofa next to the window pane at Icon Milan going through my account statement. The numbers swam across the spreadsheet; it was not designed for models to understand.

'Where do these expenses come from?' I asked Carla as I leaned on her desk, running my fingers through staggering sums. She looked up from her pristine new computer. The giant rolodex that had been the kernel of any booking table for years had suddenly taken its leave and had been replaced by technology. All the Icon branches were now linked via the same computer network; with a click or two of her mouse, Carla pulled up my statement.

'These expenses have been deducted by both Icon Paris and New York,' Carla explained. 'Courier expenses, composites, and "internet fees" – that's new!'

I was seething.

'I mean, how on Earth can they justify all these expenses when they fired me months ago?' Carla was open-mouthed with embarrassment. 'How can they give me the boot and yet continue to take money from me like this? '

'I don't… I don't… I don't know what to say…' Carla stuttered. She shrugged and lifted both hands in the air.

I stood up stiffly and scanned the statement once more. Two Italian young men swaggered past me towards Carmela, Icon Milan's chairwoman. I immediately recognised the one with bleached yellow hair from the Penzione, with his spiky-haired punk look and loud mouth. The chains attached to his denim clinked and rattled as he ambled past. His friend's hair was just as huge, only curly. However ominous and misplaced they looked, the apprentice rogues hugged Carmela effusively.

'Who are those guys?' I asked Carla, who was probably relieved they had taken my mind off the statement. 'They're always there and about at the hotel, trying to pick up girls!'

'They are PRs, they work for the local night clubs in town. They basically make sure the VIP areas are full of models,' Carla said with a smile.

I frowned, not entirely sure about what to make of these birds of ill omen, or what business they had with Carmela. My attention shifted back to my statement and I asked Carla if I could email my agency in Paris to set things right. She showed me how to set up a Hotmail account and advised me to do so from an internet café. My parents gave us very limited access to the home computer, so when I sat behind the screen at the café, my fingers were hesitant. I came to realise that I was gaining a whole new access to the rest of the world.

'Hey!' somebody called from the booth next to mine.

I looked over to my left and noticed a dark-haired guy who was probably a male model.

'I recognise you,' He said. 'We shot the commercial for that French cream commercial last year!' He had a lilting tone of voice. I presumed he was American, judging by the subtle twang.

'I'm sorry, I don't…'

'I was among the extras. We had to pretend to watch the paintings in the museum, while you were with the main guy,' he explained.

'Oh I see! I'm Marion.'

'I'm Brandon. All the way from Mississippi,' he smiled.

'How has it been for you here?' I asked.

'Well… it's not really conclusive. It's alright though, I'm having fun. When summer is over, I'll probably head back home anyway. My visa is going to expire.'

I smiled shyly. As I was about to turn my attention back to my screen, he added 'Are you going out tonight? I'm going to Hollywood Club. That's where all the models go. Wanna come?'

Under any other circumstances, I would have declined the invitation, but I felt we were all on the same boat and there was no reason to be suspicious.

***

A few hours later we met at a small typically Italian restaurant with some of Brandon's friends, all of whom were models. They welcomed me as if we had known each other for a long time. We were all on a budget, like students, or so I imagined, just having one dish and tap water.

We walked past the queue and straight into the club. It was a huge crowded place, where the music was so loud that I felt the bass echo in my chest. The blonde punk came to meet us and escorted us to the VIP area where other models were crammed like sardines in a box, swimming in their own oily sweat. I spotted a few older men ogling the much younger female models. Most girls had a Slavic look; tall, blonde and seemingly anaemic, with high cheek bones. They smiled at everything the men told them, but I bet they did not understand half of it.

'Do you come here often?' I screamed into Brandon's ear.

'Every week. It's nothing special, the music isn't even good but we get free booze, and sometimes free drugs!'

I looked at him in dismay. He was the archetypal University quarterback: healthy, strong, and athletic. I guess he was the last person I expected to take drugs, but in the modelling industry those of us who abstained were in the minority.

As we left the club around 6 a.m. on Corso Como, Brandon wanted to get some food.

'That meal wasn't enough, and that was ages ago. I'm starved. I know just a place for a Panini. Hungry?'

'I'm OK thanks. I should head back and get some sleep,' I replied. 'But come to think of it, the small café next to my residence should open soon, you could get your Panini there.'

We strolled along the tram tracks, a few lights went on in people's kitchens and the city slowly awoke.

'Have you worked much in Milan?' he asked.

'I've only just arrived, but I'm on hold for a few catalogues. I'm hoping they'll get confirmed as I desperately need the money!'

'For a while, I couldn't understand why the agency hadn't fired me,' he said. 'I owed them so much money from the beginning: my flight, my visa, my cards, my rent… There must be something wrong with me because I rarely get bookings!' He kept looking down as we walked. 'First I was excited to be invited to every single party, but soon I realised that I was just a commodity, along with the champagne and the coke. I realised that there was a two-tier business going on when one of those old farts came on to me. Can you believe this? They just wanted to pimp me out at parties, basically!'

I was speechless. I had a hard time realising the scope of what he was saying. Model agencies in Paris, London, New York and Milan were not only distributing drugs, they also thrived on hustling their models, and stole money from the girls who did get work by deducting miscellaneous expenses from their accounts that were impossible to verify. Both situations were intimately intertwined and were a consequence of one another.

***

'Marion, your agent wants you to call her back,' Mama Teresa said as I finally came down through reception that morning. I nodded and went to the corner café and ordered a freshly squeezed orange juice, a cappuccino and a panini.

'Marion! You'll be glad you came to Milan, you're on option for the *Amica* cover and the Armani campaign,' Carla was almost breathless with pride.

'Really? How so?'

'Well you saw a photographer's rep the other day and one of his photographers put those two options on you,' she explained. 'The photographer wants to go for dinner with you.'

'Who's the photographer?' I enquired, rolling my eyes.

'Paolo Piviano.' The two words came bashing against my chest. I was lost for words.

'Are you there?'

'He's already tried the Armani trick, this guy is a total pig!' I exclaimed with a high-pitched voice.

'They all are, *Amore*.' Carla sounded jaded. 'But don't do what you don't want to do? Play along and see if you can get away with it? It would be so great to book those jobs. But again, it's your call honey.'

My whole body convulsed at the thought of having dinner with the swine. *I don't want to go, I don't want to go, I don't want to go*, I repeated to myself. But eventually, either curiosity or greed led me to the restaurant. There he was, sitting at his white cloth table, facing me. A candle flickered in front of him, reflecting in his glasses as he read a book. I paused and watched him for a few seconds. It wasn't too late, I could still run away.

'Hello *Cara*,' he smoothed. Too late, he'd seen me. I felt sick to my stomach, as I let him kiss me on both cheeks. 'I have taken the liberty of ordering for both of us, so you can try true Italian food.' He waved me to sit down in front of him.

When the food was finally served, he took my hand.

'*Cara*, you have to eat spaghetti with your spoon… and roll the fork into the spoon.'

He held both hands and guided me with my spoon and fork as if I were a child. I identified the deviant look in his eyes; it brought me a few months back and stirred all the negative emotions I had felt back then. Each spoonful of spaghetti put in my mouth by his hand filled my stomach with angst. I managed to gently push him away and admitted that I wasn't very hungry.

When it came to the inevitable, I made my well-rehearsed excuse, 'I'll just take a taxi home, thank you.'

'There aren't many taxis in this neighbourhood, but I'm staying at the hotel around the corner, we could go to my room and order you a cab,' he sneered.

How am I going to get out of this one now? I wondered. 'That's very kind of you, but I'm pretty sure I'll find a cab,' I replied with a contrived smile. My hands twisted the white napkin so hard under the table that I could have squeezed every last atom of air out of it.

As we walked along the pavement, he wrapped his arm around my waist. I prayed for a cab to show up then. No taxi. *Please God, do something.* A few cars drove past us when finally, a taxi screeched around the corner. I freed myself from his grasp and waved the driver.

'Thank you Paolo, thanks for dinner!' I told him as I wound up the window. I did not turn around, I shrivelled into my seat and closed my eyes. I was safe at last.

The following day, both options were off. I wasn't surprised, but I wasn't relieved either. Any chance of success in the business always seemed to have too high a cost. I thought that by meeting him in a public place, I would get away from any form of hassling but obviously, he took my acceptance to come to dinner as a free pass for sex. That's what it always came down to, what would you let these photographers do for the sake of your career?

'Listen, don't be upset, men will always try to get down your pants, in this business or any other. It's the downfall of being beautiful. You have to learn and use it as a weapon. You don't have to sleep with them, but you have to let them believe you will, to keep them on their toes.'

I gave her a blank stare.

'Don't worry, you're on for the haute couture shows in Rome. Come back with higher spirits, OK? You have to make this industry work for you. Play the game,' Carla added in a friendly tone.

CHAPTER 23

Marion, From Milan to Rome, July 1997

I looked through the small airplane window at the clouds that were drawing closer and closer as we ascended up into the sky, I was daydreaming about the Spanish Steps in Rome, the Eternal City, the famed heart of the Roman Empire, home of the Pope and where I would present precious collections to famous designers and fashion magazines the world over.

I went through customs and made my way towards the luggage belt. Bags of various colours and shapes popped out of the hole in the wall and disappeared as their owners collected their belongings. As the belt had cleared up, I started worrying that my suitcase had been lost. I looked around in exasperation and noticed that an old man dressed head-to-toe in black, with black sunglasses, surrounded by an entourage was walking directly towards me. A woman with a bob of blonde hair and two younger men resembling his bodyguards had a stern stare, which I did not find reassuring. I looked behind me but the place was deserted. The mafia were definitely edging towards me. Before I could even react, the old man dug his hand inside his jacket and pulled out a business card.

'Good afternoon, I have been watching you. I think that you would have great potential as an actress.' I was taken aback and did not react. 'Think about it and give me a call,' he said as he handed me a rectangular piece of paper with Franco Zeffirelli, *Movie Director*, written on it.

His austere looking entourage fell in behind him and they disappeared as fast as they had approached me. I stood there, staring at the card while my luggage passed behind my back and disappeared inside the hole in the wall.

I rummaged through my bag for my newly bought mobile phone. I was embracing a whole new era of technology.

'Mum, have you ever heard of Franco Zeffirelli?'

'Of couuuuuurse!' She replied ecstatically. 'He's not a young man anymore but back then, he made a few good movies such as *The Taming of the Shrew* with Elizabeth Taylor and *Romeo and Juliet*. Of course I know who he is. Why are you asking?'

'Well, I've just met him at the airport! He literally walked up to me, handed me his business card, and asked me to call him to discuss a potential career as an actress!'

'Call him back! I have always said that you were born to be a movie star!'

I knew that my mother's opinion was always to be taken with a pinch of salt, but I was willing to seize any opportunity that would escalate me from obscurity.

***

The fabric of the old Fiat's seats had suffered from too much bottom shuffling, coffee spillages and other suspicious bodily fluid stains. The springs dug into my buttocks through the hard packed concave cushions as rough driving through the paved roads of central Rome jerked me around. A sun-bleached, tree-shaped air freshener danced annoyingly under the rear-view mirror where the driver's glazed eyes met with mine occasionally. He had combed a long strand of hair from above his right ear, up and across his skull, like a single fence spanning a sterile desert landscape. As I rolled down my window, I admired the Colosseum, which stood proud amongst the ruins. We drove down large winding avenues streaming with cars and motorbikes, and then into smaller maze-like streets where well-dressed men and women loafed around coffee terraces sipping cappuccinos.

Finally, the taxi dropped me off in front of a quaint hotel with pots of lavender on the steps leading to the door. An elegantly dressed woman in her forties welcomed me with a smile and showed me to my room. The bathroom sink and bathtub were made of limestone and the fluffy towels smelled of lavender. It was the most charming place I had ever stayed in as a model; this was the closest I had come so far to living the glamorous life I had always dreamed of. I read the note left on my bed telling me that all girls would be fitted for rehearsal at ten a.m. the next day.

As the day drew to a close, I decided to go out for a bite to eat. I walked down the winding streets in search for a typical Italian delicatessen and ate a prosciutto sandwich by one of the numerous soothing fountains in Rome.

The next morning, after a long night's sleep, I woke up in high spirits and sat on a terrace facing the sun by the Spanish Steps. While I sipped my cappuccino, I noticed other models gathering in front of the terrace, ready for their ten o'clock appointments.

We entered a large warehouse with tracked ceiling lights and linoleum floors, which had been prised up in places revealing old floorboards. Brown curtains had been improvised by rolling cloth around the marble columns in order to keep both the sunlight and the onlookers out. Despatched to our respective stands in the large warehouse, we met with our teams of stylists and the other models involved in the show. From where I stood, I spotted Donatella Versace with her signature long bleached hair and her black eye make-up having an agitated conversation with her brother, Santo. Santo flung his arms wide and looked around him, making gestures at his watch, as if to suggest that he had a job to do and other people to see thank you very much, rather than listening to her complaints. There was a slight titter in Donatella's voice while Santo listened, turned his heels, walked towards the exit door and fired back a dirty glance as he opened it. It swung shut behind him with a bang.

'Don't mind them, they're Italian. What would sound like an argument to us, for them is actually just a normal discussion!' The stylist of Comme des Garçons interjected as she flicked a lock of hair away from her face and handed me the next outfit.

Journalists were scouring the warehouse for scoops like eagles hovering above a field filled with rabbits. A hand-held camera caught me ducking behind the clothes rail as I squeezed into my dress and the staggeringly high stilettos, which caused my feet to arch to their maximum.

'I'm never going to be able to walk in those shoes. It feels like my feet are bending backwards!' I said, but the bespectacled metrosexual female stylist with the boyish hair ignored my concerns.

She only had to worry about making sure the clothes fit, not how I was going to walk down the slippery steps. She arranged the silk dress so the slit would open right above my knee and with a vapid expression on her face, she declared me ready. I ran my hand through the organdies and fur, taffeta and cashmere hanging on the rail, and staggered towards the exit with my silts and my long slashed black and grey dress.

The air was thick with anticipation as models looked at each other, unsure of what was to happen next, standing in a queue at the top of the Spanish steps awaiting their instructions. Finally, a man with a heavy Italian accent split us into two groups and asked us to stream down the slippery steps one after the other.

'Girls, I want you to walk down the stairs to the very bottom and exit on each side to the back and get changed into your next outfit. All the designers are being shown without a break, so please make it fast. The audience will be seated at the bottom of the stairs and there will be a band playing in the middle. Don't let them steal the show, be sophisticated and look in front of you as you walk down the stairs.'

I looked down; my stomach churned at the steepness of the steps. I could hear the faint murmur among the people watching us from the bottom of the stairs. They were mostly tourists, wearing floppy Japanese hats and shorts that revealed their stubby white, legs shiny with sun screen. On the right hand side, a washed-out ochre building overlooked the steps. A young man with slicked hair leant against the iron-wrought railing of his balcony, causally smoking a cigarette. A woman with a red dress stood next to him with her hands on her hips. They were in a perfect spot to watch the rehearsal.

I moved my toes gently to make sure my blood was still circulating and carefully put one foot in front of the other, placing the sole delicately on the smooth surface of the stone. The steps were slightly slanted and rounded at the end, which made even the simplest action perilous.

By the time I made it back to the warehouse to get changed, there was an unusual buzz amongst the press and the designers. The models looked at each other in dismay.

'Gianni Versace has been murdered!' said the Comme des Garçons stylist with watery eyes.

The news came as a deafening bombshell and spread like wildfire as a pervasive humming sound quickly filled the large room. The show was postponed; the producer sent us back to our hotels and promised to give us an update later on. The warehouse was a hive of activity and panic; everyone was running around in order to fish for more information. Donatella and Santo had been ushered out by security. General chaos prevailed amongst the fashionistas; everyone was lost for words. The models got dressed, walked out and fished their mobile phones from their bags, hoping to get more details on the dreadful news. Some models burst in tears, others recoiled from the scene and made their way back to their hotels in shock.

'…Versace killed by forlorn lover Andrew Cunanan in front of his house in Miami, today…' the journalist said on CNN. We all sat listening to the details of the killing with our mouths agape, confused by the mixed rumours of mafia involvement and crazed lovers. Gianni Versace, the fashion pygmalion was down, and the rest of the fashion world was at a standstill. The whole industry had entered a state of mourning.

These were strange times, even though top models existed well before him, Gianni had taken them to a whole different level, gathered them all on one stage and polished their image as superstars.

***

The next morning, as I had a few hours before my flight, I decided to phone Franco Zeffirelli, hoping to get an appointment with him that same day.

'Good morning, my name is Marion Durant, I met Mr Zeffirelli two days ago in the airport. He has asked me to call him…'

'Let me see if I can find him, hold the line please,' said a man's voice. I heard birds chirping in the background. I pictured him as Dr Moreau in the movie version of H.G. Wells novel *The Island of Doctor Moreau*; dressed in a white robe with his face painted white, surrounded by animals. 'Mr Zeffirelli said that he has contacted a renowned casting director in London who could potentially help you. She's expecting your call. Do you have something to write her number down?'

And that was all. The ball had been pushed into somebody else's court and I was deflated. Naively, I thought that if a movie director wanted to use an actress, he could impose his choice onto the casting director. But I realised that it was just another casting. All of a sudden acting sounded like an insurmountable mission. As a model all I had to do was just show up and look into the camera. As an actress, I would have to have lines memorised and rehearsed, I would have to overcome stage fright, and act the part convincingly. I sat on the plane on my way back to my parents, overwhelmed by disappointment and low self-confidence.

***

'Were you in Rome for the shows?' asked the salt-and-pepper haired man sitting next to me on the plane.

He was all spruced up, with perfectly manicured hands and silver cufflinks on his white shirt upon which the initials GZ were embroidered.

I lowered my book and smiled, 'Well, yes and no actually. It got cancelled because of—'

'Versace's murder. I know,' he interrupted with a sullen face. 'I look after some of his family business. I'm a lawyer,' he added. 'It's a tragedy.'

'Oh wow, I am impressed. What is it like? It must be quite difficult at the moment?'

'I guess we have a lot on our hands, yes. But let's talk about you. Where are you from?'

'Avignon. My parents live there. I'm starting my University degree in October!' I smiled.

'Avignon is a very beautiful town! What do you study?' he switched from English to French with great ease.

'English Literature.'

'Pretty and wise. That's very rare nowadays.'

I looked down, for lack of words and asked, 'What is your business in Nice?'

'I'm going there for leisure; I used to sail for Italy when I was younger. My ex-team members and I gather at the Monaco boat show every year,' he said as I stared at him in wonder. 'Those were the good old days. I can only reminisce now! That's why you should fulfil your dreams while you're young.' He sipped his tea, lost in his thoughts. 'What about modelling? Do you like that?'

'I suppose I do.' I paused. 'I like the lifestyle more than the job itself. It's fast money, I suppose.'

'Modelling is a very short and ruthless career. You have to try and seize every opportunity, you need to network with the right people and be extremely diligent with your money. There is a young girl who I now advise, who used to leave all her money with her agency. It is unthinkable that such a successful model would blindly trust her agency with her assets. It's a business; you should treat it as such.'

He sipped his tea again and unfolded his newspaper. As he was engrossed in his reading, I took my novel *Memoirs of a Geisha*, and dived into Sakamoto Chiyo's peregrination. As the plane landed and people started gathering their belongings, Giuseppe pulled out his business card from his wallet; 'I'll tell you what. I am attending the Pirelli calendar launch in London next month, I think you should come.' He put his wallet back into the inside pocket of his jacket. 'Bruce Weber the world renowned photographer will be there, along with other eminent people who could probably help you with your career,' he added, as he took his luggage. 'Think about it, give me a call and my secretary will organise it all for you.'

As we parted, I realised that I didn't even know his name. I looked at his card; *Giuseppe Zampini, business lawyer* was written in gold letters.

CHAPTER 24

Marion, Milan, September 1997

After the shows, I returned to my parents as modelling work slowed down during August. We eventually went back to Rome to do the haute couture shows and all the top models gathered in memory of Gianni Versace. The shows had taken a different turn with Versace's death; it would never be the same again.

A month before I was due to start university, I went back to Milan to fly to London on board a private jet with Giuseppe and a friend of his, Pirelli's chairman. It was a struggle to sell it to my parents, but I convinced them that Giuseppe would introduce me to one of the best photographers in the world. Upon my arrival at Malpensa airport, in the early morning, Giuseppe's driver was waiting for me holding a board with my name written on it. He was about fifty years old, extremely polite and diligent. As he opened the back seat door for me, I suddenly felt like a Lady and did not dare speak at all while the Mercedes ran smoothly along the highway.

I was ushered into a waiting room and served a cup of tea while I waited for Giuseppe. The room was ornate without being too ostentatious with settees made of soft grey velvet in front of a marble mantle piece. Antique armoires with golden handles contained various awards and prices. There was a framed picture of a magnificent sailboat and I wondered if the man with the warm red jacket was Giuseppe. As I leaned closer, Giuseppe barged into the room.

'Ah, la plus belle!' he said. 'Hope you've had a good flight.'

'Very good thank you!'

We kissed on both cheeks.

'We don't have much time, our flight is at two o'clock, but we can catch a quick bite,' he said, looking at his watch. 'Do you have anything to wear for the special evening?' He put his arm under mine.

'I have a simple black dress...'

'OK, come with me,' he said as we walked out, arm in arm.

A few minutes later, the driver pulled up outside the Versace shop and let us out.

'Are we seriously going to buy something *here*?' I asked. 'It costs a fortune!' I exclaimed, kicking myself for having said that.

'Don't worry about it, I get a little rebate and at least once we get to London, the Duchess of York won't ask me who that country bumpkin is!'

'Is it really that bad?'

'I'm only joking.'

Giuseppe hurried into the shop, and randomly selected a few dresses.

'Try this one on,' he ordered as he stretched his arm towards me.

'But, but...' I stammered. 'I'm going to look like a transvestite with this frock, I am too muscular for this type of dress,' I commented as I shook my head. 'I have really broad shoulders, they won't fit me.'

'Try them on anyway,' Giuseppe said, hardly listening to my babbling.

I squeezed into the skimpy dress, had a look into the mirror, huffed in despair and opened the curtains.

Giuseppe stared at me with goggled eyes, 'You're right, you do look like a man in that dress!' I wasn't sure if I was supposed to be upset at the comment or pleased by his honesty.

'Giuseppe, let me choose one please, it'll save you time and comments,' I replied with a witty look.

He chuckled and moved aside while I made my way towards the clothes rails. I eventually found a dress that fitted me perfectly and let Giuseppe choose my boots and coat. I wondered how much the whole lot had cost; it had been so easy for him. I envied his ability to walk into a designer shop and select clothes without looking at the price tag. I felt that I permanently lived in limbo, waiting for a job to be confirmed, or for a cheque to finally hit my account.

At five in the afternoon, as we drove to a small private airport where another private jet awaited us, the car slowed down and eventually stopped in front of a statue.

'Come with me,' he ordered as he got out of the car. 'I want to show you something.'

The mausoleum was erected in memory of a soldier who had had an important role in the Italian Resistance Movement during World War II. As I read the brass plate, I immediately recognised his name — *Zampini* and I looked at him with a start.

'This is the place where my father was shot,' he said sternly.

'He was part of the resistance!'

'That's right, head of the Resistenza partigiana.'

'He must have been a brave man!'

I looked at Giuseppe as his eyes were locked on the stone.

'Bravery is a beautiful thing, indeed. But when you are eight years old and the fascists drag your father's bullet ridden body on a cart to dump it in front of your doorstep, there is nothing heroic about it.'

He swallowed with difficulty; his throat constricted as he renewed with the painful memory.

'How terrible!' I exclaimed.

'My sister and I were hiding in the cupboard when they found us. When they placed their gun on my sister's head, I swore that, should we make it alive, I would become a lawyer and hunt those bastards down with all my might... which I never did of course. I was naive I suppose.' He turned around and started walking back to the car. 'We get over things, even death. I have moved on and focused my attention on more positive things. I was a young angry man at the time. With age, I've learnt to channel anger through sport and work.' He slammed his door and looked at me as the driver started the engine again. 'What I mean is, nowadays, young people don't realise how lucky they are. Please don't let your youth go by, believe in yourself and take the bull by the horns because if you don't do it, no one else will do it for you.'

The man sitting next to me symbolised everything that stood for bravery, elegance and inspiration. We did not speak until we landed in London where a Rolls Royce was waiting for us on the tarmac.

The chauffeur wore a long coat, white gloves and a hat. There was no waiting for customs or bags, no public transport nor sharing a room with strangers. We parked in front of the Claridge's hotel where porters rushed to open the car doors. It had been an effortless trip and one could easily get accustomed to such convenience.

'Dinner is at seven,' said Giuseppe. 'That gives you plenty of time to go to the hairdresser and make yourself presentable. I'll meet you downstairs at six thirty.'

I was relieved to see that Giuseppe had booked a separate bedroom for me; maybe there were some true gentlemen out there after all. My room was large and completely cream with arches above the bed, beige and white striped wallpaper and a cashmere bed throw. Bespoke furniture adorned the room and elegant pictures in silver frames surrounded the king size bed. There were fresh flowers on the bedside table which gave the room a delicate fragrance. I took a long bath in the marble bathroom and went to the hairdresser in the lobby where Giuseppe had booked me an appointment for a blow dry.

Later on, I went down to the reception area with my straight glamorous hair and my slit Versace dress. There was something delicious about financial ease and luxury. I loved how the porters bowed to me as I walked by, I felt like a star. I prayed they wouldn't realise that I was a fraud. I was an ex-swimmer and a struggling model, lost amongst members of the British Royal family and eminent businessmen at a cocktail party. I loitered around the bar and picked at some canapés while I waited for Giuseppe.

'Good evening, may I ask who you are?' asked a ginger-haired woman as she handed me her hand. Giuseppe flew to my rescue and fastened his arm around her.

'Your Grace, could I show you something?'

Giuseppe led her away, glancing at me with goggled eyes over his shoulder.

'Who was that?' I asked Giuseppe once he had come back.

'The Duchess of York!' he whispered. 'She can be quite nosy so the last thing both you and I need is people thinking you're my lover.'

My lover. It dawned on me that however good my intentions were towards Giuseppe, I was no better than the Russians girls in

New York. The idea revolted me, I flared my nostrils as I inhaled, I held my head up, and tried to convey an impression of merit and importance. And yet, I was probably just an escort to these people, using my looks to work my way up. I realised that as Carla had wisely advised me, the best thing to do was to play along and see where it could take me.

I sat for hours brooding over the idea with four sets of forks and knives and as many glasses filled with exquisite expensive wines. The talk was of charity work, reviews on the Pirelli industry and finally a short presentation of the calendar itself. I suffered in silence, and with a smile, but I hoped I would be soon put out of my misery. By the end of the evening, I was trying my very best not to slouch on the table. I had exchanged a few pleasantries with the lady on my right but had kept quiet for most of the event, which had been rather excruciating given my personality.

As the conference drew to an end, I stood up, relieved to be released of my urbane obligations, when the lady on my right handed me her card.

'I am Nan Bush, Bruce Weber's agent. He thinks you would be perfect for his next *Vogue* story. Call me when you're in New York!' she said.

Those were almost the only words she had muttered during the whole evening, and probably the most important ones of my whole career.

I sat right back down and thanked her. A sparkle was revived in me. I wasn't an escort, truth be told I was working on my career strategy. *Giuseppe is a genius*, I thought, flabbergasted. My boredom had paid off after all. All the strutting about, looking seemingly busy and slightly aloof, had resulted in a rather fruitful evening. I was finally holding my passport to stardom.

'I'm going to New York next week on business,' Giuseppe said. 'Why don't you come along so you can meet Nan Bush,' Giuseppe said.

'I can't go...' I replied.

'Why is that?'

'My university course starts in one month's time and, more importantly, I have absolutely no money—'

'Why don't you start your classes and come later once you're organised. I am sure you can do both. English Literature – look, you're already practicing! Don't worry about it, you'll be fine. As for your flight, I'll organise it. You can pay me back later once you've earned it!' he replied with a smile.

PART FIVE

BACK TO NEW YORK

CHAPTER 24

Marion, Back to New York in Style, New York, September 1997

Giuseppe had reserved a room for me at the Four Seasons hotel on 57th Street. As I walked into the grandiose hallway, I filled my lungs with air and took in as much of the incense perfumed air as possible. It was a majestic hallway; imposing marble pillars separated the reception area from the waiting area. An elegant carpet ran through the corridor, leading to the reception desk resplendent with flower bouquets.

A porter took me to my room. The door clicked open and I discovered a luxurious bedroom with a view of Central Park. I was growing rather fond of those luxurious retreats. The room was modern and yet the wooden furniture and mix of fabrics gave it a homely, comfortable feel. I helped myself to some tea and rang Giuseppe.

'Ciao Bella!' he answered.

'The room is beautiful, you're crazy to get me one like this!'

'Well, don't get too used to it as it's only for three days. After that you're on your own!'

'Where are you?' I asked.

'I am in a taxi to my second business appointment. Why don't you get comfortable, organise your meeting with Nan Bush and I'll pick you up for dinner at seven tonight?'

'Sounds like a great plan! See you then!'

And I hung up.

***

At ten a.m. I was in the back of the taxi taking me downtown to Nan's office feeling slightly jetlagged and cloudy. As I leaned my head on the headrest, I felt both the power and energy of New York were insignificant compared to the giant buildings that towered above me. The taxi pulled over and dropped me off in front of a red brick building with iron staircases winding down one side of it. I double-checked that I had the right address and rushed in through the main entrance. I paused for a moment and breathed in and out slowly in order to release some of the tension that had been building inside me since I woke up. The meeting with Nan was vital; it could boost my career and change my life entirely. I pressed on the elevator button but it did not seem to work. I looked around for stairs, but the idea of walking up eight flights put me off.

It then dawned on me that the reason why the lift did not budge was because it was there. All I needed to do was open the door, push the second gate upwards and push it back down before pressing the button. The system seemed so backward to me; but I was finally in and moved slowly and jerkily to the eighth floor.

Nan opened the door herself, greeting me with a friendly smile. She had generous blue eyes encircled by the wrinkles of a well-lived life and full lips. Her grey hair had grown out and blended in with the darker ones, most of which she had tucked behind her ears. A few rebellious ones stood straight on her head. She was dressed in black and was wearing a heavy silver necklace.

'Come on in. You'll have to excuse the mess, I'm doing a lot of filing today.'

I followed the corpulent and yet small woman through the strewn papers and stood next to her large brown desk holding my Book against my chest. She put her glasses on, fetched her Polaroid camera and set it amongst her files.

'May I see your Book?' Nan asked as she stretched her hand out. I watched her flip through my pictures slowly, deciphering every pose while I did my very best to stand as still as possible.

A fire engine siren was blaring loudly down the street outside, resounding over all the other city noises. I stared at her age-spotted hands as they turned each page and wondered what she was making of my pictures. I endeavoured to interpret each tiny movement but Nan Bush went through my portfolio stoically.

'Alright,' she said finally, putting me out of my misery. 'I'll take a couple of polaroids, which I will hand out to *Vogue* later today when I meet with the art director.'

A vivacious glee swept across my face. I was growing restless and I struggled to stand still for the picture.

'This is the address where you should go tomorrow morning at ten. Don't be late and wear your hair down,' Nan said as she handed me a piece of paper.

Two minutes later, I was back in the rabbit cage of a lift and spat out on the streets. *What now?* I thought.

On the way back across town, I wondered about Morten. I'd had no contact with him since I had left New York, and yet, coming back triggered every single memory of him. I imagined him walking down the street smiling at me with every intention to rock my world once more. As I intermingled with the crowd on Broadway, my heart started at every single tall blonde head. He was out there somewhere, breathing the same air as I was, and yet he was out of my sight.

Once back in my hotel room, I took out the spreadsheet with all the model agencies' contact details that I had compiled prior to my arrival. Armed with the promise of a story in *Vogue*, I thought I would have no difficulty finding a new agency to represent me in that side of the world. I naively believed that I could both study and travel the world when the various agencies would book me for a job. After all, I could always catch up on my English Literature studies during my travels; it would be a bit of a juggle but hopefully manageable.

Irene Models was the only one who sounded keen on meeting me the following day. The others were either too busy or too sceptical to see me. I decided to go for a swim in the hotel pool and waited for Giuseppe to pick me up.

'How was your appointment with Nan Bush?' Giuseppe asked before wolfing down the mussel he had carefully plucked out with another empty shell.

'It went fine, I guess. She was hard to read; she kept a poker face and flipped through my Book. Made no comment.' I sipped my water. 'Good news is, I am meeting with one of *Vogue*'s art directors tomorrow morning.'

'Fantastic! Any luck with ringing agencies?' Giuseppe asked as he waved at the waiter. 'Would it be possible to get a finger bowl please?' he asked the waiter, who nodded and rushed towards the kitchen.

'I rang a few but I just have a good feeling about Irene Models. Apparently the owner is a bit dodgy, though...' I said.

'What's his name?' Giuseppe asked as he plunged his fingers into the bowl to remove any trace or smell of shellfish. He then wiped his mouth with the white napkin.

'Jean-something... one of those composed French names. I think it's Jean-*Pierre*. Can't think of his last name. Something ending with 'I' like Alesi. I'm not sure.'

Giuseppe looked at me blankly, poured more water into his glass and said, 'The name rings a bell, actually. I remember reading about him in the press – something to do with sex trafficking...'

'Wow, that's *really* dodgy. I may be barking up the wrong tree. Perhaps I should try another agency!'

'They're all pretty much the same, you know. Just play it by ear, watch your back and don't trust anyone – that's what I tell my daughter!'

'I didn't know you had a daughter! I knew about your son working with you in your law firm but you've never mentioned your daughter.'

'We're not in very good terms, unfortunately. She's from a previous marriage...' He sipped some more water. 'Anyway, it's not very interesting.' Giuseppe waved at the waiter once more, visibly not planning to tell me more.

'Giuseppe...' I muttered.

He looked at me. 'Why are you so nice to me?' I asked.

He smiled.

'Well, if you say that *they are all the same*, what makes you different from the others?' I asked.

'First of all, I am not a model agent and therefore I don't see so many beautiful girls that it would make my head spin!' he sniggered. 'Second of all, I am nice because you have something I don't have.'

He made a sign to the waiter for the bill.

'What is that?'

'Youth!' He smiled and frowned. 'You're refreshing and I don't get this in my everyday life. My wife is ill, my job is serious and boring sometimes. I find spending time with people like you extremely rejuvenating. If that makes any sense,' he paused.

'It makes sense,' I replied, 'thanks for the compliment.'

I didn't dare ask about what ailed his wife. After all, I was expected to be lively and fun. I put my smile back on and followed him out of the restaurant.

***

The next morning I stood in front of the mirror; my hair was down as requested by Nan and I had managed to apply a make-up which actually enhanced my features, for once. I tried on a black dress, turned around and then back in front of the mirror, pouted, and took it off. Most of my clothes suffered the same treatment until I finally settled for tight black trousers and a flattering black sequined top with a plunging V neck. My breasts were too small to be vulgar in that top but perky enough to be shown accidently. I put my high heels on, traded them for boots, kicked them off and decided for the heels again. I stood up in front of the mirror, pulled my trousers up, smoothed them on the legs and nodded to the mirror in satisfaction.

'*Vogue*, here I come,' I said aloud to myself, dancing with excitement.

I was expecting to wait in the lounge for a long time, but I was called in at ten o'clock on the dot and ushered into the art director's office. A blonde woman with short hair and glasses stood up behind her brown art deco desk and held her hand out to greet me.

'Please have a seat,' she said with a husky voice. I sat down and clasped my handbag. 'Nan Bush is very adamant about your potential, and insists we should use you on the next shoot with two other brunettes,' she continued, then paused as she flicked through my Book.

No emotion transpired. I was fully aware that my Book was not the best she had ever come across, but her silence froze me to the spot. Behind her, rows of fashion books and magazines were lined up on mahogany shelves, covering the entire wall. She was swivelling gently on her white lacquered chair, which looked like a giant stemmed glass with a black leather inner layer. She swung her silver pen between her fingers like a metronome and suddenly held it still.

'Who's your agency?' She finally asked as she looked up and pushed her glasses back on her nose.

'I don't have one yet, but I have an appointment with Irene Models to sign a contract this afternoon,' I replied.

'I see,' she said, resuming swaying her pen. 'I tell you what. I'll talk to Bruce about the storyline and we'll keep Irene informed of the dates,' she added, with a smile, at last. She tapped her pen on her desk and put it down to rest.

I nodded and thanked her, dying to get out of her office. I wasn't sure how well the appointment had gone but clearly, Nan Bush had a great influence on the art director. I tried not to analyse the encounter too much, and if there was one magazine that was allowed to be snotty, it was *Vogue*. I walked out of the building, looked up to the sky for what felt like the first time and prayed.

As I had a few hours to kill, I decided to wander through Central Park on my way to Irene Models which was located on 60th street and Madison. I trod on the fallen yellow leaves, surrounded by vibrant beeches, red oaks, Norway maples and red-berried hawthorn trees, feeling at one with the elements. The wind caught my hair and lifted it in all directions, the tree branches saluted me as I walked past, and squirrels ferreted around the dead leaves for nuts. They scampered off as I approached. I breathed in the smell of wood and wet leaves. Lovers strolled past, hand in hand, a grandfather pointed out the hundred-year-old trees to a little boy holding a miniature sailboat. I sat on a bench to have my lunch and appreciated the scenery set ablaze by autumn.

***

When I entered Irene Agency, the receptionist asked me to sit and wait. Framed magazine covers adored the wall. I recognised some of the models, but others were unknown to me. They all looked at me with an emotionless expression on their faces. I wondered whether I should cut my hair like that model on the far right or dye it auburn like the other one next to it. They all looked so glamorous and so different from me. I felt so boringly normal next to them. Somehow, the fact that they had been groomed and immortalised by the photographer made them appear beyond reach, out of this world. On the other hand, I was well and truly alive, sitting on the red sofa as ordered, feeling my cold toes in my shoes which were too tight, waiting for a stranger to make a difference to my career. While I was daydreaming, a chubby man wearing jeans and casually rolled up sleeves walked up to me.

'Hello, who are you here to see?' he asked as he ran his hand through his hair.

'I have an appointment with Jean-Pierre,' I replied, hoping that it was the right name.

'Let me see if he's available. Do you have a Book?'

He kept a grim face as I handed it to him, then he turned around and shuffled his feet back behind the wall that divided the waiting lounge with the booking area. I could hear the phone ringing and bookers speaking tensely into their phones. I sat there, waiting for my Book to be analysed and criticised by the professional model bookers and hoped for the best, which, for the time being, was an appointment with the big boss. I wanted to impress them with the whole Nan Bush story and the potential editorial with *Vogue* it had entailed, but the world wasn't built on "ifs" and "buts". Nothing was definite so far, and I had to face it. If the *Vogue* adventure wasn't anything more than a sales pitch then and I had to accept that.

A few minutes of intense deliberation later, the chubby guy came back, chewing on a toothpick. He leaned on the veneered wall with my Book under his arm and waved at me to follow him.

'This way, please.'

As he escorted me towards the manager's office, I glanced at the booking area. It was a large open space bathed in sunlight with modern desks and busy bookers. A couple of female models chatted with their agents and discussed their pictures. Overall, a sense of quietness and order prevailed.

Chubby, who still hadn't told me his name, ushered me into the main office where a sixty year old man of small stature sat behind a large desk. He was bent over piles of paperwork, speaking softly on the phone that was cradled in his neck. As he saw us, he raised a finger, asking us to wait for a moment. I stood there, wishing I also had a toothpick to munch on.

'Marion!' he exclaimed as he hung up the phone and sprung out from behind his desk. To my surprise, he wasn't much taller standing up. He wore pale denim jeans and a black turtleneck. His tanned face was as withered as a prune and his mouth was wider than Aerosmith's lead singer –Steve Tyler.

'Please have a seat,' he said in French. 'How long are you in New York for?'

'Well, actually, I only came to meet with Nan Bush and Vogue. My plane leaves tonight at ten.'

'Wow, that's a quick trip. You should stay,' he said as he lit up his cigarette. 'Stay and see some clients. If *Vogue* comes through, they'll all follow like sheep.'

Blank. *Why do all French smoke?* I wondered.

'It's silly to come the whole way to New York and pack up when you're on the right track,' Jean-Pierre added as he put his feet up on the side of the desk, revealing his cowboy boots.

'Because I can't afford staying longer,' I admitted half-heartedly.

'Don't take your plane, stay at our models' flat and reimburse the agency when you start working. We'll put it on your account.'

Part of me wanted to see what would happen next, but overall, I cringed at the idea of staying in a models' flat again and dreaded the numerous castings yet to come. Prune-face was staring at me, expecting an answer. I considered what awaited me after my plane ride back home and reluctantly accepted his offer. There were still three weeks to go before University started and I had promised my parents to be home then.

'Unfortunately the lady who takes care of the apartment is on holiday and will be back tomorrow. I'm afraid I don't have the keys,' Jean-Pierre said as he peeped inside the drawer and fumbled for the keys. 'You're welcome to stay at my place – I have a spare room,' he offered. 'Just take a few items with you and leave your heavy bags at the agency, you'll get all your belongings tomorrow, along with the keys.'

What should have been perceived as a kind offer sickened me. I had wised up to his sort.

'It's very nice of you,' I lied. I had to think quickly. I thought of Giuseppe who would certainly not mind helping me a bit longer. 'I have a friend in town I can stay with tonight.'

I could read the disappointment on his face. It was clearly going to be a balancing act between keeping Jean-Pierre interested enough to provide me with work while physically keeping him at arm's length. 'But we could go for dinner together tonight if you're free,' I offered triumphantly.

'Fine,' he answered as he stubbed out his cigarette frantically. 'I'll pick you up at eight tonight.'

***

I knew that Giuseppe had only taken an extra room for me until that day and I was at a loss as to where I would sleep if I stayed longer in New York. Giuseppe was in his bedroom when I returned to the hotel. As he opened the door, I stormed in, rather agitated.

'Wo, wo, wo!' he exclaimed.

'Giuseppe, I'm in trouble. Irene's owner, the notorious pervert has asked me to stay in New York…'

I paced around his bedroom.

'That sounds good to me, so far!'

'It doesn't, actually. He knows I have nowhere to stay and offered me to stay with him.'

'That's the best way to check if he's actually a perv!' Giuseppe laughed.

'That's not funny!' I fumed. I started prowling again. 'I offered to go for dinner with him tonight, not to blow my chances.'

'Well, I hope you don't assume I am going to pay for your hotel room forever!' he said as he undid his tie and removed his pants. Before I knew it, Giuseppe was in his underwear, leaving me speechless. He walked to the bathroom and came out wearing a bathrobe. '*Vogue* wants to shoot you. You have found an agency. Therefore, you don't need my help anymore.'

I was dumbfounded.

'You can share my bedroom if you don't have any other alternative but I can't keep on paying for everything. My daughter is the same, she takes me for granted and doesn't know where the limit is.'

He sat in the room settee and took out *The Financial Times*. 'Now if you'll excuse me, I still have some work to do.'

I looked at him, stunned. He glanced back at me over his reading glasses. 'Don't you have a dinner to go to?' he asked, and resumed his reading.

I suddenly felt terribly sad and lost. More precisely, I felt trapped. If I accepted to stay with Jean-Pierre, God knows what he would do. On the other hand, I did not feel comfortable sharing a bed with Giuseppe either. He may be old, but he was a man with desires. I was stuck in an extremely awkward situation. I could feel tears welling up and my throat constricting with angst.

When Jean-Pierre walked into the hotel lobby, I was sitting on the sofa. As he made his way to the reception desk, I ran swiftly after him and called his name. He turned around and smiled.

'Are you ready?' he asked.

I nodded and smiled.

'I haven't had time to go home and get changed, so if you don't mind, we'll quickly stop by my apartment. I am dying for a shower and I need to slip on something smart.'

The words "changed" and "shower" pricked something inside me. There I was again, confronted by the same ambiguous situation. I struggled to hide my disappointment and followed him into his car.

***

The driver dropped us off in front of Trump Tower. Jean-Pierre entered the building first and I tagged along, looking a bit off-colour. A few young people were gathered on the ground floor by the main sofa. One of them walked up to Jean-Pierre.

'What are you guys up to?' Jean-Pierre asked the young man.

'We're going to Puff Daddy and the Family's concert with Donald,' the young man replied.

'That sounds cool!' I remarked.

Jean-Pierre turned around to look at me with a surprised look. 'Harry, this is Marion, she has just joined our agency. Marion, this is Harry, one of America's finest tennis players.'

'Want to join us?' Harry asked us.

'Sure!' I replied. I then turned to Jean-Pierre and said, 'Are you coming?'

'I am quite tired actually; you guys go and have fun…' Jean-Pierre replied, disappointed and turned on his heels.

I could tell that he was upset but I was smiling at my ingenuity. That young lad had saved me from an inextricable situation. I now fully expected Irene model agency to give me the cold shoulder but it was a risk I was ready to take, as I didn't feel safe being alone with Jean-Pierre.

We made our way towards the elevator and the whole flock was crammed in the lift up to the skyscraper's top floor – Donald Trump's flat. I wasn't sure who Donald Trump was but I gathered that if the tower bore his name, he was certainly rich and influential. Donald himself opened the door and greeted us, resting a golf club on his shoulder. He was a tall bulky man with strawberry blonde hair and bushy eyebrows. His witty eyes narrowed as he took notice of me.

'And *you* are?' he asked, pouting.

'Marion, a friend of Jean-Pierre, from Irene Models.'

'I see, but he's not here?' he asked as he scanned the corridor with his piercing gaze.

'He was tired, I think. These guys invited me to come along with you, I hope you don't mind.' I was becoming a bigger fan of Puff by the minute.

'Come on in,' he grunted.

The entourage I was now part of were largely absorbed with looking around the flat, while Donald largely ignored us and fiddled with his golf club. When he putted the ball gently into the hole, everyone clapped and cheered. I felt like I had entered Aladdin's cave – gold was everywhere: the door handles, the kitchen taps, and there was even a fountain made of gold. As I approached the large windowpane to admire the breath-taking view of New York City, my eyes were drawn down to the street and the cars below. I was seized by giddiness and pulled back. Donald's entourage was scattered all over the living room

'Right, I'm ready! Let's go,' Donald said with a rallying effect.

A few minutes later, I was sitting in Donald Trump's limo with his friends, drinking champagne. New York was full of twists and turns. Within a few minutes I had gone from rags to riches. This was a once in a lifetime experience and it would never have happened if I had stayed home in Provence.

Busta Rhymes frantically swung his locks around, rapping *Fire It Up* with a fierce voice and a large aching grin. He wore white overalls and jumped up and down on the stage like a jack-in-the-box. The crowds cheered and danced, surrounded by heavily armed policemen. It was an amazing performance, if a bit ear-blasting, but Donald's security man who was as wide as a wardrobe, whispered in Donald's ear, 'For your safety, it would be best to go now, sir.'

As Donald stood up, we all followed. I noticed the dour stares from the people surrounding us and I wondered what Donald represented to these people.

'Does that mean we're not going to see Puff Daddy?' I asked Harry.

'It's not very safe for Donald here,' he admitted. 'Donald is a powerful man and being in a crowd for too long may be dangerous.'

I nodded as if I understood, but clearly I did not know what was really going on.

As the evening drew to a premature end, I was left with the question: where to sleep? I didn't want to go back to Giuseppe after his last speech. I looked through my phone's contacts, I stalled on the name "Kate" and I remembered what she'd said on her postcard about moving in with her boyfriend. I glanced at my watch; it was close to ten o'clock. In any other situation, I would have thought it inappropriate to call anyone so late at night, but it was New York and she was the only friend I could think of. The phone rang a few times, but no one picked up. As I was about to give up, a voice answered.

'Hullo!?' said the voice. I could hear music and laughter in the background.

'Kate?'

'Speaking.'

'This is Marion. I'm back, I'm in New York…'

'Oh wow Marion! Where are you?' Kate asked.

Light was at the end of the tunnel, at last. We chatted gleefully and I explained to her that I was looking for a place to stay that night.

'Well, we're having a bit of a party here, so it may not be the best place to crash, but you're welcome to join us for some laughter and some booze!'

***

Twenty minutes later, I was pressing the buzzer at 26 Church Street in the West Village. Kate let me in and shouted my name as she saw me climb up the stairs. She was radiant, wearing a simple cream dress, high heels. Her eyes shone. We hugged and giggled for a while on the landing.

'Come on in!' she said. 'I am so glad to see you again!'

A few other models were gathered in the living room around the coffee table. A male model with messy brown hair and clear green eyes wrapped his hands lovingly around Kate.

'This is my boyfriend Pete,' said Kate with a smile.

He kissed her and went away to fetch himself another drink. Unnoticed, Morten sat on the sofa, staring at me while he sipped his beer. When I turned around and suddenly noticed him, my heart missed a beat. He stood up and hugged me tightly.

'How are you doing?' he asked.

'I'm good, thanks,' I paused, slightly taken aback. 'I wasn't expecting you to be here tonight…' I mumbled.

'Always up for a good party!' He then emitted a deep guttural laughter. 'Pete and I have been friends for a good while now,' he said with his arm casually draped around Pete's shoulder, messing his hair in a playful manner with his free hand.

'I'm only just back in New York. I had to get away—'I mumbled.

'Guys, why don't we head up to the Bowery?' Pete asked. 'We're running low on booze!'

Before I had a chance to get my head round it, we were out of the door, stampeding down the stairs into the streets.

***

They took me to a new place they'd found called the Bowery Bar. It was booming with house music; a bald DJ wearing sunglasses was jamming his records and nodding his head to the beat in front of a trendy crowd of rather drunk youngsters. Fortified by half a dozen beers, Morten regaled the table with colourful anecdotes about his latest advertising campaigns and untold behind the scenes stories. He expounded the theory that the dirtier and drunker he showed up at photo shoots, the more of a star he was. Morten was like perpetual-motion machine: his limbs swirled constantly like a windmill. I cocked my head in contemplation, drawn in by his aura and perfect features. Morten craned over the table and reached out for a glass filled with vodka and cranberry juice.

'Hey, that's mine! Keep your hands to yourself,' Kate told Morten, fluttering her hand in a dismissive way.

Morten smiled back with a wanton face. With a cringe of apology, he grabbed a bottle of vodka and threw it back like there was no tomorrow. He then stood up and made way towards the gents. I spotted him a few minutes later, hovering around the dance floor. He made circles around the table, visibly inebriated, getting closer to us with each swing. He ended up sitting down next to me, shuffling and grinning. He fastened his arm around my shoulder and whispered praises in my ear, which were half muffled by the blasting music. Everything I had felt for him before was reignited within me. I don't know how he did it, but Morten had me wrapped around his little finger. I was simply magnetised by his underlying pain and utterly bewitched by his God-given beauty. The sound of my name on his lips was an exquisite torture. His sweet talking led to long, lingering kisses, with no respite for long minutes. Everything in the room seemed wrapped in gauze. I felt dissociated from the people surrounding me as if our physical contact had severed me from the rest of the crowd. I searched his face for a glimmer of true emotion as he ran his fingers through mine. His blue eyes were blurry and slightly unfocused; his chin was spotted with scattered tufts of beard. *He's just a lost soul*, I thought.

He lifted his glass to my lips and poured the liquor inside my mouth, while he licked my ear and kissed my neck. It was one drink too many. That was the last thing that I remembered. I came around later, curled up in a corner of the club, utterly confused by the floor tile in front of my face. Its irregular tar-like surface oozed with dirt and spilt alcohol. My head was spinning dangerously and the contents of my stomach threatened to come out if I moved an inch or even breathed.

'Are you OK?' asked the bouncer. 'You're gonna have to sober up somewhere else young lady,' he said as he helped me up and out of the club.

I staggered out on the curb and gathered all my strength to hail a cab. When I finally succeeded, the uneven roads didn't spare me. I tried to unwind the windows but they were locked. I looked around but couldn't demean myself by throwing up in the taxi. I grabbed the collar of my jacket, and threw up in spasms, my insides yielding to the rough driving. The driver was so busy honking and swerving that he did not notice a thing.

As I wobbled into the Four Seasons' lobby, one hand rummaged in my pocket for the room key, while the other tried to contain my warm bodily fluid inside my jacket. The card was nowhere to be found. *Damn, I've lost the key*, I thought. I straightened up and asked the receptionist as normally as possible for an extra card to my room. She noticed that my body was slightly askew and my appearance suspicious. She beckoned the porter over to accompany me to my room.

Once in the lift, the porter pretended he hadn't noticed my condition, despite the fact he was standing right next to me. A strong stench of alcohol and puke emanated from my whole being. I was so embarrassed I wanted to vanish into thin air. I perceived a warped image of myself as I looked into the mirror.

Thankfully, Giuseppe had already gone to work by the time I staggered into the room. He had made the bed perfectly, with the four corners precisely tucked in, and the whole room was immaculately tidy. I smiled at his old fashioned habits and thought it must be due to too many years spent in boarding school.

I stumbled into his bathroom and ran some water in the bathtub. I removed the soiled jacket and threw it into the water to let it soak for a while. The foul odour sickened me once more. I unbuttoned my shirt and scrapped the detritus into the toilet bowl. I clung firmly to the sink to take my pants, my shoes and socks off. Just before my legs gave way under me, I stumbled to the large bed and threw myself flat on it. I lay there on my stomach like starfish, my face squashed against the pillows. I could smell my own halitosis and moaned in disgust. When the shivers started creeping on me and my whole body shook uncontrollably, I crept under the bed sheets and rolled myself in the foetus position, thanking whoever had invented the thick mattress.

Giuseppe woke me up with a start as he closed the bedroom door behind him. My eyes fluttered open painfully and tried to focus as hard as possible on the blurry image of Giuseppe.

'There you are!' he said with a sprightly tone of voice.

I grunted and managed a faint 'Hello!'

He stepped into the bathroom and sulked right back out. 'What are your clothes doing floating in my bathtub?'

I hauled my sick self straight up in the bed, rubbed my eyes and replied in a faint voice, 'We had Chinese last night, before going out and it did not agree with me.'

'I did not know Chinese food reeked of alcohol like that,' he replied while he started fumbling through his documents in the desk drawer.

'*Busted!*' I thought. 'We went to Puff Daddy's concert last night and I may have had too much to drink,' I managed to say.

'Appalling. Absolutely disgraceful, young lady!'

'I am sure it happened to you when you were young…'

'Actually, I have always had the decency not to inflict it on anyone!' he rapped out.

I could tell in his tone of voice that I was starting to rile him.

'Giuseppe, you're not my dad, you know!' I replied, brazen-faced.

Giuseppe slammed the door shut as a reply to my insolence. I slouched back onto the fluffy bed and went right back to my previous state of lethargy.

I had no recollection of the previous night. I felt as if I had been robbed of hours of memory. The last thing I remembered was how Morten had grabbed my hair and almost gobbled me alive with kisses. Then he had vanished, literally. He had left me alone with my drunken stupor, along with Kate and the others. After that, all I remembered was throwing up in my jacket in the back of a taxi. He had good reasons to be tetchy. I would have kicked my own bottom if I could. In a daze, I pulled myself out of bed, hoisted myself into the bathroom and washed both my clothes and myself as best I could.

An hour later, I was stooped on the bench of a gloomy laundrette, gazing at the spinning washing machine. My pulse throbbed in my temples and my mouth felt as though I had eaten buckets of sand for breakfast. My whole body felt as jostled and wrung out as the clothes whirling in the machine. Somehow, laundrettes had always depressed me; they were haunts for lost souls and toothless beggars. I glanced at all the other lonely beings surrounding me: single mums struggling to make ends meet, bachelors in want of a girlfriend, students without a dime and a homeless man wrapped up in a raincoat that was so stiff with dirt, he could have made it his tent for the night. The homeless guy sat at the rear of the shop, eagerly pouncing on a stale sandwich ditched by someone the week before. And then there was me, as lonely as a cloud, taken for a punch bag by a crazy gorgeous Swede who thought it appropriate to barge in and out of my life, deepening the wound in my heart a little more. I turned my head away from the homeless man and realised that my machine had stopped spinning. My clothes were as flat as paper against the tumbler's inner wall. Flashes of memory in front of my eyes between me and the unmoving machine. After a night of drinking and being played, I felt the void within me widening.

My daydreaming was interrupted by my mobile phone ringing.

'How was the concert last night?' Jean-Pierre asked.

I immediately recognised his sleazy voice and could picture his prune-face cringing and wrinkling as he spoke.

'It was good,' I answered, then covered the receiver with my hand and cleared my throat. 'We did not stay long though.'

I fumbled for my lip gloss in my bag.

'Are you up for some appointments this afternoon?'

Even the laundrette's begrimed window revealed what a sore sight I was, 'I guess so!' I replied while grimacing and pinching my cheeks hoping to bring some colour to my face.

'You have created quite a flurry of interest around you.'

'Have I really?' I asked, dubiously. I looked up and stifled a victorious *"Yes!"* as I was too worried to disturb the laundrette's prevailing dejection with effusions of joy.

'*Elle, Glamour, W,* Peter Lindbergh, Demarchelier, Gilles Bensimon… you name them, they all want to see you.' Jean-Pierre was particularly laudatory. '*Vogue* dictates what's fashion-forward and on the pulse. The others are mere followers. This is your moment!'

I have heard that before.

'Do you have something to write on?'

'Sure, let me grab a pen…' I replied as my hand hastily searched my bag for something to write on. I extracted my Filofax and jotted down the various addresses.

'When you're done, please come to the agency to collect the keys to the model's flat.'

I hung up, surprised that he still wanted to see me after letting him down previously.

September was a much milder month to walk the streets than the cruel December that greeted me when I first arrived last year. I fell in behind the average denizen trudging Broadway on his or her way to work and walked in rhythm with the pulse of the city. Scaffolding blighted the buildings, drills disembowelled the roads, fire engine sirens wailed, taxis and cars weaved their way through the streets, and thick fumes escaped from the guts of the city. Lady Liberty brandished her torch, the financial centre bustled with bankers, the Staten Island ferries sailed back and forth, the Empire State Building was scraping the skies, and I was on my way to my castings. I felt as though I was part and parcel of the city life. I had put my best foot forward and it was another normal day in New York City.

Each appointment had an eerie feel about it. The clients all welcomed me into their offices with the same glib smile. My haphazard encounter with Nan Bush had triggered a premature ascent into the higher echelons of fashion. Some took the time to understand what was arresting about me; others thought I had wangled my way into fashion, judging by their slanted looks. But they all took the time to look at my pictures and politely saw me out. Time had stopped while *Vogue* was making their decision whether or not to use me.

I walked back to the hotel, feeling deflated. I was now coming down from the adrenaline high of the meetings and was starting to feel the sleep deprivation of the previous night. Giuseppe had gone back to Milan and I was now on my own. I was given the keys to the models' flat on the corner of East 86th street and 2nd Avenue, the farthest I had gone so far.

It was a small three bedroom flat, surprisingly it had recently been refurbished with wooden floors. It wasn't spacious but it was comfortable enough. It was only for four weeks before going to university in mid October, but at least I was on my own, which was a real plus. From the kitchen window I looked down at the gym fanatics exercising relentlessly at all hours of the day and night and tried to ignore them. I was exhausted just watching them; I could sense their bodies going into overdrive, their muscles heating up, their joints stretching out and the stench of sweat pervading the gym floor. Overall, I loathed the mind-numbing waking-up-gym-work drill. But within a few days, I took to the same routine: I woke up at six in the morning, jogged absent-mindedly on the treadmill looking at the red building in front of me by the window, determined not to put on weight this time and went religiously to all my castings and attended dinner parties with Kate. I was back into the inevitable model's routine. Jean-Pierre kept his distance or had set his sights on younger prey, but as I walked into the agency that morning, he beckoned me to follow him.

'*Vogue* called back,' he said with a grave voice.

I held my breath and waited for the news.

'They haven't found the two other girls they wanted to do the story with. So I'm afraid it's postponed. Unfortunately.'

I was speechless. *Vogue* had the power to turn any model's career into gold, yet they could not find two other brunettes in the whole wide world to do the story with me. I shook my head in disbelief.

'They'll never shoot it, right?' I asked with an imploring tone, desperate to be wrong.

'Don't be negative, they might, you never know.'

'That's the trouble; you *never* know...'

My eyes brimmed with tears. As I looked down, drops fell on my lap and weaved through my trousers. The dark patches formed by the tears stood for all the blotches and blows I had collected from the beginning of my career.

***

The next day, my body refused to get out of bed. The doctor came and swore nothing was wrong with me.

'Are you sure I don't have any fever?' I asked.

He nodded.

'Virus of any sort?' I asked again.

He nodded once more. 'You're just exhausted and you need to rest,' he advised.

I was definitely not cut out for modelling, however trivial it sounded; I just could not cope with the highs and lows of the industry. I felt as if I had been stretched out beyond repair.

A phone call woke me from slumber. Kate had split up with her boyfriend and was looking for a roommate.

'I was wondering if you would be interested in sharing my flat with me?' she offered.

'Well, I need to go back home soon. My uni starts mid October, I have promised my parents!' I said half-heartedly, thinking back to the night when she, Morten, and Pete had left me all alone in a near coma on the street. It somehow reminded me of when Lucie had called to borrow my triathlon gear when I was crippled two summers ago.

'Three weeks is better than nothing, it'll give me time to get my head round things and find someone else once you're gone. And who knows? You may work like hell and never leave!' she laughed.

That's how I accepted. I was too desperate for company, too weak or too stupid to stand up for myself and have a go at her for leaving me behind. I knew that it wasn't the smartest financial move to make, but I was desperate for company. Her flat had two bedrooms – hers was the largest one with a double bed, and I moved into the smaller one with a single bed. Without realising, that set the tone for our friendship. When I lay down, I had the suffocating sensation that the walls were closing in on me. I shut my eyes, tuning in with the distant beat of the house music playing in the gay neighbourhood every evening.

I lay in my coffin of a bedroom at night and on the couch during daytime. The only time I ever went out was for castings, which were becoming scarcer by the day. I dreaded stepping out onto the street, as I knew that it was conducive to spending the money, which I did not have. I let the late September chill brush my face as I stood by the open sash window, imagining myself as a wanderer of wild landscape, standing alone, leaning naked into the cold wind towards an unknown destiny. Faced with the immensity of the city, I felt compressed to nothingness.

Kate found it convenient to have a roommate who shared half the rent and only occupied a third of the flat. It had only been two weeks but each cent spent felt like an arm and a leg. Since the beginning of my career, I had never felt financially independent nor comfortable; being a rich model was a very distant idea. On top of gladly taking my money, Kate could neither cook nor clean and pretty soon her ex, Pete, started barking at the door once a week, and eventually every night, followed by his personal belongings. They were at each other's throats constantly but always kissed and made up the following day. Their relationship rollercoaster was too much for me.

One evening, as I struggled to fall asleep, Kate's shouts were so loud that she managed to be louder than the night-life frenzy of the Saturday evening outside. Worried, I ran to her bedroom and, to my surprise, she was holding Pete half way out of the window.

He was pleading her to calm down and let go of him. So she did. They both looked at me with crazed eyes and shut the door on me. The next morning, they acted as normal lovebirds, except that Pete's left arm displayed four bruises inflicted my Kate's angry claw. It had convinced me to put off revising the rent arrangement; I didn't want to be the next one to be flying out the window. At first it had seemed that butter wouldn't melt in her mouth, but Kate was actually capable of a good deal of spiteful rage.

I had been the flavour of the month – filling my diary with appointments, getting small jobs, all on the promise that *Vogue* was going to make me their next rising star. But after that job got cancelled, the illusion of success had shrunk down to almost nothing. No one booked me anymore, I roamed the streets to castings all day and crashed on my couch in the evening dreading the following day. I had been on a steady diet of rejection for over a year and was standing on the nadir of my career. I thought it couldn't get any worse.

***

'I have a job that pays very well and could help put your finances afloat but…' Jean-Pierre said as he scratched his chin. 'But we have to think whether it would be a good thing for your career or not.'

'I am all ears.'

'Have you ever heard of the magazine *Photo*?'

He took a cigarette and lit it.

'Yes, it's for photography amateurs…' I replied, with a searching face.

'I mean,' he exhaled his smoke, 'have you seen the pictures in *Photo*?'

'Briefly,' I replied, pensive. 'There is quite a lot of nude in it, if I recall correctly.'

'That's right but it's artistic and it pays really well.'

He dragged on his cigarette, his lips squeezing around it. I realised that it wasn't pep talk; it dawned on me that Jean-Pierre may have been paving the way for a dodgy scheme.

I sat up and asked with a raised brow. 'Are you insinuating that I should pose for *Photo*?'

'Well, actually, no. I was thinking of German *Playboy*.'

'Ger-man-Play-boy?' I rapped out. 'I don't think so!' I was astounded. 'I am not pausing naked in some dirty magazine for some perverts to …'

I was lost for words. I stared at him intensely and stood up.

'Why would I demean myself by doing that?' I turned around and marched across his office towards the door.

'It's totally your choice, I am not forcing you into anything, but they pay twenty thousand dollars for a one day shoot.'

My hand stopped on the doorknob. I turned around.

'How much did you say?'

'Twenty thousand dollars,' he repeated as he took another puff of smoke, as cool as a cucumber.

I released the door handle, stepped towards him, and I looked down.

'I am not comfortable with the idea but again, the money wouldn't hurt.'

'Think about it. If you decide to go ahead and do it, I'll phone up the photographer and the art director to confirm.'

***

When I returned to the apartment, Morten, Pete and Kate were making dinner. I froze, taken aback by his presence. As usual, he put his best charming smile on and greeted me.

'Hey, girl! How have you been? Last time I saw you, you were as drunk as a skunk; we couldn't move you out of the club!' he guffawed.

'I don't see what's so funny,' I replied curtly.

'Well, it was quite funny actually – you were totally out of it.'

'How could you possibly think it was funny that you guys all left me alone, half-conscious in the streets?'

'*You* are the one who said you were fine. *You* pushed us away and wanted to be on your own!' he replied with a concerned look.

'I don't remember!'

I walked past him and dropped my bag in my bedroom.

Morten followed me and stood in the frame of the door.

'Come on, don't be such a pain in the neck, come out and play with us.'

I did not want to turn around and face him. I pretended to tidy up my room but there was only so much I could do in such a confined space.

'All right, I'm coming!' I exclaimed as he stood there, staring at me.

I sat down on the sofa, half-angry, half-embarrassed, and accepted the glass of wine Kate handed me.

'*Skol!*' They all said as they clinked their glasses.

'Our ancestors used to drink out of their victims' skulls, you know,' started Morten.

'Another one of your theories?' Pete joked.

'It's true! After a battle, the two clans – or what was remaining of them – would gather around their leaders while they drank the wine of truce.'

'How civilised!' Pete laughed.

'Well, it dates back to the barbarian times…'

'Because you have evolved since?' I managed to squeeze in.

Morten glanced at me and continued.

'They would bang the skulls so hard against each other that the liquid would go over and mix one into the other; should there have been poison in the brew, both would have been poisoned.'

'Why don't you try the wine first tonight, Morten?' Pete joked.

We all laughed.

'That's why you should always look into people's eyes when you clink glasses with someone; you never know what their intentions are.'

'You took it to a whole new level by bringing the drink to my mouth!' I snapped, unable to avoid alluding to the outing at Bowery Bar.

'Come on Marion,' interrupted Kate. 'Get over it now.'

'Easy for you to say,' I snapped.

CHAPTER 25

Marion, Goodbye New York, October 1997.

I inevitably took the booking for German *Playboy*. My bank account was as empty as an idiot's mind and Kate was already counting the dollars I owed her. I had to try and recover some of my debts before I left New York. I gathered my strength and focused on the money. *No one can ever know*, I told myself as I walked towards the studio. I imagined my mother's expression if she ever found out. I tried to not even think about my father's disappointment. My brothers may have found it cool, but I would worry they'd show the magazine to their friends. I pledged to myself not to mention it to anyone. I was hoping I could separate my mind from my body for a few hours.

The studio was a large warehouse and the photographer's assistants were setting up the lights and decor. The make-up artist was yet another male presence, which did not prompt me to relax and sink into the new role I had been given.

'Darling, don't worry about it. It's just a job. Think about the money. What do you think I am doing? I am not exactly going to boast about working for *Playboy*,' the make-up artist said. I cringed at the name once more. 'Everyone here is doing it for fast money. There's nothing wrong with that.'

'I suppose you're right,' I replied, not totally convinced by my own words.

Frank, the make-up artist, had grown up in the Bronx. He knew about scarcity and hard work. 'I haven't robbed or killed anyone for the money I am making today, so I guess I have nothing to be ashamed of,' he said as he smeared liquid latex on my body. My sexuality was in the process of being reified and I stood naked in front of an emotionless man while the latex hardened. Gradually, the cast imprisoned my limbs; it felt as if I had been feathered and tarred.

'What do we have here?' asked a tall bulky man with dark hair and a French accent. He turned to me and smiled. 'Hello Marion, I'm Robert, the photographer.' I replied with a stiff smile.

I would have shaken his hands if I could.

'I have just finished the first layer. What do you think? Do you want another one?' Frank asked.

'I think it's fine. I like the fact that it's everywhere except on the nipples. It's quite sexy,' Robert said with a lecherous smile. I felt sick to my stomach, and kept on staring in front of me, sinking into my statue role.

'Latex is quite difficult to remove and the skin needs to breathe, so let's make this quick.' Frank was growing concerned.

I was pushed across the room like a figurine where the assistants helped me hop inside a mirrored box.

'Marion, can you please try and spread your legs apart?' Robert asked coolly, as if he had asked me something as mundane as passing him the salt. I looked up at him with beseeching eyes as he brandished his camera and pointed the lens at me. 'That's right! Spread them a bit more, don't be shy!'

I cringed and hesitantly put my feet against the side of the box. It was as bad as a gynaecologist routine check up, only worse – I was wearing latex and he was taking pictures.

'Are we almost done?' I asked, wondering how much longer I had to endure the torture of being tarred, boxed and fantasised upon.

'I can smell you...' Robert mumbled behind his camera, making the sexy *mmm* sound effect.

My whole being shuddered at the comment and then, unexpectedly, giggles set in. My body shook with nervous laughter at the irony of the situation. Winning the modelling contest was supposed to take me through the milky way of fashion, but the bottom line was that the route I was on was a very short route indeed, leading to a shameful dead end in a box.

***

I walked back to the flat with my arms across my chest, pressing my collar against my throat, staring absent-mindedly at the pavement. Once again, I felt I had been pushed so far out of my comfort zone that I stood on the verge of a very deep cliff.

'I'm home!' Kate said as she barged into the flat.

I turned my head very slowly towards her, black mascara smeared underneath my eyes.

She startled as she saw me. 'Gosh, you look awful!'

Kate knew just how to lift my spirits – not. As a reply, I turned my head back in front of me, my arms still folded across my chest. Kate squatted in front of me, gently held my hand and locked her eyes into mine.

'You don't want to tell me what's wrong?'

'Today…' I began, hesitantly. 'Today, I felt at my lowest in months. I did a photo shoot naked, smeared in latex, in a box.'

'You did what?' Kate asked with a surprised look on her face.

'I needed money, so I paused for German *Playboy*,' I blurted out. 'I did it for the money,' my bottom lip quivered. 'Does that make me a whore?'

My chest heaved as I burst into tears. They were hearty tears from the depths of what remained of my soul.

'That doesn't make you a whore at all,' Kate said in a reassuring tone but could not find a word that would qualify it better and lessen my guilt. 'I haven't posed for *Playboy*,' she confessed. 'But, I have come across a very famous photographer who did ask me to pose naked once.' I looked at her, wiping the tears off my face with my sleeve, smudging the mascara across my face. 'He made it clear that if I wanted the story to be in *Elle*, I had to "give it to him", whatever that meant at the time – I never found out because I left.'

I was growing more and more interested in Kate's story. 'Well, at least you have your conscience,' I said.

'I wasn't implying that. Most men in the industry will try to get in your pants, that's all.'

'What does that make us for staying?'

'I personally have no qualifications, and modelling is all I know. So I try to not ask myself too many questions and to take the jobs as they come. When you come to think of it, we don't work every day and we make more than most people. If it means revealing a bit of flesh here and there, so be it.' Kate, stood up. 'Care for some tea? You must be cold after running around half-naked all day,' she winked and giggled.

***

Morten had got into the habit of sleeping over lately, for free. At first on the sofa, but he soon found his way to my room. Nothing ever happened between us, I had become a very comfortable eiderdown to lay his head upon. As I lay awake that night, I grew aware of his long limbs curled up around me, of the snake-like grip stifling me. I wanted to get my body back, I resented being mere tits and arse. I wanted to break free of any kind of bondage, be it a contract or a box.

The next morning, I walked into the accounting department, determined to extract every last remaining cent out of my account. A chubby lady with greasy skin and thick glasses stared blankly at the screen and finally muttered a few words.

'There is no money on your account, I'm afraid,' she said.

'I just did a big job yesterday,' I spoke hesitantly while moon face gawped at me. I realised that I was making it sound grander than what it really was. 'I was wondering if I could get an advance on the payroll?' I looked down. 'I need the money,' I mumbled.

'But there is no money on your account,' she repeated sternly, looking at me over her glasses.

'I don't understand?' I faltered and shook my head.

'The job was twenty thousand dollars. Take off twenty-five per cent for the agency fee and another twenty-five per cent for tax, that's fifty per cent in total. That leaves you with ten thousand. Ten thousand dollars minus the rent for the past few weeks, the composites, the couriers, and your work visa equals to minus two thousand dollars.'

I was taken aback. 'Are you saying *I* owe *you* money?'

'That's right!' she replied as she folded her arms onto the desk and looked at me fixedly.

If there was any pride left in me, it had just been instantly deflated to the size of a nut. I took the statement she handed me and left her office sheepishly. My blood felt like it was seeping out of me, my muscles shrunk, and my brittle bones became dust. I did not exist anymore. The carrion feeder had finished me off for good.

***

When I sat on the plane a few days later, on my way back to my parents, I was resolute never to go back to New York. Kate was terribly upset that she had to pay for the rent on her own, with the two boys sponging off her. It felt wrong, worse than a divorce where the house was under her name and the kids turned out not to be mine. If I hadn't left, Morten would have eventually ended up destroying me. Our relationship was stale and negative; nothing good could possibly come out of it. Work was counterproductive as ever and I felt like a water mill spinning above a dry river.

Somehow, thinking this through thoroughly made me feel better. I sat uncomfortably, in the dark, with my reading light over me, while my neighbours snored, shoulder to shoulder, all squashed into their seats. I took advantage of the solitude to gather my thoughts. I pulled down the little plastic table, placed a piece of paper in front of me and laid down the pros and cons of my career in black and white. It still did not help me with the question – what to do next?

PART SIX

PARIS & VERSAILLES

CHAPTER 26

Marion, Monique Makes Her Move, Paris June 2002

My mobile phone vibrated on my desk, as I was studying for my final Master of Arts exam. I was in my last year of university. Whenever it was possible, I took on a few modelling jobs. It was enough to finance my studies and be independent from my parents, but not often enough to disrupt my studies. A hoarse voice greeted me.

'Hello Marion! My name is Monique. I run a model agency called Number One Agency. Jean-Pierre from Irene has passed on your details to me. I'd like to represent you.'

I was speechless. I was not expecting to hear about Jean-Pierre and even more surprised that he would try and help me in any way, after all this time. He had sounded rather casual and calm when I told him I was going back to France. He was probably relieved.

'Now, I am not sure whether you have found another agency since, but I'd be happy to meet you and discuss a potential work arrangement,' Monique added.

'I am not based in Paris, I live in Avignon at my parents...'

'When are you coming to Paris next?' she asked.

'Well, I hadn't really planned—'

'Is there any way we could meet and have a chat? Jean-Pierre told me that you had a very commercial beauty and that's precisely my line of expertise. I think that there is a large market for older ladies – not that you are old of course, but you look very womanly and mature – and ladies nearing thirty can't relate to models who look like kids.'

I'm only twenty-two! But why the hell not?

I went back to the living room where my parents were watching the national news. I sat down, racking my brains to find the best possible way to announce I had to go to Paris.

'I am going to Paris next week,' I mumbled.

My parents had hardly heard me.

'What was that, Darling?' my mother finally asked.

'I have to go to Paris for a job on Thursday.'

My parents looked at each other in disbelief.

'What about your final exam? It's just around the corner! Hope you're not skipping too many classes?' My mother exclaimed, visibly saddened as her dream of seeing me teach was so close and so fragile.

'I'm only going for a day Mum, I'll be back in the evening.' I stared intensely at my parents, but all I could read was disappointment. 'You know I take a few jobs here and there to pay for my studies, this is nothing different.'

***

As soon as my plane landed in Paris, I called Monique and arranged to meet at a café close to her agency on the Île de la Jatte in the western part of Paris. Before our meeting I decided to go to a hair salon to get my hair straightened, as I would usually do before castings and jobs.

'Why would you want to tame such beautiful mane?' Julia, the hairdresser asked me. She was a very sensuous girl with mixed origins and curly hair.

'Because, most people don't like it, especially in my line of work.'

'What line of work would that be?' she asked as she raised her brow.

I hesitated. 'I'm a model,' I replied. I avoided her glance and stared in front of me in the mirror. I had always been worried that the title "Model" would pigeon hole me as stupid, or worse, would trigger mockery. Julia's eyes lit up.

'I would have loved to be a model, to travel and be pampered...' She said, day dreaming as she pulled on my hair with her brush. 'Do you enjoy the lifestyle?'

'Yes and no. I love the fact that I'm independent. I don't work on a daily basis. You think it's all easy money and lots of travelling… but I resent the loneliness and the unstable income.'

Julia listened but wasn't convinced. 'I see!' she replied.

An hour later, as I handed my credit card to Julia, I heard a loud roar. Two motorbikes zoomed past, turned in the street and pulled up in front of the hair salon. The two men clad in leather got off their vehicles. One of them crossed the street while the other walked into the salon, holding his black racing helmet with one hand and his lock with the other. He was handsome and tall with short dark hair and brown eyes. A light flickered in his eyes as he locked them onto mine. For what seemed a long moment, we stood there, under each other's spell. It was as if time had stopped. I was captivated by his charming smile and everything around us seemed to disappear far off into the background.

'Can I help you, sir?' Julia asked, bursting the romantic bubble.

'Sure, erm…' he said, somehow distracted. 'Would you have time to cut my hair now, please?'

'Certainly!' Julia replied. 'I'll take payment from my customer and be right with you.'

The young man left the salon in order to place the lock on his black KTM bike.

'I don't know what's wrong with this machine today, it's been playing up all morning,' said Julia as she swiped my card again. 'Please take a seat. I won't be long…'

Julia invited him to sit down on the seat next to me. As he removed his jacket, a subtle whiff of aftershave mixed with leather emanated from him. He rolled up the sleeves of his shirt, he had great arms. He looked all strength and health. He leaned forward, with his elbows on his lap and his legs apart, firmly rooted to the ground. I glanced at his face and noticed the perfect curve of his nose overshadowing his full lips. His prominent cheekbones and strong jaw line gave his face a chiselled look. I found his presence soothing and reassuring. We exchanged glances but didn't dare say a word.

'Right, it seems to be working now. Marion, would you like to try your card again, please?'

As I exited the salon, I turned around and shyly smiled at the young man. A light wind caught my hair and made it swirl around my face as we locked eyes. A mild sensation of sadness suddenly invaded me as I walked out of his life.

***

As I approached the café, I noticed an older woman with salt and pepper hair waving at me as she stubbed out her cigarette.

'You must be Marion,' she said with a yellow grin.

'And you must be Monique!'

'I have ordered an espresso, would you like one?'

'I'll have a cappuccino, actually.'

Monique waved at the waiter and ordered a cappuccino for me and another espresso as she handed back her empty cup. She extracted a cigarette from a blue pack that had a picture of a black gypsy dancing. As she inhaled, her tired vocal cords made a whistling sound, her mouth formed an O and she exhaled thick pungent smoke between us. I held my breath and prayed the smog would dissipate as fast as possible.

'I'm sorry, does the smoke disturb you?' she asked as she waved her hand.

'It's OK,' I wheezed.

'Jean-Pierre has told me great things about you!'

I doubt that, I thought. 'Oh really?'

'Let me tell you more about my agency and why it is different from the others,' she said as she stirred the lump of sugar into her coffee. 'Most of my girls are older, more mature and mainly commercial. I sell models who represent the real consumer, and not just the young or the wealthy. I am trying to convey an eternal sense of beauty.'

As I listened to her rhetoric on aesthetics, I thought it ironic that they were coming from such a hag. I was at a loss as to what to believe or to say. After Monique delivered her speech, and downed her espresso, she caught sight of some traffic wardens and dashed off to her badly parked car.

As I subtly looked for my phone to check the time, I realised that it was missing. I rummaged frantically through my bag, and then spilled the contents of my bag on the table at the café. I searched my jacket. Nothing.

Shit, shit, shit! I thought, running my hands through my hair. I slouched back on the seat and stared at my belongings lying on the table. I tried to think about where I could have possibly left it.

'I don't remember taking it out of my bag.' I mumbled to myself. I cringed at the thought that it had been stolen. My whole life was in that phone, including my credit card pin codes.

I went into the café and fed the phone booth with a few coins. I dialled my own phone number. Obviously, if it had been stolen, I doubted very much that they would pick up, but I couldn't think of anything else to do. It rang a few times until a male voice replied.

'Allo?' the voice asked.

'Who is this?' I asked, fidgety, ready to bark.

'Richard.'

'Richard… Richard?' I racked my brains but I couldn't think of who he was. 'How did you get my phone?' I asked in an aggressive tone.

'Because you left it behind at the hair dresser's this morning and I thought you might call it to call to get it back,' Richard replied.

It finally all made sense. I was at a loss for words for a short while.

'Thanks for picking it up…' I hesitated, softening up. 'How can I meet you to get my phone back?'

'Well, I live in Versailles, but if you want, I can bring it back to you today.' His voice was calm and gentle.

'The thing is, I have a flight tonight and I need my phone… today. Can I possibly meet you somewhere, please?'

'What time is your flight?'

'Ten.'

'I'll meet you there at eight? Which airport?'

'Orly, West Terminal. Are, are you sure?' I stammered. 'It's quite a long way from Versailles.'

'It's all right, I'm off duty today and with my bike, it's easy.'

'Off duty? What do you do?' I was running my finger on the phone booth's window.

'I am a military policeman,' he replied.

My finger stopped. 'Really?'

Out of all the existing jobs, I wouldn't have picked that one. I had always felt that policemen were part and parcel of the state machinery, along with postmen, school teachers and politicians. There were not real people made of flesh and blood; they were part of a bigger design. Richard was very much alive, gorgeous to say the least, and he happened to hold my life in his hands. Three good reasons to see him again.

I paced back and forth on the sheltered part of the pavement in front of south terminal, while the rain poured down. Despite the driving rain, I heard the roaring sound of a motorbike. As I turned my head, I noticed two bright headlights driving towards me and come to a halt. Richard jumped off his bike, ran towards the covered area where I was standing and removed his helmet. His brown eyes shone as he smiled.

'Do you have time for a coffee?' I asked him with a shy smile.

'Sure!' he said.

His leather motorbike outfit squeaked as he walked stiffly. His boots buckles rattled along.

We huddled around a small table with our coffees. As he took off his leather jacket, I couldn't help but stare at his shapely biceps and forearms.

'Here's your phone. There haven't been any calls, except yours.'

He smiled as he handed me my Nokia. My hand inadvertently touched his and he intertwined his fingers through mine and ran his fingers along my arm. We stopped talking and looked at each other for a few seconds.

'Passengers on the flight Air France 6809 to Marseille should proceed to gate number 5 for immediate boarding,' said the announcement.

'Oh my God, that's my flight!' I said, reluctant to break the spell.

Richard did not say a word; he stood there immobile while I gathered my belongings.

'Well, I guess, that's it.' I searched his eyes. 'Bye.'

I took one step, stopped, turned around, kissed him stealthily and ran away. As I turned around to wave him goodbye, Richard put his leather jacket back on and was lighting a cigarette. He made a sign with his hand and exited the airport. I felt a pang in my stomach that prevented me from breathing properly. I ran furtively towards gate 5 where the airhostesses were waiting for the latecomers. Out of breath, I handed them my boarding pass, glanced once more behind me and headed towards the airplane.

In the rush, I had forgotten to ask him for his phone number. I could feel a knot in my throat from being so upset with myself. I looked out of the window as the plane took off. It's probably not meant to be, I thought sadly.

CHAPTER 27

Marion, Running to Richard, June 2002

After I had passed my exams and finished my degree, I made the most of my summer by going to the beach with my family and taking on a few modelling jobs thanks to Icon Milan and Icon Munich. Funnily enough, now that I had decided to take a step back from modelling, I had many agencies in Europe and a new one in Paris. *How ironic*, I thought.

One evening, as my parents and I were sat on the sofa after dinner, my eyes were suddenly drawn to the television set. Georges Orleans, the journalist, was presenting the eight o'clock news. I took hold of the TV remote and put the volume up.

'...today, a crazy gunman shot and injured many military policemen.'

I could feel my heart bouncing like a ball under my ribs. In the background, military policemen were escorting injured men into the ambulance. One of them had a bandage on his head and another one around his arm. His khaki jacket had been torn off and was maculated with bloodstains. The camera caught his gaze for a couple of seconds before he hopped into the ambulance.

'*Richard!*' I thought as I brought my left hand to my mouth. I hurried to my bedroom and searched for my phone. I scrolled down the dialled numbers and texts and then looked through my contact list with hesitant fingers. '*Richard*' There he was. *He has added his phone number to my contacts*, I smiled.

I deliberated over the idea of sending him a text.

"Saw you on the news. I hope you're OK. Would love to see you" I paused, erased the end of the message and started again. "Saw you on the news. Are you OK? Marion". I hesitated, and then pressed send. I placed my phone on my bed, and stared at it as if I expected it to jump. My phone buzzed instantly, causing my heart to jump. I threw my fingers at my phone and opened Richard's message with a large grin.

"Knew I had to take bullets to see you again! Richard."

I read it three times and replied. "Where are you?"

"Military Hospital Percy, in Clamart."

It wasn't hard to convince my parents that I had to go back to Paris. I had fulfilled my end of the bargain by finishing my studies, so my parents saw no danger in letting me go and work with Monique. After all, I was twenty-two years old; I was free. But parents will be parents so as long as I lived under their roof, I had to run it by them.

I took a flight on Wednesday that week and went straight to Richard's hospital bed. His head bandage had yellow stains and revealed a few tufts of hair here and there. His arm was held in a sling and placed on a pillow. One of his eyes was half-closed and a purple bruise spread around it. He struggled to smile as he saw me.

'How are you feeling?' I asked with a concerned look.

'My head is killing me but I'm alright,' he replied as he hoisted himself upright, grimacing.

'What happened?' I asked as pointing my finger at the various bandages.

'We were posted around a lunatic's house, watching his every move, waiting for the go-ahead to coerce the crazed gunman into surrendering,' Richard said in a tired voice. 'We barged into his house when he finally went to sleep. But the floors creaked and woke him up. He managed to point his hunting rifle at us and to shoot twice. A bullet scraped my skull and luckily missed my eye; another one went through my shoulder and shred my ligament to pieces,' he explained ruefully. He stripped the sheets off himself and grimaced as he aimed out of his bed. Clenching his feet, he forced himself to stand upright.

'Shouldn't you be lying down?'

He released his breath. 'I'm dying for a cigarette. Do you have fancy a coffee?' he asked as he walked slowly towards the door, in his hospital outfit.

I watched the curve of his muscled back as the open shirt loosened as he grabbed a cup of coffee with his one valid hand. He placed his leather jacket over his shoulders and handed me the cup. Once outside, he opened his cigarette pack with one hand and pulled one out with his teeth. The small flame of the lighter created shadows on his injured face. He looked at me tenderly despite his slanted eye and smiled.

'Are you planning on staying for a while or do I have to see you off again?' he asked.

Reddish shades of beard softened the nascent hair and aged him slightly; the young guy I had first met seemed manlier. A mole that resembled a tiny blue ink dot was cradled above his upper lip and distracted my eye.

'I am supposed to fly back to Marseille on Saturday...' I replied as my eyes darted back and forth, remembering what I had told my parents.

'Stay until then,' he said gently as he made a pathetic step towards me.

His stare became more intense. I gently caressed his cheek. He placed his hand on mine, brought my hand to his lips and kissed it sensuously. I stepped in close to him and pressed my head against his chest. We held each other in a fond embrace and kissed as passionately as his injuries allowed.

***

Later that day he was discharged and the taxi took us to his barracks in Versailles. We drove up a hill, passing the officers' houses and turned into a maze of grey buildings. It was a rather unappealing site – it looked like a council flat with its drab colours. Young men in uniforms and black boots walked back home with their khaki bags thrown over their shoulders. Kids scurried around them as they escorted them back home. A lush forest softened the concrete walls all around. It had an eerie feel of the dystopian society described in

Aldous Huxley's *Brave New World* where everyone dressed the same and worked towards the same goal. My throat constricted, I held my breath and tried not to show him my concern.

The taxi pulled up behind a military truck. With great effort Richard climbed out of the car despite the stab of pain tearing through his shoulder. We watched the taxi reverse and turn into the street. He fumbled for his keys in his trousers, he opened the three locks and pushed door number 401 with his good shoulder. It opened onto a long corridor with black and grey chequered linoleum floors. A black cat came meowing towards us and rubbed against Richard's leg.

'Hey Isis ma belle, how have you been?' Richard said as he petted his cat.

I looked up and noticed there were loose wires running along the side cupboard in the hallway. To the left there was a small, grey kitchen with a tired stove, which contrasted with the American size fridge. The kitchen was deprived of chairs and a table and its bare windows hadn't been cleaned for a while. A thin layer of black dust coated the edges. A yellow coffee machine was lit up and contained an old brew smell. Richard stood behind me silently and closed the door while Isis came purring against my trousers.

'She likes you!' he said while I squatted down and stroked the cat's silken fur.

I stepped into his living room where a sad-looking old brown velvet couch beckoned me, surrounded by two dusty palm trees. The shutters were closed, allowing very little light into the room.

'Have you just moved in?' I asked him. 'It's very… bare.'

'My wife has moved out… along with all our belongings.'

It hit me like a thunderbolt. I turned toward him and looked at him in a questioning manner.

'We're separated, if that's what you're wondering,' he said as he struggled out of his jacket.

'I see,' I replied as I also removed my coat and folded it across my arm. 'You're so young…I really hadn't expected you to be married.

'I was probably too young to get married in the first place. I had just turned twenty-one. The next four years were not happy ones.' I could feel a hint of sadness. 'She left a month ago. I told her she could take whatever she wanted. She took me at my word,' he said as he looked around.

'If you look at it on the bright side, you're not left with all the memories,' I said struggling to hide my shock.

'True, but she could have left some cutlery and some sheets at least...'

'Wow, it sounds like she was very angry with you.'

'I guess the notion of sharing becomes blurry when marriage comes to an end.' He threw the old brew away, and switched on his machine to make fresh coffee. 'She was a troubled soul anyhow.'

'How do you mean?'

'She grew up on a tropical island where people solved their problems with alcohol and violence. What started as a lively relationship quickly developed into a feisty marriage where she always tried to get the upper hand and kept it that way for years. She would talk down to me both in private and in front of others. She toyed with my feelings up until the day I finally found the strength to put an end to it, irrevocably. You should have seen her fury.' He took two cups and turned towards me, 'Coffee?'

I nodded.

'How are you feeling now?'

'Relieved,' he said with a smile. 'I was very young when I met her, she must have totally bewitched me.'

I decided to stay that night, and the night after and all the following nights. I was happy, as happy as one could be, in the empty flat of a man with a hole in his shoulder and an arrow through his heart. Unlike Morten who was only a lost boy, I had met a real man. I felt protected and loved; I even came to like the bareness of his flat. I saw it as a blank canvas onto which anything could be drawn.

As the days went by, we spent most waking hours discovering each other's bodies. Richard was a vast inviting land I was willing to discover and conquer. We spent a month refurbishing his flat, replacing the beige wallpaper with quicklime, revitalising the bathroom and kitchen walls with livelier colours, and softening the windows with warm colourful curtains, with lots of love-making in between. For the first time, I felt that I was truly building something both literally and figuratively. Of course my parents were disappointed that I did not try and become a teacher. My mother had not expected me to live in a military barracks; she hoped that I was only going through a phase and would soon grow out of it.

We only lived twenty kilometres outside of Paris, but each trip into the capital seemed like a true mission. Bumper to bumper, I grew infuriated in traffic jams and dragged my feet to every single casting Monique had organised for me. I took her up on her offer simply because I needed to make a living.

'The client really loves you, you're on option,' was Monique's recurrent sentence in order to boost my confidence. Astonishingly, my career eventually boomed. I would never have bet on Monique being the catalyst to my success, but she patiently worked her way with clients. All of a sudden, the drought in my career was replaced by heaps of work. She managed to book me for chocolate commercials, hair commercials, and many more. As money attracted money, my German agency booked me for all kinds of mail order catalogues. In the long run, I mastered the salt mines, the blinding sun and all sorts of humiliation. I could put up with it as long as I could coo with Richard on the phone at the end of my day's work. For months I spent my life on planes accumulating more money than I had ever dreamed of.

CHAPTER 28

Marion, Versailles, July 2003

The following summer, a year after I had first moved in with Richard, he was eventually sent away on a three month mission to Wallis and Futuna, an island in the back waters of the Pacific Ocean and barely visible on a world map. His squad had to contain a riot dividing the King's followers and the French locals, who were under the control of the French representative there.

'Apparently, the King's cousin has run over a little girl and thought he could get away by offering a few pigs to the mourning family. His jail sentence angered his followers,' he managed to explain through the crackling line of one of the three existing phone booths on the island. 'The trouble is, we're only eighty policemen against many more.'

'That sounds pretty dangerous. Is there any chance that you'll get any kind of back-up?' I asked softly, groggy with sleep at that early hour.

'Well, they are trying to get us some, but the rebels are preventing the planes from landing, by lying down on the tarmac.'

'But that's crazy!' I said, now sitting upright in my bed in the dark.

'Hopefully, things will calm down and we won't need to interfere,' he added. 'I've got to go, honey. There is a queue of people behind me waiting to make a phone call and I am literally being eaten alive by mosquitoes in here!' he laughed.

In his absence, I regularly met with Monique at the Plaza Athénée hotel on Avenue Montaigne in Paris, trying to delay the moment I had to go to sleep alone. I loved the amber scented hallway and its revolving doors, and she was always up for a drink. I strutted down the carpeted hallway mechanically, kissed the bar manager on the cheek and ensconced myself in one of the comfortable winged chairs while I waited for Monique. The bar married old traditional style with a tasteful modern twist; its blue lit bar and the many models sitting behind it had revamped the image of the cocktail lounge.

Monique walked in once, escorted by a couple of lanky models, one of which turned out to be Elena. I hadn't recognised her at first – her hair was longer and darker, and she seemed to have gained some weight as well. She smiled as she approached the table.

'Long time no see!' she said.

'Your English is better!' I replied, unable to think of anything else to say.

'Time flies! Where have you been?' she asked with a strong Russian accent.

'New York mainly, but finding ground in Europe thanks to Monique,' I said as I turned to Monique and smiled.

We all sat down and ordered champagne with fresh raspberries.

'What about you? What have you been up to?' I asked Elena.

'I don't model much. I paint now,' she said with a nod.

'You paint?'

'I have a small atelier in my flat. The light is very good on Île Saint-Louis; there are no buildings facing my window.'

'Very nice!' I said, wondering what she was doing with Monique if she wasn't modelling.'

We sat there smiling for a few seconds. The conversation dwindled as Monique caught a glimpse of Georges Orleans walking into the lounge. She waved at him. He was much smaller than I would have thought. He had traded his usual business suit and tie for leather pants and an open shirt. The fifty-year-old man refused to accept his age and clearly wanted to be seen as a hot young rock star.

'Ladies!' he said with a charming smile as he sat down next to Monique.

We smiled back and giggled politely. The journalist I had grown up watching, who sent me to bed at eight o'clock sharp every evening was sitting across from me, sipping rum and Coke. His presence took the conversation to a higher level. He mastered any political or current affair topic better than anyone; as a consequence, no one dared budge or contradict him. He could sense how tensely I watched him and basked in his knowledge. He was really excellent at holding court. He liked it so much that once everyone had gone home, he asked Monique to organise another dinner a week later, which she submitted to gladly.

During the following dinner, Georges hadn't anticipated that his fellow war photographer was going to steal the show. All the attention turned to the man who risked his life to witness the vileness of war and sacrificed his life for his art. We were all agape while he described his work.

As I was sitting next to Georges, I could sense the tension rising inside him. He tapped his fingers, rocked his legs, and played with his phone. The more attention his colleague got, the tenser Georges became. After slouching over his phone for a couple of minutes, he sat erect, slammed his hands onto the table, stood up and left. Everyone's heads turned around with the same bewildered gaze.

Monique ran after him. I did not pay attention to her question, but I heard his answer.

'What's going on with Marion?'

Monique made a hushing sound, grabbed his arm and turned away from us. They spoke vehemently for a few seconds until Georges freed himself from Monique's grasp and left the restaurant, disgruntled. Monique sat back in her chair, avoiding my glance.

***

'It was a very strange evening,' I told Richard over the phone.

I had managed to get hold of him, despite the crazy ten hours' difference. One of his colleagues had woken him up.

'Why was that?'

'Georges Orleans was absolutely peeved, and I am not sure why.'

'He was just probably having a bad day, that's all.'

'No, I think there was more.' I paused. 'I think he had a special agreement with Monique.'

I decided not to dwell on the subject for too long, but deep down I had a bad feeling. Those evenings spent with Monique had helped me to know her better. She was unusual and untraditional; half mother, half bawd. I liked her as much as I dreaded her; however weary I was getting of her tricks, she had been the best agent I had ever had thus far. I couldn't go into details with Richard; he was too honest to understand the reasoning behind Monique's behaviour. I had been lucky enough not to have been solicited by Mr Carillon, I was determined to keep all the men Monique introduced to me at bay.

***

I hadn't had any news from Richard in days. I made sure the phone receiver was properly placed, and I roamed sadly around the flat in the hope that he would ring me soon. I even called the phone company to check if my line was out of order, but to no avail.

A few days later, in the middle of the night I woke me up with a start to the sound of the telephone ringing. I kicked off my sheet and ran to the living room to grab the receiver from the console where it had been consigned.

'Marion?' asked a strange voice.

'Speaking,' I replied, trembling with worry.

'My name is Steve, I am calling on behalf of Richard,' he said. 'I run the restaurant where his squad eats every day. I have just seen Richard—'

'What's happened?' I said interrupted in a faint voice.

'He's fine, don't worry, but he cannot call you. He's… he's keeping the Ambassador's house and…' Steve's voice was hesitant.

'And?' I urged him.

'Well, the trouble is, the rebels are standing outside the house, preventing the people in the house getting out.'

'Are they armed?'

I started feeling unwell and had to sit down on the floor. Our cat, Isis must have felt my concern as she came purring next to me.

'I'm afraid they are. But please don't worry too much, reinforcements are on the way. I am sure that everything will be under control so.'

The line went dead.

'Allo! Allo! Steve? Are you there?' I started panting. *Oh My God, Oh My God*, I muttered. I was at a loss, not knowing what to do but wait by the phone for more information.

After two days of terrible wait, Richard finally called me.

'Oh my baby, are you OK? I've been worried sick!'

'Sorry I couldn't call. Everything is fine now.'

'Where are you now?'

'Back at the barracks. The rioters have cooled down. It was not a pretty sight, all those angry guys outside the house brandishing their machetes. But I have not become a chipolata yet!' he joked.

'Glad to hear you're safe! Did the army take over?'

'They never came. The Authorities refused to send the military. Too costly they said.'

'Too costly?' I was taken aback. 'This is disgusting!'

I was appalled, and directed my anger towards the all system. My man was just cannon fodder, nothing more. For so many years, I had been stuck in a glamorous, superficial, money-filled business filled with self-inflicted drug tragedies while Richard and his squad had been risking their lives, not for money, nor Number One Agency, but just because they were doing their job.

***

Our reunion was as intense as ever. I was waiting in the kitchen, by the window, when I heard the roar of his motorbike. My heart jumped, I sprang to my feet and stared out of the window, determined not to miss any second of his arrival. As if it were déjà-vu, his black motorbike screeched to a halt in front of our building. He turned his head towards me, as if he could feel my presence. He dismounted and marched towards the front door without removing his helmet. The wait was unbearable.

I had a large grin when he finally came through the door. He looked tanned and healthy, as if he had been on holiday, minus the riot. He took me in his arms and carried me to the bedroom.

'You can go back anytime,' I said with a smile, as I caressed his bare chest. 'I have missed you so much,' I said with tears in my eyes.

'I've missed you too!' he said as he wiped my tears gently and kissed me. He took my face with both his hands and added, 'Why don't we make a baby?'

At that very moment, I felt permanently cured from Morten and his demons. It was as if all that had ever happened before Richard did not matter. I held the most beautiful man I could dream of in my arms and I was determined to never let him go.

***

Richard and I made the most of his holiday, which was customary after such a long mission. We went for long walks by the lake behind the barracks and enjoyed our friends' company. It took us a month, and much practice, to receive the happy news. Our baby was on his way, the fruit of our passion and seal of our life.

Unfortunately, my modelling career died of a natural death with the birth of our son, Anton. My bookings became scarcer; no one wanted a pregnant model, they preferred stuffing the girls' shirts with cushions of exactly the right size. It took me a while to regain both my figure and I found so much pleasure in looking after our son that it took a long while before I felt the desire to travel away from him. Anton gave me the emotional equilibrium I had been looking for, all those years. Having a family was the answer to my questions, it was my raison d'être. I finally felt whole.

I loved being stationed in the barracks, waiting with the other wives for their brave soldiers to return. I loved the sense of community and help we gave one another. I loved it until all the money I had saved while modelling dwindled into nothing. That was when reality hit me in the face – I had to find a job, a "normal" job as my parents would call it. The trouble was that on the work market, a modelling career and a Master of Arts in English Literature were worthless.

As I sat in front of my computer to write my CV, I stared at the flashing cursor on the white page for long minutes. It basically summed up my career; a blinking dot at a standstill. I could hardly write more than a couple of lines. I grew frustrated spending my days waiting for Richard, feeling like a bored suburban housewife. I hoped I hadn't become boring to him.

Having made the decision to become a breadwinner once more, I had to hand over my nine month old baby to a nanny, who would certainly not care about him as much as I would. Then I got on to the very bottom rung of the career ladder. I found a receptionist position in a car leasing company, which hardly paid the bills, and was as dull as dishwater. I went to work every morning with a knot in my stomach, longing for Anton's babbling and Richard's love all day. Modelling had made me unfit for everyday life, I resented the work routine, the bad pay, the undermining looks I received from one group of my colleagues and the lecherous looks from others. Modelling had been an experience like no other, but it had cushioned me from the harsh reality of normal life. I felt like a once beautiful cashmere jumper that had been washed out of shape and relegated to the back of the wardrobe.

***

'Why don't you come to London?' My brother Patrick suggested over the telephone.

'London? We can't!'

'Why not? I need a PA as I'm opening a hedge fund over there and I think it would be fun to work together.'

Patrick's proposal came totally unexpected. Millions of thoughts flashed through my mind in a split second, trying to rearrange the jigsaw quickly.

'What about Richard? He has a career here. I can't leave him behind!'

'I don't know... he could do anything he wants. I have a gym project in mind. I was planning to do it with Tim but I guess Richard could join the venture. He's a good guy and I believe it would be a great opportunity for you both.'

Silence.

'Come on, you're not going to spend your life in a barracks making nine hundred Euros a month! Don't tell me you're happy there! I hear the news through Mum,' Patrick exclaimed.

'Well we are happy, we're in love, we're healthy...'

'But that's not enough, it doesn't pay the bills.'

It was as simple as that. Everything was always so black and white with Patrick. He had the money and the generosity to bring us all to a whole new exciting life.

***

'London?' Richard had to sit down when I broke the news to him. 'But… what would I do there? I'm in the French military police it's not like I can just…' he stammered.

'Well, you know how Patrick is fond of side-projects, he's planning to open a martial arts gym and would like you to be involved. He suggested we should come over to visit him in London to discuss everything. What do we have to lose? Anton is only a year old, my job is shit and it can't get any worse,' I sighed, 'and your career is not going as well as you thought since your shoulder injury.'

Richard stared at me with his usual shiny eyes and smiled.

The next thing I knew we were sitting in a cab on the way to the airport, feeling slightly sick to our stomach at the idea of trading our old life for a brand new English one. Change of jobs, of scenery, of culture, of house – so many elements that we had never imagined. It made our heads spin. We sat silently, facing each other, rocking our way to the airport, biting our lips with excitement.

EPILOGUE

Marion, London October 2005

Two years later, as I was driving Anton to nursery, down one of the streets near where we lived in Fulham, South West London, I recognised a tall blonde man stepping out of a house. I caught a glimpse of that familiar silhouette with blonde fluffy hair and instantly recognised him – it was Morten. He was on the phone and hadn't noticed me. I slammed on the breaks and brought my car to a halt.

'What is it, Mummy?' Anton asked, not understanding why I had stopped in the middle of the road.

'Hold on a second, sweetie,' I replied, my eyes riveted on the rear mirror.

Leaving Anton in the car, I walked stealthily towards him. Unaware, he strolled on looking down at his feet, and speaking into his mobile. A plane flew overhead, he turned to me and his eyes locked onto mine. He hung up his phone and smiled.

'Hey! What are you doing here?' he asked.

'I live here – I have done for two years,' I replied.

'So do I! How funny is that! You're telling me that we have been unwitting neighbours?'

I looked at him; he was still quite handsome and charismatic despite the years of hard and fast living but my body remained numb to his presence. I found him grey and dull. He hadn't changed much, but I had.

***

'Who was it, Mummy?' Anton asked.

'It was no one baby. No one at all,' I answered as I drove away.